SO HARD TO DO

SO HARD TO DO

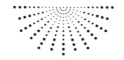

SALLY BASMAJIAN

Published in the United States by Creative James Media.

www.creativejamesmedia.com

Cover Design by Alt 19 Designs.

978-1-956183-82-5 (trade paperback)
978-1-956183-83-2 (eBook)

First U.S. Edition 2023

In memory of my wonderful mom,
Dora Lucas Basmajian
Loving, fun, generous, strong—and an indefatigable reader

1

THE BREAKUP

*J*annie sat in the sunlit living room, facing the person she loved most in the world. Only a narrow coffee table separated them, but the distance seemed immense.

"Please don't leave." Jannie took a shaky breath. "The two of us are supposed to stay together, forever."

Apart from her raspy breathing, there was no noise in the room. Was she the only one here who gave a damn?

Their bond had always been solid. So mutually supportive—steadfast, through good times and bad. A love like this should never be broken.

Jannie pitched in again. "You're the best thing in my life. My greatest mentor. My rock."

She groped for a tissue. In spite of her valiant attempt to stay calm, tears gathered and fell. She wiped one away, but not before she tasted salt.

The blue-gray eyes she gazed into seemed concerned, sympathetic, maybe even conveying hints of love. Still, there was no response. Jannie had to try harder.

"Have I done anything to upset you? Is it my

messiness? Or because I quit therapy? I'll do anything to fix this. Just tell me."

She began to cry. Her torso rattled from the intensity. Only now, as she felt her heart shrivel in defeat, did she know for sure—the perfect love they'd shared had died.

A reassuring hand patted her the way someone would pat a dog, with kindness but promising nothing. Jannie hunched her shoulder away and looked down, trying to control her sobs.

After a few moments, she heard, "You'll manage. You're almost thirty years old. It's time, sweetie."

And with that, her beloved mom picked up her bag, opened the door, and left.

Suze tried her best not to show her elation, but happiness frothed like champagne mist throughout her whole body. She hadn't felt this alive in years. Today was the start of an exciting new chapter, and she couldn't wait to get going.

The hardest part—leaving Jannie's lovely condo—was accomplished. Now, at age fifty-eight, Suze intended to get a job. Once that was achieved, she'd save up a nest egg and maybe even acquire a beau, eventually. It didn't matter that her hair was silver and she'd been a homebody for most of her adult life—Suze felt invincible. Her heartbeat accelerated at the prospect of the adventures that lay ahead.

Jannie was a darling and Suze would certainly miss her. But her grown-up daughter needed to get on with her own life, before it passed her by. Even though Jannie had attained success in business, she was far too dependent, as if she were still a little girl in grade school—a sad, eccentric little girl who'd had many social and academic challenges to overcome, and had done so brilliantly. Suze had been there every step of the way and couldn't be prouder.

It was time. Jannie needed to flap her fledgling wings and prepare to soar. Like Suze planned to do. Starting now.

Her new apartment was a tiny jewel, high up in a dated but sturdy tower on the slightly seedy western edge of Toronto's Annex. The window let in streams of sunshine that bounced off a copper-colored parquet floor. She had just the one room, plus a sliver of a galley kitchen and a minuscule bathroom. It was a far cry from Jannie's executive condo farther uptown, but it suited Suze perfectly.

Before the move, knowing that space would be limited, she had jettisoned most of her old possessions. She now owned things that could serve multiple purposes. Her couch folded out into what the salesperson had assured her would be a comfortable bed. Her dining room table doubled as a desk. Her laptop provided all the entertainment she'd be treated to, given there was neither room for a flat-screen TV nor budget for cable fees.

She felt lighter in possessions and in spirits than she had in years. There were enough beloved relics from the past—an ancient Turkish rug, her all-time favorite novels, her set of mixing bowls—to give her comfort. Everything else in the shoebox apartment, and in her life, was brand new. The future beckoned, and in the friendliest possible way, too.

Her cell phone rang to the tune of *Que Sera Sera*—Jannie's ringtone. A sensation of loving dread whooshed up the back of Suze's neck. She pictured her daughter's brown eyes streaming with tears and her uncombed, black curls corkscrewing crazily. At the age of twenty-nine, Jannie was the image of her long-departed father, who had been quite a dark and handsome looker in his day. She'd also inherited some of his theatrical ways, although not his demons of addiction, thank the Lord.

"Mommy!"

The depth of emotion Jannie packed into the single word was impressive. She started with a sonic boom on the first syllable and swooped the second one upward until it concluded on a warbling "eeee" sound.

"Jannie, darling," Suze said, deepening her voice to its most soothing alto.

There was no response but she heard wheezing sounds that were reminiscent of their late and not so adored tabby cat struggling to bring up a hairball.

"Dear? Are you okay?"

"No." Jannie hiccupped loudly.

"There, there," Suze said, as if Jannie were three years old again, with a boo-boo on her knee.

More inarticulate noises squelched through the phone. Suze dug the fingernails on her free hand into her palm. Jannie could get through this. Transitions had always been a problem for her, but if Suze stayed firm they'd both make it to the other side.

"I'm so lonely."

"Hey, I live in Toronto, too. Only a short subway ride away." She gave herself a mental kick. Given any encouragement, Jannie might decide to hop a train and visit, and if she entered this apartment tonight she might never leave.

"I mean," Suze said before Jannie could leap at the opening, "we're going to be able to visit each other easily in the future. Now, though, I need to meet with my super and give him the last of the money I owe him. There are so many chores to take care of, I had no idea!"

Sobs rattled into Suze's ear—deep, ragged, ugly. Her

poor, poor daughter was so distraught. Suze wondered for a nanosecond if she should back down and invite Jannie over for the evening.

She stiffened her spine. "Listen, sweetie, hang in there. Make something to eat, and watch a movie. Maybe a comedy?"

"There's nothing to eat. I ate all the chocolate. And the potato chips, too."

"You did what?"

"You know I'm an emotional eater. I couldn't help it. It was like the food jumped into my mouth."

Suze held out the phone and counted silently to five. Her grown, executive daughter was backsliding to a much younger, less stable version of herself—the kid teachers said would never make it. They claimed she was too impulsive and much too easily distracted. But Suze insisted Jannie would succeed and dedicated herself to helping her daughter rise above—way above—all the dire predictions. Jannie could get through this.

"There are plenty of healthy things in the fridge. I left you a couple of casseroles. Heat one up."

"But you always make dinner."

Suze grimaced. She'd been so focused on supporting Jannie with academics and then with getting ahead in her career, she'd neglected to teach her daughter basic life skills. She'd helped Jannie achieve worldly success but created a domestic disaster.

She opened her mouth to offer assistance, then closed it firmly. No, she wouldn't drop everything to run over and rescue Jannie. It was time for her daughter to learn how to survive on her own.

"You can't go wrong. Put in a casserole, shut the door, and press the reheat icon on the display console. If you smell anything burning, hit the off button. You'll be fine."

"Seriously? You're going to let me kill myself in a nuclear meltdown?"

"Jannie, you've heated things up before. And why don't you pour yourself a glass of white wine? There's an open bottle at the back of the fridge. Now, sorry, dear, but I'm late. I love you."

No answer.

"Jannie?"

"No, you don't. You can't possibly love me."

Suze steeled herself and said, "Sure do. Tons and tons and forevermore. Now, off you go. Talk soon. Bye!"

And before she could hear Jannie make another anguished moan, Suze clicked off.

She spent the next hour pacing back and forth in her tiny apartment. Several times, she picked up her phone and stared at the directory, thumb hovering above Jannie's name. It took every bit of willpower she had not to press down on it.

Jannie slumped on her sofa, thinking about the past. Mom had insisted—against the advice of all the teachers—that Jannie could handle an academic course load and had worked with her for hours every night at the kitchen table to ensure she succeeded. Mom had coached her on how to handle baffling social encounters, translating nuances that always escaped her. Consoling Jannie when she'd been jilted by various boyfriends who'd only dated her because they'd thought she'd be so grateful she'd be easy. Being there through thick and thin.

Jannie glanced at the clock. She'd been crying on and off for hours. Her nose felt as if someone had scrubbed it with steel wool and her eyes were burning slits of pain, but she hadn't eaten a proper dinner and her stomach coiled in knots of hunger.

As if lured by an irresistible force, she emerged from her couch cocoon and wandered into the kitchen to forage. She opened the refrigerator and located the healthy casseroles, pre-baked by her mom. Way too many veggies for a sad day like this. There were bound to be some tastier items in whatever was left of the junk food stash, so she rifled through the kitchen cabinets and grabbed a box of ready-to-nuke popcorn, with extra buttery flavoring. Mom was right; of course she could handle this. Jannie removed the plastic outer wrap and placed the snack-to-be in the microwave. She punched a few buttons. When the interior light switched on and the turntable began to rotate, she cheered and left the device to do its job, while she went to run a much-needed bath. It was time to enjoy two of her favorite things: eating junk food and lolling in a piping hot tub, simultaneously. A sensory delight right up there with sex, and unfortunately there had been none of that lately.

Anyway, on such a blue day, even the dreamiest man couldn't offer the same comfort as a bath. Jannie turned on the water and added fragrant oil. She paddled it around with her hand, mixing well, and then waited until the bath was a third full before dispensing the salts. This was an art form, something only a true bubble artiste would ever understand.

She took off her jeans and t-shirt, stripping to her underwear and keeping her back turned to the foggy mirror. After the day she'd just had, she'd be a wreck— Rudolph-red nose and crimson eyes to match.

She was testing the temperature of the rising water when, out of nowhere, an alarm wailed. Jannie's heart lurched. She threw open the bathroom door, only to be assailed by louder-than-ever sirens and beeps, and also by a cloud of acrid smoke. Oh, God, the popcorn! She never should have turned her back on that infernal death machine.

From the towel rack, she tugged a washcloth free, plunged it under the running faucet, and held it to her nose, still raw from crying. She charged blindly into the smoke and ran to the kitchen, stubbing her toes on the edge of the doorway, but not stopping. Even through the smog it was easy to see the microwave—her hoped-for snack had gone up like a torch and was burning with fervor. Should she risk getting third-degree burns by trying to yank the blazing thing out? Or just pull the plug?

As Jannie gingerly stretched out her hand, someone pounded on her condo door. Maybe Mom was here to rescue her! Jannie turned her back on the fiery appliance and ran toward salvation. She flung open the door.

"Oh, Mom, save me! Please!" She gasped mouthfuls of fresh hallway air.

"Stand back." The baritone voice was calm and certainly didn't belong to her mom, but at the moment Jannie didn't care. It was wonderful to have help from any source, so she obeyed and stayed put while her mystery rescuer followed the smoke trail into the kitchen.

After an interval, he called out, "All clear."

Jannie walked back into her suite. The air was breathable again because the hero of the hour had opened the windows. The alarm, which had been shrilling all that time, fell silent.

"Thanks." Jannie blinked the grittiness from her eyes and did a double take. He was gorgeous, in a slightly older gent kind of way. Tall, olive-skinned, hazel-eyed, with a thick head of dark hair and a full beard.

"No thanks needed." The man glanced away, amusement crinkling his eyes. "But maybe you want to cover up a bit?" Behind his beard, his lips twitched into a crooked grin.

Jannie looked down at herself. In the hubbub, she'd forgotten she was practically naked. It was beyond awkward, but at least she was wearing the good underwear.

She snatched one of Mom's doilies from the coffee table. Holding the lacy morsel in front of her breasts she slunk toward the bathroom, planning to grab her robe.

"This is so embarrassing. If you'll just wait a sec while I put something—"

Jannie opened the bathroom door, only to be hit by a tsunami of water and suds. It was as if the dam between here and hell had broken, and the force of it made her knees buckle. As she lost her grip on the doily, she cast a final, agonized glance at the hunky baritone guy. Then, she closed her eyes and sank into the raging torrent.

2

THE MORNING AFTER

*I*t was a glorious morning. Suze lay in her converted sofa bed, feeling contented as the August sunlight streamed through her high-rise window. Yes, maybe she needed to buy curtains, and maybe the salesperson had exaggerated when he'd told her that the discounted couch was going to astonish her with its advanced lumbar technology, but all was well in her world. She was embarking on her new adventure, with no one to worry about except herself.

She swung her lower body over the edge of the mattress, thwacking one ankle on a metal support. As she rubbed away the pain, she looked ruefully down at her flannel granny nightie. She would have to buy something more glam one of these days—something lacy and clingy and *so* not age-appropriate, as if anyone would be there to admire her in such a sexy little number. But maybe, in her shiny, reinvented life, miracles were possible.

There were nine steps from her sofa bed to her microscopic kitchenette. She opened the fridge door, careful not to hit the opposite wall. Yesterday, she'd had just enough time to buy a few staples and now she selected plain, nonfat Greek yogurt and fresh fruit for her breakfast. She didn't yet own a coffee maker. Instead, she boiled water on her two-burner stovetop and made do with store brand orange pekoe tea, liberally laced with honey that she squirted, with a satisfying thwop, out of a plastic bear.

Suze sat at a desk that doubled as her table and began to munch away happily. While she ate, she opened her laptop and scanned the international news. The world at large was in a sorry mess—horrid wars and steadily encroaching global warming. Awful, really, and it made her feel insignificant and helpless. With a sigh, she turned to local stories. The threat of a teachers' strike continued to dominate the coverage. City councilors bickered. Disgruntled Torontonians howled. Nothing unusual there, and Suze was about to turn her computer off, when a small item practically jumped off the screen at her. The headline read, *Priceless Stamp Collection Damaged by Flood.*

In itself, not so interesting. But in the photo that accompanied the article, there was a distraught and familiar-looking man. And behind him, a building that also looked very familiar. It couldn't be—was this even possible?

It was Suze's former home. The condo. And it had happened last night.

It wasn't like Jannie not to have phoned. She called several times a day. Something as momentous as a flood in the complex would have sent her scrambling for her iPhone immediately.

Suze grabbed her mobile and tried to turn it on. Nothing. She'd forgotten to charge it last night before she went to bed. No wonder this had been such a serene morning—until now.

Belatedly, she plugged it into the charger and turned back to the computer screen. Yes, there it was. Tyler

Howard, aged twenty-eight, had been devastated when a flood from an upstairs condo, caused by a careless neighbor, wreaked havoc on his home. Among the items being examined for damage was his great-great-grandfather's priceless stamp collection, which included a fine specimen of something called a 12d Black Queen Victoria. This stamp alone was said to be worth hundreds of thousands of dollars.

The yogurt in Suze's stomach curdled. There were many units in Jannie's condo. Surely, the flood could have occurred in a different section, caused by someone else. No way could Jannie have had anything to do with it. Of course not; that would be preposterous. Jannie might not be a model of mature independence, but she'd never caused a disaster that had made the news. And if she had, then why wasn't the message light blinking urgently?

The morning, which had gotten off to such a positive start, was looking much less rosy now. Suze had to get to the bottom of this. Her appetite was gone. She placed her dishes in the sink, leaving the cleanup for later—which was totally unlike her—and ran to get dressed.

Most of her belongings were still nestled in neatly packed cardboard cartons. Suze foraged in one that was labeled *Casual Clothes* and pulled out a t-shirt, a pair of skinny jeans that had belonged to a ten pounds lighter Jannie, and a black, high-necked athletic jacket. She found seen-better-days-but-at-least-vaguely-supportive-on-the-top-and-panty-line-free-on-the-bottom undergarments in another box and dressed quickly.

She grabbed her minimally charged phone. Should she call Jannie? No! She had to give her daughter the benefit of the doubt, even if Suze *did* intend to sneak over there and see what had happened. Before heading out the door, she ran to the bathroom and gave her hair a vague brush, frowning at how pale her skin looked next to all that silver. There was no time to fix things with properly applied makeup, but she dabbed on some lip gloss. That would have to do.

She took the subway to the St. Clair West station, walked briskly eastward, and arrived at Jannie's Forest Hill building in less than half an hour. In this part of the city, everything seemed more refined. Aristocratic uptown trees deigned to bend slightly in the breeze, and neat gardens nestled against impressive stone houses.

Suze's heart swelled. Jannie had done well for herself to be able to afford a condo in such an upscale neighborhood. All those years of caring for and coaching a daughter who'd needed special help to get through school had paid off. Maybe Jannie couldn't cook, but she'd overcome many obstacles, not to mention the labels the educational system had tried to foist on her. Now, if only she hadn't caused the flood.

Outside the condo, all was quiet. There were no signs of calamity. The building appeared as it always did—solid and dignified in its brown-bricked, understated elegance. No rivulets of water gushed forth. No ark floated by on the front lawn. Perhaps Suze had been mistaken. Maybe she had misinterpreted the news photo and the flood had happened elsewhere.

Still, she should check, just to be sure. And to be a good parent. But not let Jannie know, ever, that she'd dropped by to investigate because she questioned her daughter's competence.

Suze approached the oak and glass doors. They swung open, propelled by the sturdy arms of Ernie, the building's longstanding doorman. He beamed at Suze, as if he hadn't seen her for weeks.

"Madam Suze, how lovely to see you! You're looking

radiant!" Ernie took her hand as she crossed the threshold. He led her into the glass and marble lobby as if she were made of fine porcelain, then took a step back and executed a gallant half-bow.

"It's good to see you, too. I know it's only been a day but it feels like a year." She smiled at Ernie, who blushed pinkish red. The rosy trail spread upward from his cheeks and traveled high into the dome of his nearly hairless head.

"So all's well?" Her normally calm voice held a hint of a quaver.

Ernie's pleasant expression drooped. "No, ma'am. It wasn't a good night." He seemed to catch himself, and hurried to add, "But everything is fine now."

Suze peered at him. Ernie began to study the marble floor as if it were suddenly the most interesting thing in the world.

"Tell me."

"Ah, Madam Suze, I'd rather not. You've moved on. Our little affairs shouldn't trouble you."

"I need to know. Please. I swear I won't tell Jannie."

"Hmmm. May I tempt you with a cup of coffee and maybe a cookie? Chocolate chip, your favorite?" Ernie moved in the direction of his reception desk, still avoiding Suze's gaze.

"No coffee until you tell me what's going on." She tried to scowl at him, but he was so sweet; she just couldn't.

In the distance, a bell rang. "Ah, please excuse me." He bustled away.

Ernie would never give up an opportunity to schmooze with her unless things were dire. Unbidden, her trembling fingertips rose to her temples, which were beginning to throb. She closed her eyes and squeezed her head gently, trying to think more clearly.

"You appear to be in need of assistance." A warm male

voice broke her reverie. It held a faint hint of a hard to place accent.

Suze turned around, dropping her hands. She gazed up into intelligent, rather narrow, hazel eyes set under straight brows. Dark brown hair, flecked with gray, and a beard and mustache, neatly trimmed but more substantial than the spiky stubble that many men his age—late forties, maybe—still persisted in sporting. His lower lip was full and sensuous. His long, straight nose pointed slightly down. Altogether dreamy. And that voice.

"You look like you've had a shock," the man said. "Could I offer any help?"

Back at his desk, Ernie made a show of rustling through papers and waving the phone about, as he murmured occasional remarks into it. He took a break from his frantic activity for a moment, placed his hand over the voice piece and said, "Madam Suze Foster, allow me to introduce you to Mr. Aram Krikorian. Condo 5D. He moved in a couple of weeks ago. Very nice gentleman."

"Thank you, Ernie, for this introduction," Aram said, smiling at Suze. "He's our building's expert, so if he says I'm a nice gentleman, it must be true. Now, please tell me how I may assist you."

Suze swallowed. What an attractive man Aram was. How charming, too. Perhaps too much so. She made an effort to breathe more slowly and tried not to stare pop-eyed at him. Maybe she could even summon up a few coherent words.

"I, well, I don't know how to broach this subject. But was there perhaps a slight flood last night in this building?"

His face was solemn, but his eyes twinkled. "You want to know because . . .?"

"I just want to make sure my daughter, Jannie, wasn't anywhere nearby if it occurred."

"Ah, what a shame."

"What do you mean by that?" Suze grabbed the sleeve of his well-tailored black jacket with both hands and pulled him toward her.

"What I mean is—but we shouldn't stand in this public space, discussing business that isn't meant for all ears." He dropped his voice as a young couple emerged from the elevator and passed through the lobby, making their way to the door. "Why don't you come to my condo? It's on the same floor as your daughter's, if Jannie Morris fills that role in your life. Strange, I see no mother-daughter resemblance."

His eyes drifted from hers, to her cheekbones, to her mouth. She let go of his arm and swallowed with difficulty.

"Um . . ." she began, not sure if going to a strange man's condo was a proper way for a lady—even one of a certain age like herself—to behave.

"Ernie will vouch for me," Aram said. In the background, Ernie's head bounced up and down in verification. "And, we'll leave the hallway door open. That way you can depart if I behave in anything less than a proper gentlemanly manner."

At this point, Ernie was making shooing gestures with one hand. Suze thought for a moment and made up her mind. Aram didn't appear to be an axe-murderer or a rapist who targeted gently bred, middle-aged ladies with silver hair.

"Okay," she said. "Seeing as Ernie is in favor."

Suze and Aram were silent as the elevator took them to the fifth floor. She studied the notices for new parking regulations, reading the fine print as if world peace depended on it. Out of the corner of her eye, she caught Aram watching her—unabashedly, intently. Oh heavens, this elevator was so confined. And, really, the air conditioning was set way too low. If only she could catch her breath, but proximity to this man, combined with worry about Jannie and weariness from yesterday's hard work, somehow culminated in an overpowering wave of dizziness.

Aram moved swiftly. As her knees gave way, he caught Suze in his whip-strong arms and, when the elevator doors opened, bore her off down the hall to his condo.

Jannie pushed her hair back and cracked open her sleepy eyes. She stared at the ceiling, hoping she'd dreamed last night's fiasco. There'd been no flood. No flaming inferno. And surely Mom hadn't moved out after all but was in the kitchen, rustling up a tasty breakfast.

She sniffed. That was definitely *not* the delicious smell of warm, flaky croissants. Nor was it the irresistible scent of bacon snapping and sizzling on the grill. It was the much less appetizing reek of musty air. And what was that roaring noise? Not the light classical music Mom usually listened to when she cooked.

Jannie shoved back the covers and sat up. All of her furniture was jammed against her bed, forming an island in the middle of the room. There were no puddles on the hardwood floor, but the baseboards showed high-tide stains. Thank God for the industrial fans Ernie had brought up. They were blasting away, drying up the last of the moisture. Hopefully there wouldn't be any permanent damage.

As bad as the situation was up here on the fifth floor, things were bound to be worse for the poor guy who lived in the condo directly below. Tyler Howard: good, quiet neighbor and cutie-muffin to boot, in a nerdish kind of way. Jannie had swamped his place, what with the sudsy bathwater cascading through his ceiling and wrecking everything, including his zillion-dollar collection of stamps. Or at least one or two valuable specimens, according to the TV reports.

Jannie sighed. It was no use pretending she didn't care. She felt horrible about what she'd done. Guilty and careless and immature. But, how insane was it that anyone would pay so much for tiny scraps of ancient, sticky paper in the first place?

It was all very confusing. If only she could talk things out with her mom; but no, she had to be strong. Be an adult, not a total jerk. And, as a first step, that meant apologizing.

She got up, dressed, and, with a straight spine and determined chin, marched down a flight of stairs to confront young Tyler in his lair. She rapped smartly on the door to 4B and waited.

After a moment, she knocked again. "I know you're home. I can hear you moving around. Please open up."

"Who's there?" The disembodied voice sounded hollow, emotionless. Like its owner was a card-carrying member of *The Walking Dead*, zombified to dustiness in spite of all the recent in-home precipitation.

"It's me, Jannie Morris. From upstairs. You know— your elevator buddy. Oh, and the cause of the awful flood. I've come to say sorry."

No response. All sounds ceased. The apartment had gone as quiet as a tomb.

"Hey, Tyler," she said in a wheedling voice she hoped was equal parts adorable and persuasive. "Please open your door."

"Don't want to see you," he said. "Go away."

"Please? I feel terrible about what happened last night."

Again, silence.

"Tyler?" Jannie stuck out her tongue at the door. "C'mon, Tyler!" She looked at her iPhone. Great, now she was going to be late for work.

Taking off a shoe and balancing on the other foot like a flamingo that's decided the water's too cold, she knocked on Tyler's door with her high heel. Rat-a-tat-a-tat-a-tat. The noise was obnoxious.

The door flew open, and Tyler appeared. He was close to Jannie's age. Short, slight, and brown-skinned. He wore huge black-rimmed glasses and was packed nicely into his geeky blue t-shirt and tattered jeans. Also, he appeared to be hopping mad. Not just figuratively, either—he jumped from foot to foot in a fury of epic proportions. Jannie kept a firm grip on her stiletto in case she had to use it.

"Who the hell do you think you are?" Tyler yelled, still bouncing.

Before she could respond, his hand flashed out. He seized her shoe, wresting it away from her with a strength that belied his small stature. Instinctively, she reached down and grabbed her other one. He brandished his captured shoe at Jannie. She shook hers at him. They were Jedi warriors, with designer footwear instead of lightsabers.

"Give me back my Miu Miu!" She glowered at him.

"Your *what*? Are you making fun of my cats?" He brandished Jannie's precious pump in her face. Behind him, three felines made a dignified entrance, tails wafting sinuously, ignoring the two crazy humans locked in mortal shoe combat in the doorway.

"I'm not meowing, idiot. It's a Miu Miu. Designer shoe. Bought in Paris. Put it down."

"You put yours down first."

"No. Let's put them down together. Count of three. One, two, three."

She matched Tyler's movement as he lowered his Miu Miu to the floor. With the tender love of a mother for a newborn, Jannie arranged the pair of them just inside the door and, barefooted, entered Tyler's condo. He didn't protest. He also didn't utter a word of welcome. He stalked out of the reception space and into his living room, where he plunked himself down on a cat-fur-covered couch.

Jannie walked around, looking at the ceiling and the walls. Most of Tyler's IKEA-style furniture had been pushed into the center of the room. The water damage was impossible to miss, and although there were electric fans blasting away, she knew he was in for some expensive repair work.

She chose a dry-looking armchair and sat, facing him. "I'm very sorry, Tyler. I really don't have words for this situation. I know I've messed up big time."

He said nothing. His eyes darted around the room, taking in the damage, looking everywhere but at her.

"Your stamp collection—"

"Who cares about an old stamp collection?" Tyler's eyes continued to flick, this way and that.

That was a surprise. How could he not care about the collection?

"Will it be okay?"

"I guess so. I didn't see any water in the stamp cabinets. An expert's coming over later to take a look, just to be sure. Mom's orders." He rolled his eyes.

"I don't get it. You know I'm really, really sorry about the flood. I'll do whatever I can to set things right." Jannie crossed her heart. "But tell me, why don't you care about the stamps?"

"Not my thing. Stamps, I mean. Just inherited baggage. Never liked'em, myself."

Jannie felt a sense of immense relief, as if she'd just stripped off her Spanx at the end of a long day. At least now she knew she hadn't destroyed a cherished possession.

But his face was crumpled, like he was trying not to cry.

"Tyler, tell me. What else got wrecked?"

He slumped on his furry couch, surrounded by his feline friends. His hands moved in a nervous rhythm as he stroked a large, white angora.

Finally, he whispered something.

Jannie leaned forward, cupping her hand to her ear. "Excuse me?"

"Posters," he said, in an almost inaudible mutter. His face turned maroon.

"Art prints?"

"Wrestling posters. WWE. Dragon Gate. Lucha Libre." He looked away, the ruddy tint in his cheeks deepening.

Really? Pro wrestling?

But who was she to judge? He'd owned something that he'd evidently prized, and she'd gone and wrecked it. She hung her head.

Finally, she said in a low voice, "Are they replaceable? Can I help you get new ones?" She'd do whatever she could to fix this, as long as these posters were available somewhere on Planet Earth.

"Dunno. Maybe." His words were almost drowned out by the constant roaring of the fans.

"I'll do my best. Whatever it takes." She rose to attention and brought her right hand smartly to her forehead.

"Really?" Tyler stood in front of her, a trifle too close for comfort.

Jannie felt crowded, but held her ground. "Of course! And I'll never leave the taps on again. I swear."

She reached a hand out to him to seal the deal with a shake, but he backed off. His eyes darted away again, almost as if it pained him to look at her.

"Why don't you make me a list of everything I ruined?" Jannie said. "I promise I won't let you down. Besides, you know where I live."

"Ha ha." There was no mirth in his voice at all. He gestured her toward the door.

Jannie put on her shoes, grimacing at how dirty the bottoms of her feet were, and left. She hoped he'd be okay. But he'd looked shattered—and it was all her fault.

3

PLEASURE AND BUSINESS

*A*fter fainting in the elevator, Suze didn't bounce back to full consciousness immediately. She hovered below reality's surface, wafting on pleasant waves of lassitude. She was safe and reclining on a piece of furniture that was exquisitely comfortable. Her nostrils quivered as she inhaled the agreeable muskiness of fine leather.

"Ooh, the salesman didn't lie. This really *is* the best bed ever." She stroked the hide possessively, like a cheetah with a newly acquired gazelle.

Aram cleared his throat. Suze's eyelids flickered but didn't open. She was deep in an excellent fantasy brought on by her fainting spell, and she smiled as she savored the scent of manliness and money.

"Rich Corinthian leather." And again. "Rich Corinthian leather," rolling her r's and chuckling at her horrible Montalbán imitation. She patted the well-bolstered couch. "Mm. You're a lovely bed, you are."

"I'm glad you approve of my sofa," Aram said.

"Heavens!" Suze's eyes fluttered open. Her hand flew to her gaping mouth.

She tried to sit up straight but moved too suddenly, almost catapulting herself off the couch. Another surge of wooziness hit her and she boomeranged backward onto an overstuffed cushion. With efficient athleticism, Aram shot from his matching leather chair and caught her head before it made contact with the wall.

He maneuvered her into a safer position, keeping his hands on her shoulders. Even though his touch was chaste and solicitous, her face grew toasty warm. Deep down, she began to feel a sparking of an unfamiliar sensation—something inside that had lain dormant for years.

How inappropriate. Cheeks still flaming, she tried to regain her composure.

"Please tell me I haven't been too ridiculous. Was I babbling?" She searched his face for clues.

"Babbling? I wouldn't describe it quite that way. Waxing eloquent on the merits of my sofa is more like it. You seem to admire, let's see, its *'buttery texture and cushiness,'* if I've quoted you correctly." The words sounded so silly in Aram's baritone, with its tantalizing hint of an accent.

Suze closed her eyes for a moment. Gracious, how absurd she'd been, and how dizzy she still felt.

"Could I trouble you for a glass of water?" Even though she wasn't particularly thirsty, she wanted a moment of privacy to collect her thoughts. And to suppress the twinges of her awakened libido, if that's what these strange feelings were. She was tingly and light-headed and supersensitive. Euphoric, too, for some reason.

"Yes, of course." Aram walked across a worn but beautiful Persian rug, past an exuberant Riopelle (was it actually an original?) hanging on the opposite wall, and disappeared through a doorway into another room. Suze took the opportunity of finger-combing her hair to remove any traces of bed-headedness caused by her encounter with the couch, and then grabbed a magazine (*Fortune*) from a stark but expensive-looking wooden coffee table to fan her hot skin.

It was as if Aram knew Suze needed a few minutes to compose herself. He was gone longer than it normally would take for such a simple task. By the time he returned, bearing a single glass of water with a lemon slice affixed to the rim, she felt almost back to her usual collected self.

"Thanks. And sorry for fainting. And for babbling. And, for, you know—well, making you carry me, Mr. Krikorian."

"Aram, please."

"Yes, Aram, of course. But as I was saying, I'm sorry for making you pick me up—oh, dear, I mean carry me here—before I hit the elevator floor. I know I'm not a lightweight."

That was only somewhat true. Last time she'd weighed herself she'd clocked in at 122 pounds, but she must have felt much heavier in her dead-weighted state. And, she was sincerely sorry to have created a scene that had forced him to get physical.

On the other hand, it had all been rather thrilling. A less athletic man might have fumbled and bounced her head like a dribbled basketball off the elevator floor, or dragged her body down the hall by her feet. With Aram, even through the haze of her fainting spell, Suze had felt sinewy muscles buoying her, steely and secure. She hadn't been held like that for years. In retrospect, she only wished she'd been fully conscious so she could have appreciated it.

"Me, Jane," she whispered, before taking a sip of water.

"I beg your pardon?"

"Um, Jannie. We need to talk about my daughter Jannie, remember?"

"Oh, yes, her unfortunate fire, followed by her even more disastrous flood."

"Fire? What fire? Heavens, don't tell me. Not the microwave?"

Aram's face was deadpan but his eyes danced. "Yes, she told me she had difficulty popping a bag of Orville Redenbacher's finest. Instead of Extra Buttery, she got Extra, Extra Burnt."

"My fault. I should have shown her all the functions before I moved out."

"With all due respect, Suze—may I call you Suze?" Aram said, and waited for her nod, "A child can figure out how to make popcorn. It wasn't your fault."

"She's helpless in the kitchen. That much at least *is* my fault. I've done way too much for her over the years."

"Perhaps. But she's all grown up now. Seems intelligent enough, too. She'll catch on. At least, I hope she does, before she causes any more damage to this building. I have my property value to consider."

Judging by Aram's crinkly eyes, he was joking. He really was a handsome man, and she did like his thick beard. But it was hard to gauge his expression, with the facial hair partially obscuring his lips. The lower one was full and sensuous, but she could barely see the upper one through the moustache. It would be nice to know if his mouth was perfectly shaped, like his aquiline nose and his streamlined ears. And his well-spaced eyes.

Suze shook her head. She had to pull herself together. This business about Jannie was serious.

"Was there major damage from the fire?" she asked.

"No. I smelled smoke, and was at Jannie's apartment

within seconds. The fire was confined to the microwave. I had no problem putting it out."

"I'm so glad you were there. Jannie was lucky. But, then, how on earth did the flood happen?"

"Jannie's bubble bath overflowed while she was busy firefighting. Could have happened to anyone. Shame, though. Poor Tyler downstairs has some major damage to his place."

Suze gulped. "Just how bad is it?"

"Nothing that can't be replaced. Don't worry. I checked with him personally. He's a business associate of sorts and a family friend. The stamp collection was mostly offsite at a secure facility."

"Oh, thank God."

"Why not ask Jannie herself about all of this?"

"I can't. She hasn't confided in me. As you said, she's a grown woman. I really shouldn't pry."

"Well, rest assured, I won't mention you dropped by. In fact, I won't even hint that I've had the pleasure of meeting you."

"Thanks. I owe you. I really do, for saving Jannie from an even worse fate. And for rescuing me, when I collapsed in the elevator."

Aram was silent for a moment. Suze read concern and inner conflict in his eyes. What had she said to cause this?

The next moment, it became clear, in a gratifying kind of way.

"Suze, you're welcome. And I'd like to have your permission to call you if you'll be good enough to share your contact info with me. I'd love to get to know you better, maybe over coffee, if that's okay with you?" He spoke with an old-fashioned courtliness, seeming to choose his words with care. His accent was more discernible.

Suze found herself short of breath. This polite, capable, handsome, *younger* man wanted to get to know her better? Somehow she managed a nod.

"Of course, I'll keep our communication entirely secret," he continued. "But I'll also keep an eye on Jannie for you, just in case anything else goes awry. I won't be intrusive. She'll never know you were here today—at least, *I* won't be the one to tell her."

Suze rose and offered her hand to Aram. He clasped it, and she felt her pulse flutter wildly. It continued to accelerate until she collected herself, withdrawing her hand. Without glancing at Aram again, she walked rapidly away from him and out the open door, hoping she appeared poised but fearing exactly the opposite was true.

As she sped homeward on the subway, she was finally able to draw a deep breath. Jannie would be fine. Aram would be there as a benevolent neighbor, overseeing her safety. Suze could relax, for now.

Strangely, though, she felt the opposite of relaxed. Her nerve endings twanged like strings brushed by a harpist's hand. This sensation was not the result of moving to a new home, or her recent fainting spell, or the pickle Jannie had gotten herself into.

No, it was related to Aram. There was something about him. Just what, Suze wasn't sure, but she looked forward to finding out.

Fire, flood. Next, it'd be locusts. Maybe a plague, too.

Whatever the case, Jannie had to stop feeling sorry for herself, and even sorrier for poor Tyler, and get her butt to the office. There were posters to replace and those Miu Mius to pay for.

As she zipped out of the underground parking in her newish red Mini, she reviewed her priorities. First, get a detailed roster of desired artwork from Tyler. Then, start working on replenishing his collection, without delay. She owed him and she was going to make things right.

At the corner, the amber light changed to red and she slammed on the brakes. As she waited for the signal to change to green, she drummed her fingers on the leather-wrapped steering wheel and tried to slow her too-rapid breathing.

What was it her therapist always said? *"Handle one thing at a time, Jannie. Just one thing at a time."*

But it was so easy to get distracted. Adele was wailing away on the iPhone, amplified by spiffy new car speakers, and the music was beguiling in its insistent achiness. To forget her troubles, Jannie started to sing along, checking first that her windows were tightly closed. Mom was the only person who'd ever appreciated her singing—who'd never criticized Jannie for not knowing the proper lyrics or, even worse, being almost tone deaf.

God, she loved her. Mom was her rock. Jannie blinked hard, trying to keep the tears back.

A car horn blared, and Jannie jumped. She shrugged a wry apology at the old lady driving a beat-up Mazda, turned Adele off, and drove onward, eyes focused resolutely on the road ahead. Within fifteen minutes, she arrived at work, locked the car and took the elevator up—way, way up—to Blasters, Budgie & Masterman, or BB&M as it was normally called in Jannie's crazy world of broadcast and digital ad sales.

Jannie had no idea how—with a mishmash of a useless Arts degree—she'd gotten this lucky in her career, but at BB&M she'd somehow found the ideal outlet for her unorthodox thinking and her bulldog tenacity. She loved it here.

And to think the Guidance Counselors and so-called experts had once claimed she'd be lucky to get any kind of job at all. All those labels they'd tried to stick on her— ADHD or whatever the disability-of-the-day happened to be. In the end, none of them had stuck. Her mom had been a dragon, refusing to let Jannie get pigeonholed and underestimated.

"Good morning, Bethany," she called out in a cheery voice as she entered the all glass and flash reception area.

The girl behind the crescent moon-shaped desk looked up with a sullen expression on her face. Her futuristic Dutch boy haircut swung in a shiny black arc. "It's Bonnie. Remember? I introduced myself to you last week. Bethany left a month ago."

"Sorry, Bonnie." *Quick, think. What would Mom tell me to do?* She tried a brighter smile. "Maybe it's because the two of you look so much alike."

"Sure. She's platinum blond. I'm brunette. We could be twins."

Jannie pondered for a second why Bonnie's tone had turned ever more sour. She straightened her shoulders. "Well, *Bonnie*, I'll try to remember next time. Oh, and I've got a nine o'clock conference call with Total Movers. I would die and go to heaven if you'd fetch me a latte."

Jannie didn't look back but continued walking to her workstation. She only had twenty minutes to prepare for her call, and she had to refresh her grasp of the TM numbers.

Compared to the glitzy reception area, the sales floor was fairly basic: modern and open-concept with no dividers at all. The morning buzz made it almost impossible to concentrate, but the noise-canceling earphones she sometimes used tended to flatten her hair. Jannie wished she had one of the prized private offices, but she hadn't reached that lofty a level. Yet.

At the next desk, Joelle gushed about her weekend. She'd gotten engaged Saturday night, apparently, and there was a gaggle of young women clustered around her, admiring her diamond. Jannie gave it a glance and offered up a quick "congrats." Joelle was the closest thing she had to a friend at work, and normally she would have tried to join in the chorus of *oohs* and *aahs*. But it was almost time for the conference call, and she didn't have a moment to spare.

Still, she registered it was a sweet-looking ring. Small diamond, but chosen with love. Jannie felt a flash of despair. It had been a long time since she'd met a nice guy. Her last boyfriend had broken her heart into tiny pieces when he dumped her a few years ago. Told her he'd had it with her bulldozing ways, and that if she didn't know by then what he was talking about, then good luck with the rest of her life. She still wasn't sure what he meant, and even though she called and texted him repeatedly, he never explained—just blocked her from ever being able to contact him again. She shook her head, trying to dispel the old, negative thoughts and self-doubt.

Not much had happened since then on the romance front. Until last night. That new neighbor had potential. Absolutely dreamy, and so what if he was a bit older? Older men were more considerate and worldly and knew how to treat women with respect. And Aram was *hot*.

She broke herself out of her daydream. The call to Total Movers was only minutes away.

"Take the party elsewhere, please!" she said to Joelle's ring-admiring entourage.

"Oh. Of course. Sorry we're disturbing you before

work hours even start," one of the bevy said. Nasty tone. Dirty looks from all as they moved away, stuck to Joelle like bugs on flypaper, toward the staff kitchen.

Jannie ignored their hostility, picked up her phone, and got down to business.

4

SHOPPING LISTS

*L*ooking for work wasn't what it used to be. The days of newspaper listings and job boards at employment centers were over. Suze sighed as she turned on her computer. Searching through internet engines was going to take some getting used to.

She'd never had a spectacular career, mostly because she'd never really wanted one. In her younger years, she worked in administrative services, supporting aspiring execs. She transferred many of those skills to motherhood, and happily gave up her job in order to raise Jannie and make a home for her. A stable one. Suze was vigilant about that, determined Jannie's upbringing be as unaffected as possible by the vagaries of her dad.

Although early in the marriage Desmond seemed reliable and Suze never doubted his love for her and Jannie, he failed them over and over. The gambling. The drinking. The endless cycle of broken promises. And finally, dying before he could engineer his usual miraculous financial turnaround.

No wonder Suze bestowed so much love on her

daughter; she needed to protect her only child. And when a young Jannie was identified as a special needs student, Suze transformed into a fierce tiger mom. Singlehandedly, while Des battled his own demons, Suze fought the system —refusing to let Jannie be conveniently labeled or inappropriately drugged or streamed into non-college-bound subjects—and with this unstinting and unwavering support, Jannie had beaten the odds. She was a grateful, loving daughter, too, purchasing a condo and insisting her mom move in with her when Suze had run through almost all of the proceeds from the sale of the family house.

The hard years were over. Somehow, Jannie had scraped through academically and was more than succeeding in business. Suze was ready to begin her own, independent life. She had a few thousand dollars in the bank. First and last months' rent were covered. Now she had to land some work, and sooner rather than later.

She sat in front of her computer screen and scanned some placement ads—database administrators, computer systems analysts, financial experts. She couldn't relate to anything she saw. She had no qualifications, and she didn't have the faintest idea where to start.

Maybe she should unpack a few boxes and look for a job tomorrow. Plus, there were those dirty breakfast plates to take care of. She left her desk and walked the few feet across her tiny studio to the sink. After she'd washed and put away the dishes, she glanced at her watch—late morning. Maybe she'd call to see how her daughter was faring. Perhaps Jannie would tell her about what had happened at the condo last night.

"Hello. Jannie?"

"Oh. Hi, Mom." Jannie sounded preoccupied.

Suze heard a vague jumble of office noises in the background. "Am I catching you at a bad time?"

"A bit. I'm working on a new business pitch. I don't have time to chat."

"Understood. Everything okay?"

Silence for a moment.

"Everything's fine. I think you were right. It's time I become more independent. I don't want you to worry about me." Jannie's voice sounded falsely bright.

"You sure?"

"Yes, Mom. I'm sure. Now, I really must fly. Talk tonight, okay? Love you."

"Love you, too." Suze ended the call.

Interesting. Jannie was withholding information about last night's disaster. Was she trying to protect Suze or deliberately cutting her out of her life? And why did Suze feel sad—didn't she want Jannie to assert her independence?

She mulled this over as she opened up a cardboard box labeled *Summer Clothes* and started hanging some things up and placing other items onto the built-in shelves of her small closet. After she'd emptied all her boxes, she stood back and took stock. Bits of raggedy this, lots of faded that. How could she possibly go to interviews? Suze flipped through the hangers, shaking her head. No one was going to hire her if she showed up wearing any of this stuff.

Only one solution: she needed to go shopping. She wouldn't buy too many pieces—maybe a skirt, a pair of black pants, a few shirts. Definitely a versatile jacket, or two. If she had several interviews for a job, she couldn't very well show up every time wearing the same thing.

There was no time like the present to get moving. She scribbled a list, grabbed her purse, and walked to the subway station.

Ah, downtown Toronto! The glittering boutiques, the tall, shadow-casting buildings, the hustle-bustle of office workers surging by, dressed in the latest acceptable fashions for the workplace. Suze—her head whipping back and forth—tried to take note of what the women were wearing as she walked toward the intersection of Queen and Yonge. They all looked so well put together but she couldn't figure out what made their outfits work. She would need help from an expert.

The multi-storied department store resembled an impregnable citadel, restricted to those who at least had a clue about fashion. Suze paced on the sidewalk for a few minutes, gathering courage, before placing her hand on the ornate brass door handle and entering.

Inside, after consulting the directory, she took the escalator to Women's Fashions. New fall arrivals were everywhere. The displays swirled with rich pumpkins, deep clarets and royal purples. Black was resplendent—aisles and aisles of black in a bewildering assortment of garment options. And what a wealth of textures: woolly and nubbly and velvety fabrics that begged to be stroked and savored. All so luxe. And so very confusing.

"May I help you, Miss?"

Suze continued to flip through a rack of discounted shirts.

"Miss?"

The single word question was repeated twice more. At long last, Suze realized it was being addressed to her. Funny, she hadn't been called *miss* by salespeople for at least a couple of decades. Her hair, which had begun its evolution to silver in her early thirties, had put her squarely in the *ma'am* category too many years ago to count.

She looked up into the guileless brown eyes of a saleswoman. The pretty young clerk was dressed in black pants, a button-down shirt, and a well-cut gray jacket bearing a tag that read, *Madeleine*—much like how Suze wanted to look for her interviews, minus the name badge. Not flashy, but crisp and businesslike.

"How rude of me," Suze said. "Yes, I desperately need your help. And my name is Suze, by the way. Here's the thing. I'm job hunting. Can you, by any chance, clone me into a replica of you?"

The saleswoman laughed. "Well, not exactly, and you're way too gorgeous to be me, Suze, but we can certainly put together a good business wardrobe. Let's get started."

"I have a list." Suze held it out like she was offering up a burnt sacrifice to the fashion gods.

"Excellent. Quite a few items here, I see. Are you about a size six? Hmmm, you're tall and slim. Maybe a four. Do you have a budget?"

"Yes. I have to put together an entire wardrobe for five hundred dollars or less."

Madeleine, who had started walking toward the new fall arrivals, stopped in her tracks. She took a sharp right toward the sale racks.

"I'm going to look for things that can take you from summer right through winter. This may require a bit of digging. Why don't you take it easy and rest in a dressing room? I'll bring selections to you."

"You're an angel."

Suze followed Madeleine's pointing finger and sank onto a bench to wait. She'd been dazzled by the array of colors and styles. The prospect of spending money when she was just a few notches above broke was beginning to overwhelm her. She tried to quiet her pounding heart by taking deep, controlled breaths. There was no way she'd allow herself to faint for a second time that day.

Someone rapped on the changing room door. Suze rose, grateful she hadn't swooned, and admitted a beaming Madeleine, who bore a hefty armload of clothes.

"Okay, I've brought options in a couple of sizes and I've found every item on your list."

"Where on earth do I start?" Suze asked, her voice shaky.

Madeline chuckled. "Don't be frightened! I'll hand you things, and you try them on. Promise, I'll give you my honest opinion as to what looks good on you."

"You really *are* an angel." Suze smiled in relief and reached out to receive some of the clothes. "I can't tell you how thankful I am for your help."

The next hour was a kaleidoscope of colors, shapes, and lengths. Madeleine's resolutely cheerful approach buoyed Suze's spirits, as she tried on one item after another. Before she knew it, she was standing at the register behind an impressive assortment of pieces stacked high on the counter, as Madeleine began cashing her out.

"You're taking the six in the pants, and the four in the white shirt, right?" Madeleine verified. Suze swallowed and nodded.

"And the two jackets, plus the skirts and the blue pullover that looked so incredible with your eyes?"

Again, Suze nodded.

"You're smart to take advantage of these sales prices. You're getting over sixty percent off on most of this stuff. I can't believe how well you've done. You aren't much above your original target." Madeleine gestured at the cash register display, which showed a figure of over seven hundred dollars.

Suze closed her eyes. She fought off a wave of anxiety, and refocused on Madeleine's open countenance. This girl would never steer her wrong.

"Maybe I should pass on the second jacket?" Suze asked.

Madeleine put a hand over her heart. "You mean the Anne Klein? The one that goes so well with both the skirt and the pants? It's an investment piece! And a steal! You'll kick yourself later if you don't snatch it up."

"What about one of the skirts? Maybe the burgundy one?

"You'll never find another BCBG skirt at that cost. I swear. Never in a million years." Madeleine crossed her arms over her chest and gave Suze a stern look. "Trust me, Suze, you're investing in classic pieces that will never go out of style."

"Well, okay, then." Suze eased her store credit card from her wallet. It felt brittle and cold in her trembling hand. "If you're sure."

"Of course I am." Madeleine's voice was once again bright and encouraging. She rang up the purchases and handed Suze back the card, then hoisted a very full pair of brightly logoed shopping bags over the counter.

"You'll knock 'em dead at the office. But . . ." Madeleine broke off, giving Suze an assessing look.

"But what?"

"Suze, I feel we've gotten to know each other well this afternoon. So I'm just going to say it right out loud. I think your new wardrobe needs support. You know, the kind of boost that comes from quality undergarments." She leaned forward and continued in a low tone. "You don't want to droop in those new tops." Madeleine's voice rose to its usual level as she continued, "Oh, and at least one pair of heels. And a purse."

"No, no. I have a handbag. See?" Suze transferred the shopping bags into one hand so that she could dangle her purse in front of Madeleine's eyes.

"Well, at the risk of sounding harsh, it's seen better days. And that was likely long, long ago in a distant galaxy. Listen, lingerie is on the fifth floor, and shoes and handbags are on the main level. You need to dress to impress. Remember fashion's mantra: accessorize, accessorize, accessorize."

When Suze eventually left the department store, she carried four shopping bags, jammed to the brim with her new office wardrobe. Her hands were indented almost to cuts by the string handles. If only she could afford a cab to take her the short distance home.

But she'd just spent more than double her budget on sales items and lingerie. All stuff that couldn't be returned.

She still had enough money in her bank account to pay next month's rent, and she could afford groceries for the next few weeks. Barely. After that, if she didn't have an income, things would get ugly.

No worries. Tomorrow she'd start her job search. Everything was going to turn out just fine. She'd be hired for sure now that she'd be dressed for success.

And when she saw Aram again she'd look fantastic. Not that this would be a reason for overspending, of course. And besides, she hadn't overspent. Like Madeleine had said, her new wardrobe was an investment.

It was going to pay off. Soon. It had to.

"It's a deal! Can't thank you enough. BB&M truly appreciates your business." Jannie hung up, leapt from her chair and pumped both fists in the air. They didn't give her the salesperson of the year award for nothing.

Her stomach rumbled and she glanced at the time. Late lunch, again. She walked past Bonnie, or was it

Bethany, on the way out and gave her a friendly wave. What's-her-name bit into her tuna salad sandwich, twitched a shoulder and made some kind of grimace. What did that expression mean, anyway? Jannie wondered if she should feel offended.

And, yikes, the reception area reeked of seafood. It was so unprofessional. Disgusting. Jannie made a mental note to issue an all-staff email later with a list of foods that should be declared off-limits. Blasters, Budgie & Masterman was a place of business, not a fish market. She internally debated saying something, but she didn't want to come across as insensitive. Instead, she pulled a My Burberry atomizer out of her purse and gave the air a hearty spritz.

Another solitary lunch hour loomed. It seemed to happen a lot these days, people drifting off for lunch before Jannie could invite herself along. She would have loved to share her success stories with the gang. They could have learned something from her approach, and she'd have enjoyed celebrating her wins.

She grabbed her phone to call Mom. Maybe the two of them could meet up for a quick lunch, and Mom could give one of her comforting pep talks. Jannie caught herself just as she was about to connect. Slowly, she put the phone back in her bag. Trying to be independent was hard. Lonely, too.

It was no use standing around feeling sorry for herself. She'd take a healthy walk to the store and stop at the deli on the way back to pick up a non-odorous snack. Tyler had sent her his list of the posters she'd destroyed when she'd Niagara Falls-ed his condo. There was no time like right now to start her mission to replace them.

Jannie walked quickly along the sidewalk, shivering as the first hints of autumn goose-bumped her bare arms.

When she entered the poster store, she paused, feeling like she'd just landed on an alien planet. Artwork, illuminated by cheap fluorescent tubing, hung from multi-level racks as far as her eyes could see. The air smelled strangely of dust and Cheetos.

There appeared to be only one other customer: a bespectacled, older gent who was flipping through posters, a reverent look on his face. Curious, she walked closer and peeked over his shoulder. He was staring at a photo of a swimsuit model young enough to be his granddaughter. Jannie moved away, but not before giving him a sharp "tsk!" that made him jump and scurry off, rat-style, down another aisle.

There didn't seem to be any salesperson to confer with, so she wandered randomly until she stumbled upon the sports section. She pulled out a printout of Tyler's emailed list, broken down by country and organization. The more exotic Japanese posters might not be available here, but she'd be surprised if they didn't have some of the American ones.

First on Tyler's list: an image of Hulk Hogan in 1989, wearing a white shirt and stomping across the ring. She flipped through the racks. No, there didn't seem to be anything quite that ancient here. But she really didn't have the faintest idea where to begin to look. She wasn't the kind of girl who knew one wrestling superstar poster from another. She needed guidance.

Jannie strode to the sales desk and found a *for assistance, please ring* tarnished silver bell. From her purse she pulled a tissue, which she wrapped around her well-manicured fingers, and gave the ringer a few sharp taps. The shrill dinging echoed throughout the store, but no one came. After a pause, she persevered. Lunch hour didn't last forever. She'd pound on that bell as long as it took.

"What's your problem?" a cranky voice demanded.

Miraculously, help had arrived in the form of a skinny, whiter-than-white man-boy of about twenty-five. He wore a t-shirt with more holes than fabric, jeans halfway down his butt, displaying Pokémon boxers, and high-top running shoes. They looked expensive. He looked pissed off.

"I was just following the directions on the sign. It says to ring for help."

"Yeah, right. So you thought your annoyingly persistent Hunchback of Notre Dame bell performance would get my attention." It wasn't a question. And it was pretty damn rude.

"Listen, I'm in sales, too." Jannie looked at his name tag and added, "Frodo."

"Oh, so you're just like me. Working for minimum wage in an environment that Health Canada would call toxic and not be wrong. Dealing with ignorant customers who don't know their ass from a poster of one."

"Okay, so not quite like you. But, please, I do need your help." She switched over to a beseeching tone and pulled at her curly hair—the damsel in distress appeal.

Frodo considered. Then he heaved a sigh.

"Well, I'm here now. What's your lame pleasure?" he said.

"Hulk Hogan. 1989. White shirt. Got one?"

"Oh, yes, miss, please walk right this way. I have at least ten of them neatly hung and framed over on that wall."

"Really?"

"No, *not* really, Miss Pro Saleswoman. We're not a vintage store. And we don't carry anything that valuable."

Jannie felt as if she'd been slapped. She took in shallow breaths, like she always did back in math class when she had no idea what the teacher was talking about.

"Do you have to be so sarcastic?" she asked in a small voice.

"No. I just like being that way. But I'll tell you what. Give me your business card—I know you must have a sterling silver case full of embossed ones on superfine stock, right? I'll do a search later through some of our sources and call you back. It's likely going to run you around three hundred bucks or so, though. Plus a private commission to yours truly for doing the spadework. Say fifty bucks on top? Any objection?"

It seemed steep but she'd promised Tyler. And this amount of stress wasn't healthy. Her forehead was beginning to sweat. Her confidence was leaking away, like air from a pinpricked balloon.

No matter what, though, she had to keep her word. And maybe Frodo, as feisty as he was, could help her.

Jannie nodded sharply and upshifted to business mode. "Frodo, today's your lucky day. I'm going to give you this list, and *you're* going to earn commissions of fifteen percent on each item you find for me. We'll deal strictly in cash, and you can pocket the profit. Sound good?"

Frodo dropped his belligerent attitude and stared at her with widened eyes. He studied the list, pursing his lips in a tuneless whistle.

"Twenty percent. Nonnegotiable. And five hundred cash, down." He lifted his chin.

"What?"

"Listen, you want me to do a job for you. And I'll do it. But I need seed money. Your wish list is long and looks like it's going to run you into the thousands. Work with me here."

Jannie gazed at him, her head tilted on one side. She hoped she wasn't being fleeced. But he had a point. In his place, she'd want a decent cut and some bucks up-front, too.

She held out her hand. "It's a deal. I'll be back tomorrow on my lunch break with the cash, and then we're on."

He looked at her hand as if it were covered in witchy warts. After a moment, he bumped it gingerly with his knuckles.

"Deal," he said and flashed a sudden, brilliant smile at her. Then, like a ghost in a haunted mansion, he backed into a murky aisle, and faded out of sight.

5

AN EVENING OF REGRET

*B*uyer's remorse. Suze had never before experienced its disturbing mixture of self-loathing and guilt. Her head ached, and her stomach twisted in despair.

She'd always been so practical. It had been her late husband, Desmond, who'd come home laden with expensive gifts, whenever he'd had a rare good night at the tables.

On one occasion he bought diamond earrings for Suze and a designer dress for ten-year-old Jannie. Jannie's eyes lit up with delight when she saw her new frock. Even though it was an inappropriately ostentatious gift for such a young child, Suze didn't have the heart to take it away, but she returned the earrings to Birks the next day. Desmond never asked where they'd disappeared to, and with the refunded cash she was able to pay the bills for the next few months, when Lady Luck once again deserted him.

Now, she looked at her new clothes, price tags still affixed, spread across her extended couch bed. She, Suze Foster, had lost control of her spending for the first time in her calm, collected life. Why, oh why, had she bought two jackets when one would have sufficed? And no employer would give a fig about the state of her underwear, but Suze had gone and splurged on new bras and panties. As if she'd ever have cause to display them.

Her thoughts turned for a moment to a certain tall, dark, bearded man. She gave her sore head a stern shake.

All right. So the lingerie bottoms couldn't be returned. She shifted the small stack of them to one side. And technically, nothing else could be, either. All the items had been on sale, even the smart, black purse.

Suze stroked it. Nice. Definitely not Corinthian leather like Aram's couch, though.

Ah, Aram. His kind, intelligent eyes, crinkled at the corners. His strong arms, flexed as he'd carried her into his condo. His—

Enough of that. It was time to get organized. She made a pile of one of the jackets, a skirt, and a couple of tops. With trembling hands, she also shifted both lacy bras and a wisp of a nightgown she hadn't been able to resist, in spite of its irrelevance to career-seeking. All of these were expendable.

Suze checked the time. Just before five. No point in waiting any longer. She grabbed her cell phone, looked up the store's number, and called.

"Good evening. Women's Fashions," a professional, female voice said. It sounded like Madeleine's.

"Yes, hello. Is that you, Madeleine?"

A pause.

"No, I'm afraid Madeleine has left for the day." The voice was now pitched lower, with a touch of a Scottish brogue.

"Oh, I could have sworn . . . well, never mind. The thing is, I visited the store this afternoon and Madeleine helped me select some wonderful items. Unfortunately, I overspent my budget, and I want to bring some of them back for a refund."

A brief silence. Then, "And were these items on sale, ma'am?" The Scottish cadence was more noticeable.

"Yes."

"Well, then, as we used to say in Scotland, mony a mickle maks a muckle!" By now, the Scottish accent had grown to outrageous proportions.

"What does that even mean?" Suze demanded. "You're not making sense!"

"Now, ma'am, haud yer wheesht!"

"Listen, we're getting nowhere. Let me speak with your manager, please."

There was no response, but the phone line didn't go dead. Instead Suze was forced to listen to about sixty seconds of Paul Anka singing Nirvana, followed by a raucous ad for the store's summer clearance sale. Both were unbearably grating. Her patience was deteriorating.

Finally, "'Allo? 'oo ees thees, *s'il vous plaît?*"

This new, over-the-top French-accented voice also sounded like Madeleine's. Suze frowned, wondering if she was being paranoid. Maybe, maybe not. She gave the woman the benefit of the doubt and in a few tight but polite sentences, restated her case.

"Eet ees zo, 'ow you say, *malheureux.*" Was there a suspicion of a giggle in the voice?

"Yes, very unfortunate, and I do understand the store's policy. I also realize that Madeleine didn't force me to buy anything. But—I feel I was pushed a bit."

Downright frostiness now filled Suze's ear.

"Ah, no, Madame, I'm sure zat Madeleine would nevair, evair pooosh." Suddenly, the zany French accent disappeared as the woman continued in a no-nonsense voice, "In any case, I'm afraid that sale items are all final, no-return transactions. Is your bill marked that way?"

Suze looked at the receipts. All of them were stamped in bold lettering: "Final Sale/No Returns."

"Yes, I was just hoping—"

"Ah, Madame, one 'oo 'opes is one 'oo mopes. Old French saying. Also, one 'oo buys zee garment on sale, must nevair, evair wail. And—"

"I get your point. And Madeleine—yes, I know it's you on the other end—I'll drop my request. But you've let me down. You took advantage of me. And I'll nevair, evair return to your store."

Suze clicked the off button on her phone. She looked at the neat stacks of clothes. Then, with the enthusiasm of a condemned man walking the green mile, she fetched a pair of scissors and began cutting off the tags.

"Good evening, Miss Jannie."

"Hi. You're working late."

Ernie was so diligent—on the job at all hours, with an unfailingly pleasant manner. After a hard day of working alongside hostile lazybones, it was refreshing to see him, at his post with a friendly smile on his face.

"And you're holding a leaking bag. Allow me."

He must have been such a gifted boy scout: he was always prepared. From under his reception desk, he whipped out a plastic sack and engulfed Jannie's soggy Cantonese takeout.

"Thanks. I promise not to create a disturbance tonight. No fires or floods, anyway. Speaking of, have you seen Tyler this evening? I need to talk to him."

"Yes, but you may want to take your food straight to

your own kitchen first." He hefted the reinforced bag of food and handed it back to Jannie.

"Good idea, Ernie. If I sprinkled oil all over Tyler's priceless stamps or beloved posters, I'd send him right over the edge."

Jannie laughed. Ernie didn't. His smile seemed strained. As she took the elevator upstairs, she pondered his reaction. If only Mom were here to explain.

Jannie placed the bag on her counter, but not without taking a good, long inhalation first—deep-fried yumminess. She began to drool but walked resolutely out of her condo and rode the elevator down one floor.

"Rat-a-tat-tat, Tyler. You in?"

No response.

"Ernie told me you're there, so open up, already."

The door cracked open. Baleful dark eyes behind oversized black frames stared out past her. Tyler's rather sweet, brown face was expressionless. "Wassup."

"I'm here to report on my progress. You know, our poster quest."

He swung the door wide. "Enter."

Jannie looked around. Not much had changed. Total dehumidification was still at least a few days away.

"Sit, if you like." Tyler swept a fluffy, white cat into his arms and plunked himself onto the couch, staring straight ahead. Jannie scooped up a puffy tortoiseshell kitty and sat beside him, angling her body so she could see his profile.

He puzzled her. She'd befriended other guys on the spectrum, especially back in Special Ed hell, but Tyler seemed so remote. Obviously, he was more into wrestling than girls, but she was kind of pretty, with her curly hair and chocolatey eyes and curvaceousness. Normally her efforts at flirtation got some kind of reaction. But Tyler continued to look away, patting his cat in a repetitive motion.

"Do you know that Mad Blankey came into existence in 2012 when Tozawa renamed the Blood Warriors?" he asked.

Say what?

This had to be wrestling-related. Not her area of interest in the least, but Mom had coached her endlessly in social skills, and her sales managers had taught her how to fake empathy when she needed to.

"No, Tyler, I didn't know that. Is Mad Blankey a favorite of yours?"

He nodded vigorously, looking at the water-damaged ceiling.

"Tell me about it." Jannie's stomach growled but she sat still, trying to catch his eye and hold it. She sensed Tyler wanted to share his passion with her. Hungry as she was, she didn't have the heart to tell him she could care less about wrestling. Plus, she owed him. And he *was* rather endearing in his geeky, awkward way.

He drew a breath and launched. "Mad Blankey isn't an it. It was a them—a unit. I was a real fan of theirs. Couldn't stand it when they disbanded after losing to Jimmyz in a five-on-five elimination match."

And he was off, into conversational realms absolutely foreign to Jannie. As he talked, he stroked his Persian buddy almost to complete flatness. Jannie sat still and listened, looking at his angled face, happy to see the hint of a smile that lifted the corner of his mouth.

To a point, she was fascinated. He was a true wrestling fanatic and the only person she'd ever met who followed the Japanese circuit. But she was also starving, and that greasy Chinese food was going to taste a lot better hot.

At a pause in his monologue, she interjected, "Wow,

Tyler, you know tons about wrestling. So you'll be happy to know I've started replacing your posters."

She gave him a quick rundown of her plan that involved Frodo's participation. Tyler nodded his understanding. Jannie removed Mr. Tortoiseshell from her lap and started for the door.

"Come back tomorrow?" Tyler said. "I know lots more stories about wrestling."

He looked hopeful, even though he gazed off into the distance as if Jannie didn't exist.

Something unfamiliar stirred, deep inside. A kind of kinship, a weird, sympathetic vibe. It had been a while since anyone had needed her. And Jannie's Mom-less condo was a very lonely place.

"Sure, Tyler. I'll be back," she said, as she closed the door, narrowly avoiding squashing a cat's stripy tail in it. "See you tomorrow."

"Remember to turn off your taps," he said, and Jannie heard him chuckle as he engaged the deadbolt.

That was so sweet. Solemn little Tyler had made a joke.

Jannie took the elevator up to her floor. Mmmm, she could smell that Chinese takeout as soon as the doors opened. Her mouth watered, and as she hurried along the corridor she almost started to slobber.

"Hello, Jannie."

Oh, lordy. It was Mr. Gorgeous, the new neighbor— her savior from fire and flood. He exited his condo and joined her in the hallway, as if he'd been watching for her to arrive.

"Good evening, Aram." She'd tried for a low, velvety tone but the result was more like a gargle.

She fidgeted with her keys. She didn't want to open the door and let him see the chaos inside or know for sure that the oily egg rolls and crab Rangoon perfuming the hallway air were hers.

"Is all well this evening?"

"Yes, thanks. Nothing to rescue me from, so far."

He was the most good-looking man she'd ever seen. Luxuriant locks. She bet that's how a Harlequin Romance would describe his hair. And under the full beard, maybe even a cleft chin. And most definitely, a sensuous lower lip. *Ooh la la.*

As she mused in an X-rated way about his mouth, Jannie remembered something from a book she'd read where the heroine had a habit of biting her lower lip. It drove men mad.

So she tried it. Nibble, nibble.

Aram just looked at her. His breathing didn't accelerate. His chest didn't heave.

She tried again. Nibble, nibble. The prolonged silence was beginning to be uncomfortable.

"Are you all right, Jannie?" Aram finally asked. He studied her.

Well, *that* hadn't gone so well. But she'd never tried to flirt with an older man before. Maybe they needed something more obvious.

She attempted to look coyly up at Aram through her eyelashes. This wasn't as easy as all those romance authors made it sound. She felt her forehead contract, her nose wrinkle and her upper lip pull away from her teeth in her effort to do the impossible.

"Jannie, are you having an allergic reaction? Shellfish, maybe? Isn't that crab I smell coming from your condo? Do you carry an EpiPen?"

She stamped her foot in frustration. It was supposed to look fierce and cute, but she could tell from Aram's face that he was way more startled than turned on.

"Sorry, Aram. No. No allergies. I just need to get home to whip up dinner. Beef bourguignon," she said inanely, trying to fake that she'd never be caught with faux-Chinese fare and that she actually knew how to cook. Which, now that she thought of it, Aram knew she didn't. The recent microwave fire would have been a big hint.

He nodded. He seemed to be struggling not to laugh. "That sounds delicious. Have a good, safe evening. Do take care of that lip."

Great. The most spectacularly good-looking man in the world thought she had a rampaging case of herpes simplex. Fifty shades of frustrated, she headed straight to her kitchen, opened her Kung Pao and chowed down.

Later that evening, Suze sat at her computer, polishing her resume. She needed to knock the socks off a prospective employer, but having not worked outside the home for over a quarter of a century (was she *really* that ancient?) she was finding it difficult to come up with compelling material. Based on what she'd typed so far, the socks on any future interviewers were likely to stay firmly attached to their feet.

It wasn't that she didn't have skills, and she'd always worked hard. Yes, much of her experience had been inside the home, but in her time she'd headed up parent-teacher liaison committees and volunteered at countless school fundraising events. She'd even been an unpaid support aide in a few classrooms over the years. She was good with people, and she was a master of organization. Plus, in her more distant past, she'd done secretarial work for some very demanding bosses.

Just before midnight, Suze gave her work a final read-through. She'd done the best she could and had been honest in her self-assessment. Yes, she was detail-oriented, dependable, and meticulously polite. Yes, she had experience working in administrative roles. And, yes, she could submit references upon request, providing that the bosses she'd had all those years ago were still alive.

Tomorrow was going to be a big day. She needed to get a good night's rest, because in the morning she'd start applying for jobs.

She was ready. Also, highly motivated. She had a new wardrobe to pay for.

Her phone started to play *Que sera sera*.

"Darling!"

"Hi, Mom. I know it's late."

"That's okay. Are you all right?"

"Yes. Fine. I ate too much Chinese food tonight, though. I miss your cooking so much! Oh, and you, of course, too."

"I miss you, too, sweetheart. How's life at the condo?"

There was a pause. Suze hoped Jannie would tell her about the disasters on the home front. She wanted to console and advise. Be an accomplished mom for a few minutes, not a desperate, fish-out-of-water career seeker.

"Everything's great. Made a big sale today."

"Congrats! I know you're a star at the office. And I'm glad things are fine."

"Yeah." Silence, apart from both women breathing into the phone.

"Sure you don't want to move back in with me, Mom?"

"I'm sure. I'm happy to have a daughter who actually wants me to, but, no, sweetie, we need to move on. Both of us. It's going to be hard at first, but we'll get through it, right?"

"Guess so." Sniff. "Yeah, you're right. I just miss you."

"Why don't we get together Saturday morning for a catch-up chat and coffee?"

"Sure. I love you tons, Mom."

"Love you, too, darling. Hang in there, okay? And see you Saturday."

Suze clicked her phone off. For a moment, she cradled it to her heart. Then, she attached it to its charger, turned off her computer, and got ready for bed. Not in the new lacy nightgown. The old granny one would do. It had been given to her years ago by a much younger Jannie. The fabric might be worn, the style may be American Gothic, but it still felt like a hug when she put it on.

6

OFFICE SNAKES AND LADDERS

*J*annie could barely breathe; the office air was so thick with tension. Joelle reached across the space separating their desks and patted her on the shoulder. In return, Jannie attempted a brave smile. Sisters in arms, they'd had to outwork and outshine others, namely men, to climb BB&M's corporate ladder. In spite of many advances for women, the place still oozed testosterone.

Apart from the coffee machine's occasional burble and Bethany-Bonnie's raspy nail filing, the place was dead silent. They'd heard the rumors. A re-org was imminent. Heads were gonna roll.

All of them needed their jobs, even annoying Bethany-Bonnie. And especially Joelle. She had an upcoming wedding to pay for, and she happened to be Jannie's only office confidante. Jannie crossed her fingers, making a wish that the two of them would survive the purge.

At nine thirty it started. A flurry of pings as every computer on the sea of desks registered an all-staff email. Jannie read it, her heartbeat galloping and her mouth suddenly dry. Yes, there was going to be a re-org. BB&M was counting on everyone to maintain a professional attitude during this turbulent time. Before noon today, staff members were to be called, one by one, to be informed of how these modifications would affect them personally.

Joelle cradled her sparkling diamond between finger and thumb as if it were a tiny, spiky baby. She twiddled it, a look of terror on her face.

Jannie thought frantically about her own finances. Those posters were going to take a huge chunk out of her emergency stash. She might last two months without a paycheck. After that, she'd be in big trouble.

Maybe a prayer would help. She closed her eyes and begged the Big Sky Guy to spare them. All of them. Even tuna-hoovering, emery board-wielding Bethany-Bonnie.

At last, an office door opened. An unfamiliar woman poked her head out. She wore a silk sari, and the deep pinks of the lustrous fabric set off her milky tea skin to perfection. Her dark eyes were wideset under a perfectly round, red bindi on her forehead, and her mouth was curved in a neutral smile.

Human Resources, for sure. She had that marshmallow-on-the-outside, granite-hard-on-the-inside look about her—the type who would hold your hand while she fired you, all the while secretly checking her watch. There was a quota of people to axe, and she only had so many hours in a day; tick tock, and all that.

And so it began.

Mark got called in by HR-Lady and the door closed behind him. Five minutes passed. He emerged, head down. Were those tears glistening on his cheeks? In his hands he toted a cardboard box. He trudged straight to his desk and began to clear out his personal belongings. Nobody went over to commiserate—HR-Lady was in her doorway, a pleasant expression on her face, but with scary laser beams where her eyes should be.

Sachin was next. He was gone the same amount of time, but his hands were empty when he rejoined the group. Jannie stared at him, hoping he'd tell her what was going on, but he sat back down at his desk and began to clack away on his keyboard like a castanet player at a flamenco party. Whatever he'd learned, he wasn't sharing.

In succession, three more male names were called. Two emerged with boxes and started cleaning out their work spaces. The third returned to his desk and began to copy Sachin's computer keyboard virtuosity. Tappety, tappety, tappety. *Olé!*

Jannie felt like screaming.

HR-Lady poked her head out again.

"Joelle? Joelle Weinzweig?"

At the next desk, Joelle leapt springbok-like from her chair. She took four jerky steps, then turned around to grab a pad of paper and a pen from her desk. She promptly dropped both, made a sound halfway between a guttural moan and a nervous giggle, and abandoned her stuff on the floor as she marched in dirge rhythm toward her destiny.

Jannie retrieved the pad and pen and replaced them on Joelle's possibly former desk. As she did, the opening notes of the only classical piece of music she knew popped into her head. Beethoven's Fifth: da da da DAH. It was fate knocking on Joelle's door, and soon it would be Jannie's turn.

She tried to think of a more optimistic tune, but the only snippet that came to mind was an inappropriate one from the rude but classic song *Baby Got Back*. Once that was lodged in her head, she couldn't shake it. On her chair, she shimmied to the imaginary beat. It really was irresistibly catchy, and somehow it made her feel less doomed.

Joelle seemed to be gone for ages. It was almost lunchtime. Jannie's stomach rumbled. She opened her desk drawer and began to rifle around for a sustaining snack. When she was hungry, she was never at her best.

She found a few loose candy bar wrappers; alas, all empty. She tossed the old foil bits into her wastebasket, then layered tissues overtop so that nobody could see the evidence. What else could she find? She felt something promisingly crinkly, maybe a packet of cookies, and angled her hand way back into the narrow top drawer to get hold of it. Without looking, she popped open the cellophane and crammed the contents into her mouth. How disappointing—it was just stale old saltines. Now she had a mouthful of salty cracker crumbs that were rapidly turning into wet concrete, and she was so nervous she couldn't swallow.

The office door opened. Joelle emerged, calm-faced but evading the many pairs of eyes that raked over her. She wasn't carrying a box. Jannie would have shouted "hurrah!" if her mouth hadn't been stuffed full of solidified saltines.

Joelle sat down at her desk. She waggled her hand at Jannie in a *comme çi, comme ça* gesture, before picking up her cell phone and texting someone—probably her fiancé—with flying fingers and furrowed brow. Whatever news she had, she wasn't sharing it with the prisoner in the next cell. Which was fine with Jannie because she was struggling to choke down the cracker boulder—and failing. She applied a fist to her solar plexus and whacked herself a couple of times. This didn't help.

The sari-clad woman reappeared in the doorway.

"Jannie Morris?"

Oh, freaking hell. Not now.

"Be right with you," Jannie called out in the bright tone of an indispensable employee. Or that's what she wanted to do, but instead she said, "Vree righ wiv oo," while spraying cement-like cracker globs across her desk. Fortunately, none of her spit balls hit Joelle, who looked at Jannie and shook her head, before putting the phone down to come over and smack her hard on the back. That helped. Grabbing her water bottle, Jannie bolted toward the HR lady, with dread in her heart and cracker fragments sprinkled over the rest of her body.

"Please take a seat, Jannie. I'm Shivani Ratnaswami, from Head Office HR," the woman said in a kind, patient voice, as if talking to a slow learner. Jannie would know; she'd been labeled one by school system officials throughout her undistinguished public school years. Until this moment, she'd always thought the joke was on them.

She wiped a fleck off her lapel and tried to smile in a professional way, hoping her front teeth weren't encrusted with cracker dough. Her upper lip began to twitch. It seemed to be in synch with Sir Mix-a-Lot's explicit lyrics, which were still jammed into her head like the most vicious and determined earworm ever.

"This has been a very difficult morning for everyone," Shivani said. "It isn't going to be easy for you, either. I hope you're a strong woman."

Jannie's lip tic accelerated. Her heart thumped, banging against her ribcage like the beating of a mad bongo drummer. Her whole body started to shake.

She braced herself, waiting for this faux-benevolent woman to fire her big butt out of the job she loved.

Day one of job hunting was going well. Suze spent the morning delving through internet postings, applying for positions that she was fairly confident she could handle. She rattled off cover letters for reception jobs. She responded with enthusiasm to ads for personal administrative assistants. She even ventured beyond her comfort zone, sending applications to places such as call centers and restaurants.

Right now, the thing to do was to get work experience, any place, anyhow. She could afford to be fussy later on, once she had established some current, marketable skills—and paid off her clothing bill.

Out of the blue, around mid-afternoon, bingo!

"Hello, may I speak with Susanna Foster?" a polished but sultry voice asked.

"Speaking. And, please call me Suze."

"Really? Susanna is so much prettier. Give it some thought, why don't you? Anyhow, Suze-Susanna, I'm calling from C.S. Adventures. You submitted your resume this week for a phone service position. Are you available for an in-person interview?"

"Yes, certainly. When and where?"

"Let's say, Starbucks, corner of Queen and John. Tomorrow morning, ten o'clock. Does that work with your schedule, oh-please-let-me-call-you-Susanna?"

Suze pursed her lips. "Yes. And how will I know you, Miss . . .?"

"Devine. As in 'I heard it through de grape-vine,' ha, ha. First name, Lola. I have red hair, I'll wear a purple dress. And you, Susanna?"

"I'll wear a black jacket and skirt. My hair's gray."

"I have no words for this. Well, yes, I have one: frumpy. Ah, well, it's a phone job. At least your voice sounds young."

"I've been told I'm—"

"Don't believe what friends tell you. Take it from me: lose the gray. But, let's see how you handle yourself as a conversationalist. We'll confab *mañana*. Ta-ta for now, deario."

Click.

Suze stared at her cell phone. Lola Devine didn't speak like a typical boss, but Suze couldn't afford to be fussy. Maybe C.S. Adventures wouldn't be an ideal opportunity, but nothing ventured, nothing gained. Starbucks was an eminently safe meeting place. Suze would treat the experience as practice for more serious interviews and not worry too much about the outcome.

She turned again to her computer. Unbelievable! She'd received an email from another company, BeefIt Incorporated. They wanted to see her tomorrow afternoon. How wonderful—two interviews on one day! Now, what exactly was the BeefIt job about? Suze scanned through her application emails. Ah, yes. BeefIt was a lifestyle company seeking an "outgoing and personable receptionist." Maybe she wasn't the world's biggest extrovert, and she certainly couldn't hold a candle in this respect to Jannie, but Suze knew she would definitely qualify as personable. And she'd done reception work in the past. This job might be perfect.

It looked like career searching might not be as hard as she'd dreaded. Already, in under a day, she'd made great progress.

Suze typed a quick acceptance to BeefIt, then clam-shelled her laptop. Enough was enough for day one.

She gave herself a congratulatory hug, grasping her upper arms and squeezing tightly, before getting to her feet and finding her purse. It was time to take a healthy, reviving walk. Get to know her new neighborhood better. Enjoy the last of late summer's heat.

And try not to think about how much she missed Jannie. About how not seeing her daughter brought actual pain to her body. And how she hated the loss of their mother-daughter catch-up sessions each evening over tea and Suze's homemade cookies. They'd wear comfy, stretched-out old sweats and yack with each other during commercial breaks of whatever reality show they were currently following. So cozy.

Her thoughts turned to Aram. Who had quite a different effect on her, and who hadn't called her yet about that coffee. Not that she'd expected him to. Not this soon. But still.

Suze moved to study herself in her mirror. A shower and maybe a change of jeans and shirt would be good. That, plus a fluff of the hair, a dash of deep pink lipstick, and a spritz of Clinique Happy and she'd be fine. Oh, and she'd wear some of her new, lacy lingerie. Because you just never knew. A streetcar might hit her, and there were the ER doctors' sensibilities to consider, and although it was highly doubtful she'd actually run into Aram in this part of the city, well, it was a possibility. And it'd be nice to feel womanly and appealing and vital again. She should celebrate her inner core of divine femininity that she had hidden from the world and from herself for so long. Shouldn't she?

Jannie's insides twisted themselves into knots tighter than those skinny jeans she'd stopped wearing two sizes ago. She staggered as she walked back to her desk, clutching the cardboard box Shivani had given her. People stared, but at the moment she didn't give a rat's ass. She was barely in her body at all—soul-deep crazy from the news she'd just received.

"Oh, Jannie." Joelle was the only person who even bothered to get up from her chair. Other co-workers—the ones who weren't packing their boxes and sobbing— fixed their gazes on their screens, smirks contorting their faces. Thank God for Joelle, who pulled the carton from Jannie's hands, dropped it on the floor, and twined her arms around her.

Jannie sank into the comforting warmth of Joelle's fit body. The embrace was bliss, like being hugged by Mom. Joelle's honey hair smelled vanilla-y. She patted Jannie's back as if she were a little child.

"There, there. There, there."

"Joelle, I—"

"Hush. Don't speak. Relax and breathe." Joelle kept up the patting and the reassuring cooing for a few more moments.

"Joelle—"

"Shhhhh. It's okay. It's not your fault. It's random. Half the folks here have been let go."

"But—"

"And I'm sure it's not because of your results. You've always been an overachiever."

"Yes, and—"

"And sometimes life is unfair." Joelle pulled back and put her hands on Jannie's shoulders. "I can't believe they're letting you go. You're our number one revenue source. Oh, you poor baby."

Jannie let out a little whimper of gratitude. She wanted another hug, but Joelle only stood there with her head tilted to one side. From the way her brows crowded together over the bridge of her nose, Jannie figured her friend was either going to burst into tears or say a few choice words about HR. Reading expressions was not as easy as the experts said it was.

Finally, Joelle said, stumbling over the words, "Jeez, I wonder—Jannie, this may not be the time or place, but perhaps it's a people skills thing. In your next job, you could try to be kinder to your co-workers. That's the one and only reason I can think of for you getting axed. You can be a bit of a tough cookie sometimes, you know."

"I can?" Jannie reached up and removed Joelle's hands, one by one, from her shoulders. The room temperature suddenly seemed much cooler.

"I'm so sorry to mention it at a time like this," Joelle whispered. A tear tracked its way down her cheek, and she began to wilt, like the neglected aspidistra in the pot behind her.

"Hey, it's okay, Joelle. You're right. And, apparently, Head Office has noticed I'm a hard ass, too." Jannie paused, trying to control her breathing. "That may be why they've sacked Ryan and promoted *me* to Branch Manager." She broke into a tremulous laugh that bordered on hysteria.

Joelle gasped, put a hand over her heart, and lurched away.

Jannie gazed after her and shrugged. She'd tried to tell her. Joelle was the one who had leapt to conclusions. But at least she'd talked to Jannie—no one else had bothered—and Jannie was willing to overlook her lapse of judgment in giving such weird advice. Besides, at the moment there were other priorities, like gathering up stuff from her old desk and placing it in a carton, so that she could move into the big window office next to where Shivani continued to do her dirty deeds.

Her ribcage swelled. She was twenty-nine years old and

in charge of forty-five people. Sure, that was way fewer than there'd been earlier in the day, but it was still pretty damn impressive.

So much for all those psychologists and teachers who'd said Jannie should consider entering the food service industry, if she was ever capable of holding a job at all. She'd achieved the impossible. She was at the top of the sales game, and she had the private office and cushy salary plus perks to prove it.

She smiled kindly but meaningfully at Bethany-Bonnie as she walked past reception. Instantly, B-B put her emery board down on her desktop. When Jannie pointed at it, she picked it back up, then dropped it into her wastepaper basket.

Jannie nodded graciously and moved on. It was a rush like she'd never experienced before.

7

TAKE THIS JOB AND . . .

*S*he wore a crisp white shirt, black skirt and jacket, pumps. Bare legs—no longer as white as a fawn's underbelly, since Suze had applied the self-tanning product she'd remembered Jannie recommending. Hair conditioned to a silvery moon sheen and finger-combed in a businesslike but youthful style. Killer lingerie, to please the soul and inspire confidence. And her new handbag, large enough to concuss any would-be mugger and, more practically, to carry resumes.

Suze was officially ready for her first interview.

She strode into the café, head up and eyes scanning the crowd. There was a heavenly scent of roasting coffee beans, but even from afar, Suze detected an overlay of weighty French perfume—maybe Yves St. Laurent's Paris —wafting toward her. She followed her nose to a table in the corner, and knew right away she'd found her quarry.

Lola Devine's burgundy hair flamed in comic book contrast to the pansy purple of her tightknit dress. She sat, tapping at her iPhone with extravagant, hot pink nails. A double espresso, endangered by her barely buttressed breasts, rested on the tabletop in front of her.

Suze paused for a moment, sizing Ms. Devine up. In spite of the woman's extraverted flashiness, she was beautiful—a supersized replica of Barbie. Or perhaps, with such strong facial features, more like Barbie's boyfriend, but only if Ken'd had a chance to raid Barbie's closet and makeup collection and borrow one of Midge's bouffant wigs. Expert cosmetic touches exaggerated Lola Devine's high cheekbones and made her Dresden blue eyes pop under dark eyebrows that slanted outward and upward like mirror-image French accents. *Aigu* and *grave*, Suze mused, trying to remember which was which, as she gathered the courage to introduce herself.

She took the plunge. "Good morning. Ms. Devine?"

The woman looked up from her iPhone, cast it aside, and leapt to her feet. She towered over Suze, who, at five foot six plus a couple extra inches with her heels on, wasn't used to feeling diminutive.

"Thank you, Sweet Baby Jesus. You're *so* not a snooze, Suze! What stunning hair. Rocket ship platinum—never again describe it as gray," Lola said, giving Suze a thorough up and down examination with her mink-lashed blue eyes. Apparently satisfied with what she saw, she grabbed Suze's right hand and seesawed it in a terrier-on-mouse kind of shake.

"Thanks. It's nice to meet you."

"Yes, you're a lucky girl. I believe it's everybody's fantasy to meet *me*." Lola winked, making her fake eyelashes flap like ostrich feathers wafted by a salacious burlesque performer.

Suze couldn't help herself; she laughed. There was something oddly charming about this larger-than-life

Amazonian apparition. Suze settled herself into her chair and prepared to be interviewed.

"When can you start?" Lola asked, glancing at her diamond-encrusted Chopard watch.

"Any time, but don't you want to ask me questions?"

"I'm sure you'll do. Pleasant voice. But, since you're a woman who likes formalities, we'll try a bit of Q and A. First, however, you must have some coffee."

In her chair, Lola Devine turned her body, moving the prow of her breasts in the direction of the barista and almost sending her own espresso cup flying in the process. Raising her voice to a level that rose above the ambient café noise she barked in manly tones, "Tommy, an espresso for my friend, *per favore*."

Behind the counter, the barista saluted as if Lola were an officer of the highest rank. He started preparing the order, ignoring the customers who were following protocol by lining up in orthodox fashion. Nobody seemed the least bit upset. They were too busy nudging each other and staring at Lola Devine to take much notice.

Lola turned back to Suze, and said in a much more feminine register, "All right. Here we go. Tell me what you do for excitement."

"Well, I just moved into a new apartment, and I'm looking forward to doing a bit of traveling in my future, once I've saved up enough money."

Lola feigned sleepiness, yawning and fanning her lacquered mouth with a languid hand. "You're cute, and I like your sexy voice, but your answer stinks. Try again."

"Yes, well, it was a very odd question. I was expecting to talk about my customer service skills."

Lola's right eyebrow shot even more steeply temple-ward. "C.S. skills, eh? This should be good. Let's have 'em, then."

Suze smiled a thank-you at Tommy, who'd just delivered her espresso, and gathered her thoughts.

"I'm highly organized, good with people, and, from working in the past as a receptionist, I have excellent phone manners."

"Girl, in this job you *have* to give good phone."

What an odd way of putting it. Suze hesitated, waiting for clarification.

"Okay, pretend you're answering your first call," Lola said, miming a phone with one hand, pinky stretched toward mouth and thumb held over ear.

"Sure, I guess. Here goes." Suze placed her own fake hand-phone against her ear and mouth. "C.S. Adventures. How may I help you?"

"It depends. What are you wearing?" Lola asked, amusement oiling her tone like butter on hot toast.

"Um, a jacket and skirt and . . ."

"No, really. Use your imagination. What do you think I *want* you to be wearing?"

Suze wondered what she should say. Maybe C.S. didn't stand for Customer Service at all. Could it be a short form of "classy silk?" Or "cotton sleepwear?" Should she pretend she was in evening wear or PJ's?

As she pondered this, she reached for her espresso and took an incautious sip, wincing as the hot, bitter liquid burned her mouth.

"Ouch! I need water! My tongue's on fire," she said, casting a desperate look over at Tommy, behind the counter.

"Now you're talking," said Lola Devine, giving a lascivious shoulder shake of approval in Suze's direction. "Tongues on fire are what C.S. Adventures is all about."

"No, really. I have to get some water. I'm burning up."

"Ooh, burn, baby, burn—" Lola began, but Suze jumped

up and ran to the counter. She grabbed a jug and a paper cup and poured herself some ice water. After several gulps, her tongue and lower lip still felt crimped and charred, but at least she was no longer blinking back tears of pain. Head lowered, clutching her cup of water, she returned to the table.

"I'm sorry. I really did burn myself. But I'm getting the feeling that this job may not be for me."

"And you were doing so well, too, dearie," Lola said. Her expression was serious, but there was a twitch at the corner of her luscious lips.

"Just out of curiosity, what do the initials in C.S. Adventures stand for?" Suze asked.

"Maybe that's something you should have researched before you applied, my poppet." Lola patted Suze's delicate hand with one of her huge, pink-taloned ones.

"It's something sexual, isn't it?" Suze's cheeks were ruddy.

"It just might be. What would you guess?"

"I don't know. Maybe . . ." and here Suze looked all around, then leaned forward and whispered, 'Casual Sex'?"

"What? How unimaginative! Guess again."

"Maybe, 'Custom Servicing'?" Suze put her hand over her mouth as she said the words. Her blush grew rosier.

"You're getting warmer. But no. One last chance."

Suze shook her head and stood to leave. Her burnt tongue was stinging, and this interview was never going to amount to anything. She shook Lola Devine's mammoth paw, too embarrassed to look up at the woman and meet her gaze, and started edging her way out of the crowded café.

"Hey, babe! Susanna!" Lola Devine was using her man voice again.

Suze hesitated, one hand on the door to the street outside.

"Good luck with your job hunting, my sweet. Please do make sure you do your homework next time, okay? And the C.S. stands for—all together now . . ."

As one, the staff behind the bar and several of the customers joined Lola Devine as they began to shout something with apparent glee.

But Suze was out the door and already sprinting down Queen Street. Only a final sibilant hissed on the wind behind her.

"To make a sale, burrow into the customer's mind like a worm inside an apple."

It was genius. Jannie pressed Send and raised her hands triumphantly from the keyboard. Adrenaline whooshed through her veins.

She pushed back in her padded chair and rotated to and fro like a kid on a soda fountain stool. Being a boss was scrumptious. Ideas popped into her head at a frantic rate, so fast she'd soon be showing more leadership than anyone ever in the history of ad sales. Catchy slogans, new ways to snag business, tips on how to dress to attract bigger investments—she couldn't keep up with the great concepts as quickly as they occurred to her.

Someone walked into her office, unannounced, and Jannie frowned. A disturbance in the Force, breaching her heaven-sent flow of creativity. She opened her mouth to deliver a gentle rebuke, but stopped herself when she saw the intruder was a tech guy, carrying her new printer. It was important to be sensitive to the nonexecutive staff

members, and, besides, she was anxious to get her
equipment hooked up.

"I'm very glad you're here," she said, and smiled at the
printer. The arms holding it had just the right amount of
biceps peeking out from under a faded blue t-shirt. They
bulged agreeably as they placed the machine on the corner
of her desk.

"Hi, Jannie."

She peeled her eyes away from the brawny arms and
traveled her gaze face-ward. Oh, crap. Good old Kirk.
Someone she hadn't seen in ages—a fellow battle-scarred
soldier from the Special Ed trenches of high school.

"Kirkie! How are you, bud?" Jannie jumped up and
flung her arms around his body, feeling slightly creeped out
that she'd just been looking at it in a borderline lusty way.
Old friends shouldn't eyeball each other; it was so not cool.

Kirk backed away. His cheeks flamed. He passed a
grubby hand across his forehead, leaving a gray smear
right above those forest green eyes Jannie recalled so well.
His brown hair was cut differently than she remembered—
short and jagged, high on his forehead over his un-
manscaped, straight brows. His most attractive feature, his
Blue Steel-Owen Wilson kissy-face mouth, was twisted in a
half smile, as he checked out her swanky executive digs.

"I'm okay," he said. He blinked rapidly a few times,
and added, in machinegun fire bursts, "My company's on
contract here. Tech support. Working with someone you
know: your neighbor Tyler. He said to say hi."

Jannie's brown eyes widened. "No shit. You and Tyler!
Well, I knew *he* had to be a techie. And of course you were
always a computer brainiac. Hey, bitchy old Mrs. Cooke
and all those horror show teachers would never believe
we're even employed, right?"

Kirk smiled down at his sneakered feet before throwing her a bashful glance. "You've done well for yourself, Jannie," he said.

Her heart swelled with pride. She wanted to hug him again but he'd always been such a shy guy. In high school, he'd been so reclusive he'd been tested for Asperger's Syndrome—along with everyone else who was the slightest bit different. She couldn't remember how far along the spectrum they'd pinned him in the end. It hadn't mattered; every kid in their Special Ed class may as well have had a huge sticker glued to their forehead. *Weirdo*.

"Yes! And I just got a freaking huge promotion. I'm running everything now!" It was so nice to have someone to talk to who didn't resent her good fortune. There'd been some pretty sour faces lately.

"You'll be brilliant. Always have been." He fidgeted with a cable.

"Thanks, Kirkie. Coming from you, that means a lot." She couldn't suppress the grin that stretched her cheeks to the max. It was all she could do not to wriggle with joy.

Kirk shuffled his feet, looking down at the carpet. Eventually, Jannie realized he was at the end of his conversational tether and was waiting for her to move out of the way so he could get at her computer.

"Okay, I'll leave you to work your magic." She grabbed a couple of random files off the top of her desk, and walked toward the door.

As she rounded the corner into the main bullpen, she overheard someone stage-whispering. She couldn't tell if it was a man or a woman, but there was no mistaking its malicious overtone.

"Be the bug in the client's ear and gnaw right through his right frontal lobe."

Jannie couldn't have heard that correctly. There was no way people could be mocking her inspirational email.

"No, be a pernicious parasite, and swallow shit by the bucket-load in order to get ahead." There was a burst of mean, muted snickering. Someone actually snorted with glee.

They *were* insulting her.

She marched into the gathering of people, who suddenly seemed as animated as snowmen on a subzero January day.

"Ahem, staff!" Jannie drew herself up to her full height and thrust her shoulders back. "I'd like to announce a sales meeting today at 4:30, to discuss priorities for the upcoming quarter."

"How long will it last?" a worried-looking female salesperson asked, huge dark circles under her eyes. "I have to pick up my daughter at daycare."

"And I have my son's soccer final tonight," a middle-aged, stocky man piped up. He scowled, pulled his iPhone out of his pocket and started texting furiously.

"It will take as long as it takes," Jannie said, striving for a no-nonsense, authoritative tone, and walked out to reception without a backward look.

She felt a zing of remorse, but it'd had to be done. She'd coped with disrespect far too often in her life. Once it took root, things inevitably got uglier. The only solution was to nip it in the bud. Act like the boss she was.

But how lonely it was these days. No kibitzing with Joelle. No being cozy with Mom. No meaningful human contact at all.

She wandered idly past reception. She gave Bethany— or was it Bonnie?—an approving big-boss nod. The receptionist had shown improvement lately, never filing her nails during work hours and actually making the occasional effort to do her job.

"Hello, Bethany." Jannie smiled benevolently.

"It's Bonnie."

Jannie winced at the poison shooting from the young woman's eyes. Next time she'd get it right. Really.

Meanwhile, she'd try to make nice. Make Bonnie feel appreciated. Be a leader and pump up the girl's spirits in order to gain maximum results.

"Bonnie," Jannie said, in a kindly alto. "I see you have a rather messy desk. Are you aware that a clean surface indicates a serene mind?"

That was pithy. Jannie's spirits picked up a bit. It felt good to manage others effectively.

So why didn't Bonnie look more impressed? She didn't nod or smile. Instead, her shoulders rose toward her ears, and her head lowered like an angry bull's, pre-charge. She seemed to be having a hard time catching her breath; in fact, she began to huff and puff.

And then she let loose.

"My desk is messy because this fucking company fired so many fucking people that work is being dumped on me by everyone. I'm supposed to answer phones and greet visitors. How the *fuck* am I supposed to deal with all this paper? I don't even know where to start. And now you come and tell me in that bitchy voice of yours that a clean desk is a sign of sanity, and here I am fucking insane from the stress? Well, *I'll* show you a clean desk." Bonnie flung out an arm and knocked all the papers flying. A partially filled coffee cup sailed along for the ride.

Jannie took a giant leap back to dodge the blizzard of white sheets and the cascading splash. She ducked as Bonnie picked up a stapler and lobbed it straight at her head. It missed by a fraction of an inch and smashed into a partition, splintering the glass and creating a spiky supernova pattern.

"Bethany, dear," Jannie said in her calmest voice.

"It's Bonnie. B-O-N-N-I-E. What the fuck is wrong with you, anyway? Don't you ever think of anyone but yourself?"

"Yes, Bonnie. Right now I'm thinking *you* might like to take a break to cool down." Jannie wrung her hands, wondering where she'd gone so badly astray.

"Oh, I'm taking a break, all right. A forever one. From you—you horrible excuse for a human being. Now, get the fuck out of my way!"

Bonnie grabbed her handbag and her jacket. She clomped out from behind her sleek reception desk and over to the elevator, punching the button with the vigor of a UFC star. She kept her stiff back turned.

As the elevator doors swooshed shut, Jannie heard a smattering of subdued applause coming from the bullpen. Too frazzled to face the ungrateful mob, she set the reception phone to direct-to-voicemail mode. No matter what, the business must always come first. Then she bolted for the ladies' room.

As she took a last look back down the hallway, she saw Kirk slip out of reception. He shrugged in a sympathetic kind of way and gave her his kissy-face half-smile, before disappearing into the service stairwell. And for some reason, that's when Jannie began to cry.

Suze tore along Queen Street as best she could in her new pumps, leaving curious, slower-moving pedestrians in her wake. C.S. Adventures: of all companies to have interviewed with! She had been so naïve. Now, her chest ached from the unexpected cardio of her headlong dash and her new shoes pinched, but deep reserves of embarrassment propelled her forward. It was as if she'd been rocket-launched with such velocity she was powerless to stop.

Oomph! Full body contact with someone tall, masculine, and tantalizingly bergamot-scented.

"Oh, I beg your pardon," Suze stuttered, then froze.

Aram stood there, his hands on her elbows, having caught her in full flight. He looked down at her, his normally narrow eyes wide. The impact had rocked him back onto his heels and tousled his gray-sprinkled dark hair, but he was smiling.

"Suze, what a wonderful surprise," he said, continuing to hold her in a steady grip. His touch felt solid and supportive.

"Aram . . ." Suze shook her head. What he must think of her, practically bowling him over in the middle of a crowded downtown Toronto sidewalk.

"I don't know what I've done to deserve this marvelous encounter, but let's take advantage of it. May I treat you to lunch?" He swung his body around and hooked his arm through her elbow. Together they strolled toward Yonge Street, Suze's feet automatically moving forward in synch with his.

"No, thanks. I'm not hungry. And I'm very sorry to have smacked into you."

"No need to apologize. I, myself, am delighted you did." His slight accent was barely noticeable under the smooth veneer of his speech.

Suze didn't respond. She tilted her head to one side, trying to guess where he was originally from.

"I will buy you a beverage. Maybe something cold,

after your headlong flight down Queen Street? Chased by devils, perhaps?"

"Running from my own stupidity, more like," Suze said.

"I detect a story. One that needs a bubbly drink to coax it out. Come with me." With that, Aram guided her along the sidewalk, eventually leading her into a cheery, pink-stuccoed Italian soda bar.

Over pomegranate-infused, carbonated lemonade, Suze spilled out her tale of woe. At the first mention of C.S. Adventures, Aram's straight brows snapped together, and he stroked his beard with one hand as she continued recounting the details of the meeting with Lola Devine. By the time she stopped, totally unable to talk about what the initials in the company's name might stand for, he had dropped his hand and was openly chuckling.

"Ms. Devine was right. You really have to do your homework before going to any more job interviews." He used his thumb and forefinger to pull down the corners of his mouth.

"Yes, I know." Suze was pretty sure he was trying not to offend her by laughing again. "And now, this afternoon I have an interview at a place called BeefIt. Now that I think about it, that's a rather weird name."

Suze studied Aram's face. He had his cell phone out and was Googling the company. A flash of alarm appeared in those steady hazel eyes.

"You must cancel that interview. Or just not go."

"Really? That bad?"

"Worse. This is not a place you'd ever want to set foot in."

"Foolish me." Suze sipped the last fizzy remnants of her soda. "I'll cancel. And I'll start doing proper research before I agree to more interviews. But, darn it . . ."

"Yes, go on."

"I do need to find a job. I'm out on my own now. I have to succeed."

"If I can be of any help . . ."

"You have helped. You've just saved me from going to another horrible interview. And, you're keeping an eye on Jannie, right?"

Aram nodded. "As much as a neighbor can do without looking like a stalker, yes."

"It's just that I've always been there for her. And I was a good mom. It's what I know best; really, it's all I know." Suze played with the striped straw and twirled the remaining soda in her glass.

"She's a lucky young woman. But you have new priorities in your life, and I'd like to help. As an active investor—in reputable companies, of course!—I'll be a good sounding board for you. You can bounce job ideas off me. And I'll give you updates on how Jannie's doing, when I see her in the building."

"Thank you."

Perhaps it was the bubbliness of the soda that was making Suze feel light and feminine and desirable. Or maybe it was just from being with this gracious, worldly man. He was looking at her with such intensity, his eyes gazing deeply into hers.

"I've already got your phone number. Perhaps your email address would also be helpful? Ah, perfect," he said, as she jotted down the information on a napkin scrap. "And here are my contact details."

He passed an ivory-colored card across the table to Suze. His name, Aram Krikorian, was severely fonted, followed by what must be his company's name, Krikorian Investments, and then two phone numbers and an email address. It looked luxe and altogether out of Suze's league.

Placing the business card in her purse, Suze thanked him again, and left the soda shop. As she walked to the subway she felt less and less effervescent. With each step she felt poorer and shabbier and even more unaccomplished. He owned an investment firm. She was an unemployed nobody—out of her league as well as being out of a job.

8

GETTING ON WITH THINGS

*J*annie sat at her desk, chin in hands, and gazed into space. Something wasn't right. She got a pad of paper and a pen out of her desk and created two columns: positive and negative. On the left side of the page she wrote, *I am a natural leader*. She stared at that for a minute and nodded her head decisively. Then, on the negative side, she wrote, *Everybody hates me*.

It really *was* lonely at the top. Until her promotion, she'd thought nothing could be more fun than being a boss. But not one person ever dropped by her office to say hello. A whole day could pass without anyone talking to her, unless she forced them to. In fact, people scurried out of the way when she approached, like Scooby Doo and Shaggy fleeing the gruesome Swamp Monster.

She'd been staying up late reading self-help books. *How to Earn the Love of Others* had been last night's volume. She'd used her highlighter lavishly and memorized all the important tips. According to the author, she needed to do three vital things. First, acknowledge what people say by echoing their words; second, use their given names frequently; and third, mirror their body language.

She decided to practice on Joelle. It was past six o'clock, and they were the only two worker bees still at the office.

"Joelle, how's your pitch going for Pots, Unlimited?"

"Uh, fine."

"Fine, eh, Joelle?" Bullseye! Echoing *and* name use in a single response.

"Yeah, fine." Joelle—staring at Jannie's Third Eye Chakra—shrugged and took a step forward, as if hoping to head for the exit. Jannie shrugged her shoulders (mirroring!) and took a matching step forward. She was now right in Joelle's face, which was awkward, especially because Jannie had ordered the double garlic cheesy bread with her takeout pizza for lunch, and her mouth tasted less than minty-fresh.

"I'm glad you're doing fine, Joelle," she said, hoping her co-worker would say any word but *fine* so Jannie could echo it in an empathetic way.

Joelle took a step back. Jannie followed suit, but then wondered if she looked unfriendly. She compensated by taking two steps forward, ending up right in Joelle's face again.

"What exactly are you doing?"

"Um, I'm doing what you're doing, Joelle. And discussing business with you, Joelle."

"Well, Pots Unlimited is going fine."

"And I'm glad that Pots Unlimited is going fine, Joelle."

"So, if there's nothing else . . ." Joelle brushed back a stray lock of her long, blond hair.

"No. There's nothing else, Joelle." Jannie tried to brush back one of her own dark curls, but it rebounded, sproinging right into her eye. It almost dislodged her contact lens, and now she was squinting in extreme close-up at Joelle, like a hideous Disney hag up on the big screen.

"Well, then." Joelle raised her gaze so that she stared at the ceiling instead of at the place where Jannie's horn would have been if she were a magical unicorn. Then, she heaved a prolonged sigh in a very unsubtle way and excused herself. Defeated, Jannie let her slip by. The unimpressed expression on Joelle's face was the last thing Jannie saw before the elevator doors closed.

Jannie shook her head. Maybe that hadn't been a textbook example of active and engaged listening. But she hadn't yet perfected the art. If she kept practicing, she'd be sure to impress her people and earn affection—on top of the huge respect that all of them would soon have for her leadership. She was no quitter, as Mom always reminded her.

Jannie stopped staring at her wavy image in the elevator doors and surveyed the reception area. Ever since Bonnie had left, the piles of paper, stacks of mail, and interoffice deliveries were mounding higher and higher. The phone's message lights flashed, like it was prime time at a pinball parlor. A visitor to the office might think this company was floundering. Or, horrors, badly run.

If only she could hire a new receptionist. But HR-Lady Shivani was back in New York and had made it clear that, in light of the cutbacks, no new permanent positions would be approved. Jannie heaved a mighty, Joelle-worthy sigh, cast herself onto Bonnie's vacated chair, and started to sort out the chaos.

By the time she left the office, it was after nine o'clock. Her stomach roiled with hunger. Whenever she next managed to get a few spare hours, she'd learn to cook. Mom had given her all their favorite recipes and Jannie felt guilty she hadn't tried to make any of them yet. One of these days she'd do it—but for tonight's dinner, she'd have Greek takeout: salad, hold the onions, extra feta.

On her way to Condo 5B, she stopped off at the fourth floor to check up on Tyler. In spite of all the hullaballoo at work, she was one hundred percent committed to restoring his collection of wrestling posters, and tonight she had progress to report. There was enough salad to share, if Tyler was hungry, and it would be nice to talk with someone who didn't hate her guts. A girl could only take so much loneliness.

She rapped lightly on his door. "Tyler, you there?"

There was no response. But light beamed out from the slim space under his door. She cocked her head. Music. It was definitely not a raucous Dragon Gate theme song. Nor was it a moody soundscape by Joe Hisaishi or any other Japanese anime composer. It was . . . no, impossible.

Unbelievably, it *was*, Marvin Gaye. Shy little Tyler Howard was grooving to *Sexual Healing*. That was like Jannie listening to Mom's collection of Van Morrison. Like, it would never happen.

She knocked again. Tyler was probably just unwinding to some relaxing background music, and what could be better than to have his friendly neighbor drop by for some Greek food therapy to go with the sultry soundtrack?

His door opened a crack. One dark brown eye, behind a thick lens, peered out.

"Kinda busy here, Jannie," he said.

Jannie tried to push her way in. He must have jammed his shoulder against the door, because it didn't budge.

"But I've got Greek takeout. And a report on my poster progress. Let me in." She pushed harder.

"I'm not in the mood."

"Why? Not hungry? Or are you naked?"

"Not precisely."

"Well, if you're halfway decent, I'm coming in," she said.

She craved friendly human contact. It'd been a tough day, and Jannie didn't want to face her messy, Mom-less condo, overflowing with takeout bags and boxes of all possible national origins. Or another night by herself.

"It's not a good time . . ."

But Jannie summoned up the super-strength of the truly desperate and gave his door a monumental shove. Tyler hit the wall behind him, his black glasses jolting askew. He wore a thick, white terrycloth bathrobe, which contrasted beautifully with his dark skin. He pulled it tightly around his body, and Jannie wondered if the robe and eyeglasses, plus his bemused expression, were all he had on. She felt her cheeks heat up.

She was about to apologize for intruding, when a slight form, also dressed in a white robe, came flying out of nowhere like a furious Tasmanian devil high on crystal meth. The apparition brandished a bottle of wine in a threatening manner.

"Stop! I mean you no harm!" Jannie yelled, panic-stricken.

"It's okay, it's just Jannie," Tyler said, patting his terry-robed doppelganger on the shoulder. Except for the fact that this twin had skin that was as chalky white as Tyler's was acorn brown, they were much alike in shape, size, and age. And geekiness.

Jannie's eyes popped. What was *Frodo* doing in Tyler's condo? She didn't even know they were acquainted. And on sleepover terms? The gears in her brain made an almost audible click. One young man in a robe plus another young man in a robe plus Marvin Gaye. Apparently, romance had blossomed.

She slunk backward through the doorway, hugging her

Greek takeout bag, sorry she'd disrupted their intimate moment. As she reached the hallway, Tyler poked his head out, and for the first time ever looked her straight in the eye.

"I was going to tell you, Jannie. You've changed my whole life. I owe all this to you. You're the *best*." His megawatt smile lit up the corridor. Strains of Marvin Gaye faded as he closed the door.

Jannie closed her eyes and reflected. She'd been so busy at the office, what with the new promotion and all, and an impatient Tyler had reached out directly to Frodo for an update. Birds had chirped, bees had buzzed, and hearts and bodies had melded, all to the sexy vocal stylings of Marvin Gaye.

Jannie wanted to be thrilled by her unintentional matchmaking, but instead she felt a hollowness inside that had nothing to do with being overdue for dinner. She yacked out a few small sobs as she entered the elevator and rode it one floor up.

"Is that you, Jannie?"

It was Aram. The man who made her heart flutter more rapidly than a hummingbird's wings could flap—seeing her at less than her best, again. And clutching fast food yet again, too. He was going to think she was an emotional wreck on top of being a lousy cook.

"Yup, me." She hiccupped out another sob.

"You seem distressed. May I help?" He walked closer, looking hot in his casual clothes that, even if he were so much older, emphasized his fabulous shape. His chest and stomach muscles rippled through his thin t-shirt. Behind the cover of her Greek food bag, Jannie touched her own tummy. No apparent musculature there. Just voluptuous young womanhood. More than a little jiggly. Maybe he liked a wobbly woman. If so, she was highly qualified.

"I'm tired. Could really use some company." She beagled her big, brown eyes at him.

"Well, I can help out on both sides of that equation. Please come in for a restorative glass of wine. Goes well with Greek," Aram said, waving in the direction of his condo.

OMFG. Was this really happening?

"Thanks. I'm going through a lot at work, what with my promotion and all. It's like nobody wants to be around me."

"The lot of the leader is often a difficult one," Aram said, in that slightly accented, dreamy baritone. He took Jannie's arm and led her to his door.

Joelle may hate her guts, and Tyler may be wrapped up in his swoony new love affair with Frodo, but Jannie felt like she'd just won the hook-up derby. The studliest man in the world was welcoming her into his bachelor lair. Once she'd scarfed down enough Greek cuisine to give herself the required energy, she'd allow him to take full advantage of her.

Jannie had moves. And, she'd had more than enough for one day of being the boss. As Marvin Gaye's *Let's Get It On* pointed out, why wait?

9
ALL STRESSED OUT

The golden summer weather had packed it in and left town a while ago. In its place was the revitalizing snap of early autumn. The foliage responded to the unusually cool conditions by blaring out vibrant reds and yellows. Toronto was at its colorful best.

Suze—looking out her high-in-the-sky window—absorbed the changes in Mother Nature's palette, but her soul wasn't stirred. Lately, she had failed to appreciate a lot of things. Her precarious financial situation was painting her whole world a depressing shade of taupe.

Just the other day she'd handed a rent check to her new superintendent, Gleb, a recent Russian immigrant who'd developed a nasty habit of leering at her. As she left his musty basement office she felt his eyes crawling down her spine, hovering at butt level. She was relieved to pay up and get away from him, but with the surrendering of that money, she was now officially broke.

She had enough food to last for a while, sort of. Her kitchen cabinets contained a jumbo box of Cheerios, some tins of soup, and lots and lots of empty shelf space. In the fridge, there was milk and yogurt that wouldn't expire for a couple of weeks, and some wilted romaine and bendy broccoli that already had. That was it.

She'd paid her hair-raising clothing bill a couple of weeks ago. It wasn't easy to surrender the cash, but she made a point of going straight to the department store's accounting office and settling her debt in full. Then, in a show of defiance that would have made her bra-burning elders proud, she snipped up her credit card into tiny shards in front of the startled clerk and brushed her hands together in a good-riddance motion. Tossing her head, she swept out the door, determined never to return.

At the time, the gesture had felt good. It might have been wise, though, to pay the minimum and hold onto the bulk of her cash for emergencies. Homelessness loomed large.

She wasn't lazy. Every day Suze devoted hours to her job search. She always did her research now, and was careful to stick with companies that were aboveboard and well known. But very few of the Human Resources people called her back, and if they did, they dismissed her from consideration without even an interview when they learned her work history was decades old. And while Aram kept calling and offering help, and she did meet him from time to time over coffee, she kept him at arm's length. She'd so love to escalate their relationship, but she wasn't anyone's charity case.

Suze ran her hands through her thick hair, which could use a good styling. Her marvelous, adventurous life wasn't going the way she'd envisioned it. Still, she was healthy, determined, and strong. She'd get through this rough patch. All it took was faith and perseverance.

The phone rang. *Que Sera Sera*. Suze scrambled to answer it.

"Mom?"

"Yes, sweetie. How *are* you?" Suze walked over to her furled sofa bed and sat, preparing to have a comfy chat with her daughter.

"Can we move up next Saturday's coffee? I have to go to work that day."

"Really? On a weekend? How awful for you."

"Yeah." There was a silence. Both women breathed gently into their phones.

"Well, then." Suze was first to speak. "When do you want to get together?"

"How's right now?" Jannie's voice quivered.

"Of course. Our usual place?" Suze waited for a response, but heard only a muted sob. "On my way. See you in half an hour, sweetie."

Poor Jannie. She'd been logging incredibly long hours lately. That impressive promotion had placed way too much pressure on her.

And how unfair life was. Jannie was working too hard. Suze wasn't working at all. How she longed to take some of her daughter's burden. A fraction of Jannie's paycheck wouldn't be unwelcome, either.

The prospect of getting out of the compact apartment and seeing Jannie lifted Suze's spirits. She'd do what she did best: be a supportive and caring mom, boosting Jannie's morale and inspiring her to see her challenges in a more positive way. Suze had always been able to do this, putting the best possible spin on Jannie's toughest situations, from coping with academic humiliations to facing dateless Saturday nights. The strength of their mother-daughter bond could overcome anything.

Suze consulted her bathroom mirror, fluffed her hair and quickly applied some concealer to the circles that had recently appeared under her eyes. Grabbing a jacket and umbrella, she headed out the door. Rain fell in icy needles. It chilled her to the core, as she ran to the subway, wishing with all her might she could afford taxi fare.

She arrived in less than twenty minutes. In a corner of the bustling café, Jannie slumped on a banquette, eyes concealed by the waterfall of her dark hair. There was no coffee cup in front of her.

Giving the soaked umbrella a cursory shake and draping her sodden raincoat over the back of an empty chair, Suze sat across from Jannie. She took her daughter's warm hands in her own, cold and pruny from being out in the blustery rainstorm. Jannie gave a start, but sank back into the upholstery when Suze spoke.

"I'm here, sweetie."

That's all it took. Three words, said in a sympathetic tone. And then Jannie was crying, lost in a dismaying wilderness of grief. Something must be terribly wrong for her to be in a café on a weekday mid-afternoon, when she should be hard at work leading the troops and closing deals. Had she been fired?

The last thing Jannie needed right now was her mom giving her the third degree. For several minutes, mother and daughter sat silently in the stylish coffee house, foreheads touching. As Suze's hands warmed in Jannie's grasp, she felt whole again.

Memories of Jannie's childhood flashed through her mind. There had always been so much to protect her daughter from. The errant father who failed to show up on many occasions and ruined so many others by being drunk. Teachers who didn't have the patience to get to the bottom of Jannie's learning disability, labeling her as slow, and warehousing her in Special Ed to make their own lives easier. And, just a few years ago, Jannie's last boyfriend, who'd been much too much like her father to be anything but a total disaster. It had taken every last ounce of Suze's maternal devotion to help Jannie steer herself out of that trap.

Jannie looked up. Her eyes were filled with tears, but she'd stopped sobbing.

"A latte would be nice, Mom."

"Of course, sweetie. I'll get it right away." Suze patted Jannie's hands and rose.

"And a cookie?"

"You bet."

By the time Suze returned to the table, full of motherly concern and only momentarily regretting the expense, Jannie had pulled herself together. She was looking at her reflection in a rhinestone-encrusted compact and squirting Visine into her pink-tinged eyes. Suze placed two steaming lattes and a couple of sugary treats on the table.

"Thanks, Mom." Jannie reached for her coffee. "And for coming here today, too. Sometimes I feel so alone."

"Are things that bad at work?"

Jannie sighed and looked away. She picked up a cookie and nibbled it.

"I'll take that as 'work stinks,'" Suze said. "When you're good and ready, go ahead and talk. I'm listening."

"I don't even know where to start."

"Jump in anywhere. We'll piece it together like we always do," Suze said, and took a cautious sip of her latte. Good, just the right temperature.

"All right. In no particular order, everyone hates me. I know they talk behind my back all the time, but they shut up whenever I walk by. The receptionist quit, and I'm doing her paperwork on top of my own, because Head Office says I can't hire permanent staff, what with the international cutbacks. I'm still holding down a sales territory of my own, plus running the office, plus doing receptionist work, and I think I'm going to crack up."

"Sounds awful."

"Yeah, and I don't know how much longer I can handle the stress. Oh, and I've gained at least ten pounds."

"Well, sweetie, is there more stress because of workload or because of personnel issues?"

Jannie took a moment to polish off the cookie. She dabbed her mouth with a napkin before speaking.

"It's the people thing. And I don't understand why. I'm trying to be so upbeat with everyone. I send inspirational emails. I compliment them on their successes. I attempt to remember their names."

"Attempt?"

"Yeah, well, I'm better at it than I used to be. And I read books on how to influence people. I try a new theory out on them every week."

"Do you think that could be part of the problem? I mean, it might make you appear unsteady if you constantly flip-flop your management approach."

"Maybe." Pause. "I just wish they didn't hate my guts. It hurts my feelings."

"Well, of course it does. Nobody wants to be unpopular."

Suze and Jannie joined hands again across the table. They gave each other a squeeze at the same moment, and then let go and went back to a companionable sipping of latte. Jannie pointed to Suze's cupcake. Suze hesitated, evaluating her daughter's woebegone face, before giving her a nod. As Jannie bit into it, a dab of buttercream icing plus a few rainbow sprinkles ended up on the tip of her nose. They both laughed, and Suze patted the cream away with a napkin.

"Let's think of happier things. What's going well in your life, Jannie?"

"Nothing with the folks at work, although the business itself is thriving." As Jannie munched the cupcake, the worry lines in her forehead smoothed out. "Oh, but something good has happened. You'll never guess what—I've met a man!"

Suze's eyebrows rose. "Well, well. Now *this* is interesting. Do share."

Jannie licked a bit of frosting from her finger. "Don't get all nervous, but he's a teensy bit older than I am—"

"Stop right there. By how much?" There had been too many dating disasters in Jannie's life for Suze not to be concerned.

"Oh, you know. A few years, maybe?" Jannie's face was angelic. She polished off the last few crumbs and patted her stomach. It jiggled.

"And where did you meet? Work?"

"No, just, you know, around. He's tall."

"And dark and handsome, no doubt?"

"How did you know? And he seems to have a good job. It's early days, Mom. Don't fret. Just be glad for me, okay?"

"Sweetie, I'm always happy when you are. I'll look forward to meeting him," Suze said aloud, but she couldn't repress the pessimistic thought, *if it lasts*.

"Sure. You'll love him!"

"What's his name?"

Jannie stared straight ahead. Her expression was inscrutable. After a pause, she said, "Earl."

"What an old-fashioned name!" Suze hadn't met any Earls in a very long time, and none under the age of fifty. "Earl what?"

Again, Jannie hesitated. When she spoke, it was at warp speed.

"Earl Grey. I know, I know. Wacky parents, right?"

"Sweetie, they sound absolutely demented. Who would do that to an innocent baby?" Suze shook her head, and opened her mouth to ask follow-up questions, but Jannie picked up her cellphone and checked the time.

"I've got to get back. Shouldn't have snuck out when I did, but I *so* needed the break. Mom, you're the best for being there for me. As always."

"You're welcome, Jannie. Love you tons. Now, chin up, do your best, and off you go!"

Flashing a smile, Jannie grabbed her coat and purse and dashed out of the café, leaving Suze to finish her latte and reflect on the inordinate stress Jannie was experiencing at the office. On her daughter's new love interest, Earl Grey. Really, *that* was the best she could come up with? All kinds of alarm bells ringing there. Last but certainly not least, on Suze's own precarious financial situation, now made even direr by the twenty-dollar splurge on lattes and pastries.

Things had to get better. And soon.

10

THE THRILL OF THE CHASE

*A*s she boarded the elevator in her office tower, Jannie felt the back of her neck prickle with shame. She'd lied to her own mother. But Mom may have remembered Aram as a former neighbor, and he was so much older than Jannie; nowhere near the usual age range for a potential son-in-law. She'd never approve.

And, really, poor Aram didn't deserve such a ridiculous pseudonym! In the moment, though, the only thing that had come to mind was bergamot. Like Earl Grey tea— how he smelled deliciously of it. What a stark contrast to the way Jannie reeked, the last time she visited him. Damn it, she *told* the Greek food man to hold the onions. Purple-faced from belch suppression, she had to make an immediate escape or risk burping mid-kiss.

No matter. She sighed rapturously. Theirs was still bound to be an epic, romantic, ultra-sexy relationship. Classy, too.

The elevator stopped at her floor. Jannie slipped past a couple of gossiping interns and bumped into a frantic-looking Joelle, backed by four generic guys. They were youngish and balding, in a variety of shades from birch to maple. Jack, Chandran, Gord, and Mike?

"We have a problem." Joelle twisted her hands and looked imploringly at Jannie.

"A problem is an opportunity just waiting to happen," Jannie responded. She'd write that one down later.

Eye rolling all around, for some reason. The men shuffled their feet, soft-shoe-style, as if they were auditioning for a way-off-Broadway show, and looked at each other sideways. Joelle clicked her tongue against the roof of her mouth. Jannie made a mental note to have a word with her later. There should be no criticisms in front of the troops, wordless or otherwise.

"Well," Joelle said, "this *opportunity* is our biggest client is canceling a long-term contract. Printz and Popper Stores are switching their strategy, dumping TV for print."

"That's your account, right, Chandran?" Jannie threw a hawk-like look in his direction, hoping she had the correct guy.

"Yes." There was white all around his almost-black irises.

He was right to panic. If P&P Stores pulled the plug, the team's commissions would be utterly screwed for the next couple of quarters. Chandran's head would be the first to roll. Jannie's wouldn't be far behind.

"Right, well, let's get on it. STAT!"

Jannie shooed everyone away except for the hapless Chandran. He was quaking in his well-polished loafers, but she grabbed him by the arm and yanked him down the corridor. Together they'd confront the client, face to face. It'd take all of Jannie's magic to salvage the situation. Chandran, if he could pull himself together, would learn from the master.

The situation was increasingly dire. Rent was due and Suze hadn't found a job. No prospects were on the horizon.

Pretty soon she'd have to confess her financial situation to Jannie. Suze would do almost anything to dodge this. She was supposed to be a responsible mother figure, not a burden.

Could she turn to Aram for help? She'd been avoiding him lately, and she shuddered at the thought of letting him know the extent of her plight. She didn't want a handout from anyone, least of all from him. No, for now she'd tough it out.

But the Cheerios were almost gone. She was down to her last few cans of soup. If she didn't get a paying job soon, Suze was screwed.

Meanwhile, she had to face her superintendent, Gleb, the ogler with the outrageous Boris Badenov accent. Whether she wanted to or not, she had to tell him she didn't have enough cash to cover this month's rent.

Suze dressed carefully, putting on her least suggestive clothing: a non-clingy twinset with high to the neck buttons and a pair of baggy jeans. Clothes that were too big were easy to find in her closet. Lately, she'd been dropping pounds, from a combination of buying fewer groceries and worrying too much.

She descended to the harshly lit basement and knocked on Gleb's office door.

"Who is?"

"It's Suze Foster. From Apartment 2206."

"Ah. Yes, for you I come, pretty lady." There was a sound of heavy shoes thumping across a linoleum floor. The door swung open with a protesting squeal.

"Everything squeak," Gleb said. He closed it with a

flat-handed smack, as if it had been a naughty, naughty door, and trained his pale eyes on Suze, sweeping them up and down the length of her body.

"Welcome to HQ. Is heart of building." With a cacophonous squeal of metal on cracked flooring, Gleb pulled out a hard seat for her, then walked to the other side of his battered desk and sank into a well-worn, padded chair on castors. He rolled back several inches, lolled into a relaxed sprawl, and once again took full stock of Suze.

It was hard to say exactly why the man was so creepy. Apart from his unusually light green eyes, he wasn't worth a second glance—the kind of guy who'd walk away from a crime scene holding a smoking gun without anyone noticing. He had side-parted brown hair that was a touch over-gelled; his features were small and regular. But, for all the normality of his appearance, there was something about him that gave her nasty goosebumps.

"Here's the thing." She fiddled with a button on her cardigan. "I find myself short of cash. I can't pay the rent."

Oh, dear God. What a clichéd thing to say. Next, Gleb would tie her to the railway tracks.

Too bad no hero would emerge to save her.

Gleb seemed to be considering her words. He didn't move a muscle, but remained tipped back in his cushy chair, studying Suze as if she were an exotic creature at the zoo.

"Shall I say what is obvious? You must pay rent." Gleb's peculiar eyes gleamed. Perhaps he'd always wanted to play the role of villain in a melodrama. He'd certainly excel at that. All he needed was a top hat and a cape, and mustachios to twirl.

"Yes, I know. And I will. As soon as I have the money. I'm looking for work. It may take a few weeks, though."

"Unacceptable." He pronounced it "unixxiptible."

"Can the building's management company show some flexibility? You can use my last month's rent for now. I paid it when I signed the lease and I'll reimburse you soon. Could you ask on my behalf?"

"Not good idea. New tenant: you. New super: me. Both lose credibility." He snapped his thumb and middle finger. "Like that."

"Gleb, I know you don't owe me anything. And you hardly know me. But, I can assure you I'll come up with the money."

"How long?"

"Maybe a month?" Suze gulped. There was no way she'd have the money that soon.

Gleb put his head on one side and stared at her breasts, as if they were going to pipe up and offer to pay the rent on Suze's behalf. After a minute, he leaned forward in his worn executive chair and placed his stained fingertips on the desk.

"You nice lady. I give you a month, yes? But, no more. After that, it's Form N4 for you."

"N4?"

"Notice to end tenancy. Kick you out. Lady, at that point it's you or me. Guess what. Not gonna be me."

Suze looked at Gleb's reptilian eyes and saw no sign of flexibility. She nodded and rose.

"I'll get you that rent, Gleb. Soon."

"You bet your sassy ass, lady." Gleb snorted with laughter.

Holding her head high, Suze left. She didn't have a financial leg to stand on. For now she'd have to tolerate Gleb's sassy aspersions and keep as low a profile as she possibly could.

"Hey, Jannie," Chandran said out of the corner of his mouth. "What do we do if he won't see us?"

"Relax. He will. Grant and I go way back. And if he's tied up, we'll wait."

"I'm really sorry about this." Chandran batted his deep brown eyes.

She wasn't charmed. "Yes, well, you should be. P&P's our biggest piece of business. It requires constant servicing, something you apparently haven't been doing."

Chandran flinched. She didn't care; she glared at him harder. He'd let his team down, not to mention the customer. If he'd been doing his job properly they wouldn't be in this tight little corner, fighting for their lives. Jannie was barely able to restrain herself from wagging her index finger in his face.

"Mr. Popper will see you now," the receptionist said.

"Thanks, Cathy," Jannie said, and the woman gave her a pleased nod.

Jannie had studied her detailed customer history notes moments before they'd arrived and looked up the woman's name. Receptionists often had enormous influence on their bosses. Judging from the dumbfounded look on Chandran's face, she'd have to teach him this trick, along with many other sales skills he obviously lacked.

She strode into Grant Popper's office. When he waved at the guest chairs, she chose the one nearest his desk and pulled it even closer before sitting down, flinging one knee over the other in a way that was equal parts extroverted optimist and I-won't-take-no-for-an-answer stubborn. Chandran, chin low and eyes wide, sank into the other available seat. Together, they looked across an expansive, swamp oak desk at their quarry.

Jannie gave the wood a brisk rap. Chandran jumped, but the client calmly trained his gray eyes on hers. He sat up straighter and ran a hand through his curly auburn hair.

"What's this I'm hearing, Grant?" Her tone held a challenge, but there was an underlying smile in it.

"That I'm canceling. Moving my money elsewhere, to a company that is actually committed to making my investment work."

Chandran shrank further into himself. Jannie sat forward in her chair, confidence building, anticipating a fun battle. She knew Grant Popper well. He'd always relished a good fists-cocked negotiation.

"Give me one reason why I should allow you back into our premiere properties now that you've told Chandran here you're dropping us for print—a medium virtually none of your millennial target group is remotely interested in. And, incidentally, we have two of your top competitors bidding for the positions you claim you don't want, so if you're going to change your mind, you'll have to let me know right now."

And they were off, voices raised but good humor intact. Chandran got smaller and smaller by the minute, folding in on himself like a hedgehog in a hurricane.

At the end of half an hour, Jannie had convinced the client to sign on to another fifty-two-week contract, renewing all his sponsorship positions, and increasing his overall spending by fifteen percent. He fought hard for concessions. She granted him just enough to make him feel like a winner, while keeping BB&M's profit margins high.

Grant Popper was happy. Jannie could practically hear her blood singing in her veins. She gazed triumphantly at Chandran, who was slack-jawed and sweating.

In a taxi on the way back to the office, she asked, "So, what have you learned from this?"

"That you're the best freaking salesperson I've ever come across." Chandran tented his hands in a prayerful gesture and bowed to her, angling sideways in the backseat of the cab.

"Try again." She narrowed her eyes at him.

"Okay," he said. "I learned that Popper likes to barter. He seemed to actually enjoy duking it out with you."

"Right. The man's an extrovert who wants to drive a good bargain. He doesn't like things to be too easy. He needs to feel he's singlehandedly accomplished something nobody else could. And he wants to feel special. Never taken for granted."

"Weird how you have this kind of insight," Chandran muttered.

"What?" She looked at him, trying not to scowl.

"Nothing. Sorry. I almost lost us this one."

Jannie wrestled with herself. She wanted Chandran to like her, but, more than that, she wanted him to learn a valuable lesson. Keep in-depth files on customers. Become a better salesman. She wouldn't always be there to ride in on her Hi-yo, Silver steed and save his ass when things went sour.

She reached a difficult conclusion. It was her duty as his manager to deliver a tough love message. Right now, here in the cab. Not just for his own benefit. For the good of their entire team.

By the time they reached BB&M ten minutes later, Chandran's skin was a sickly shade of gray, and he clutched his stomach. He bolted from the taxi, leaving Jannie to pay the driver, and disappeared into the building before she could catch up with him.

For the remainder of the day, he made like the Invisible

Man. The other staff members seemed even less friendly than before, which was puzzling. Jannie had just saved all their butts. They should have been kissing hers. At the very least, a sincere thank-you would have been nice.

The encounter with Gleb shook Suze, making her feel dirty. The man's behavior, eyeing her as if she'd been a scrumptious dessert, had been sickening.

She took a mid-afternoon shower. The pounding water was refreshing, but she still felt sullied. What a creep that man was, to make Suze feel so cheap.

But what a slacker *she* was for not being able to pay the rent. Back to job hunting she went. She would pay her bills somehow or other. No way would she put herself at the mercy of her sleazy super.

"Hello, my name is Suze Foster. I see on your website you're looking for an administrative assistant."

"That's right. What recent experience do you have?"

"I've worked in that role and also as a receptionist."

"When and where?"

Sigh. "1992. The firm no longer exists."

Click.

On to the next ad. And the next. If she just kept at it, something would develop. She needed to be indefatigable and maintain a positive attitude. Just like she'd always coached Jannie, when things had been grim at school.

Half an hour later, Suze opened up her sofa bed and, fully dressed, crawled under the blankets. She stuffed two knuckles into her mouth to suppress the jolting sobs that wracked her body and cried for the better part of an hour, nonstop. She mourned the waste her life had been, the marriage that had started with such promise and developed into a disaster, and the effect this unhealthy relationship had had on her beloved daughter. She cried about how much she missed Jannie and the home they had shared together. About how she was too ashamed to seriously pursue her relationship with Aram, the man she thought she was growing to love. And, more than anything, she cried about the dying of her cherished dream of finally achieving a life of independence.

Eventually, she slept. It was only three o'clock in the afternoon, but Suze was lost to the world.

11

BUDDING RELATIONSHIPS

*I*n spite of ongoing office woes, the gorgeous, snappy autumn weather made Jannie want to burst into song as she strode along on her early morning walk. She crunched through the dead leaves that carpeted the sidewalk and looked fondly at her new boots. Laurence Dacade over-the-knee patent leather, no less. Sexy and tight, and altogether hot.

But they'd been expensive, and she owed Frodo big bucks. He'd tendered his final bill, which had come to a shade over five grand. Cash flow would be an issue for a while, but the posters were worth every penny. Not only had Jannie been able to fix a challenging personal situation —for the first time in her life without Mom's intervention —but she'd also played a brilliant role as Cupid. Tyler and Frodo were so sweet on each other. It was a win-win-win situation for all of them, and she was just sorry she'd had to cause a fire and a flood to achieve it.

Five minutes of walking was more than enough exercise. These boots weren't nearly as comfortable as they were glamorous. Jannie checked her watch and decided she had just enough time to drop in on Tyler, before driving to work.

"Knock, knock. You guys decent?" she called through the door of 4B.

"One second, Jannie," one of them said.

It was nice to hear a welcoming, friendly voice. The door swung open. Tyler stood there, wearing geeky jeans and a plaid shirt, a look of blissful happiness on his face. He swooped Jannie up in a bear hug.

"Hey, easy there, big guy," she said, just as Frodo appeared and flung his thin body onto theirs, creating a three-way embrace.

They staggered, wedged in the entrance to Tyler's condo, holding their multi-person squeeze. Tyler's three cats approached and stropped themselves against their legs in a frenzy of motorboat purring.

It was cozy but a bit weird, and the two man-boys showed no sign of letting go of her. She wriggled. They clutched. She wriggled some more, and said, "Leggo of me, boys," and they finally desisted. The cats scattered.

"Come in, Jannie. I just made a pot of shit-kicking joe," Frodo said.

He was rocking the same look as Tyler, all jeans and madly plaid. The two smiled at each other and held hands, Frodo's pale skin almost phosphorescent next to Tyler's deep brown.

Cute? Ridiculously so. Jannie was equal parts proud and jealous.

"Sorry, no time for coffee, she said. "But I've got your final payment for the posters." She handed over a wad of cash to Frodo, who made like a magician and vanished it.

"Woot!" Frodo exclaimed. "Hey, we can buy our new furniture now."

Jannie surveyed the apartment. Apart from multiple

feline claw marks, the furniture looked fine. No water stains at all. She said so and both of them nodded.

"Yes, well, we're thinking of upgrading the IKEA," Tyler said. "Now that we're a couple, we want to choose things together." He gave her a shy grin.

A couple. Created by her, Jannie Morris. She felt herself swelling up inside, thrilled to be recognized as a pretty wonderful human being. Those people at the office should be more grateful to be led by such a magnanimous, loving person.

Which reminded her. She needed to vamoose. Set a good example and all that.

She marched her sexy boots to the parking garage, got in the Mini, and zipped off to work, there to kick figurative ass. The BB&M team was going to close the quarter with the most outstanding sales results ever. All due to her remarkable leadership.

The empty receptionist's desk was relatively tidy, but only because Jannie had been there at ten o'clock last night, sorting through the junk that had accumulated for the past few days. If only Shivani would allow her to replace Bonnie, but all the HR woman would tell her was that no permanent hires could be made before year-end results came in. Until then, they'd have to make do with the staff they had.

"You, there!" Jannie called to whoever it was walking past her door, which was wide open—the sign of an open-minded and approachable boss.

"Yes, Jannie?" It was one of those generic balding guys. Not Chandran; this man was lighter-skinned. So that left Jack, Gord or Mike. Jannie decided to gamble.

"Mike, I'd kill for a coffee." She held up an empty mug and twiddled it by its handle. Her eyes were locked on her computer screen in a demonstration of her commitment to excellence and great time management.

For a moment there was no response. She looked up, eyebrows snapping together over the bridge of her nose. She required coffee to operate at maximum efficiency.

"My name is Gord," the generic guy said, after an uncomfortably extended silence. He leaned against the doorway and didn't reach out to take the mug.

"Really? Gord, eh? Well, that makes you," and here Jannie consulted her computer screen, "our lowest performer of the last quarter. Are you aware that your sales are down by ten percent?"

"No. Thank you for telling me. I really should get right to work to correct that," he said. And disappeared.

Well, *that* strategy for getting a subordinate to fetch her morning caffeine had been an epic fail. Jannie hauled herself out of her chair, took her mug, and walked into the kitchenette. She popped a plastic capsule into the machine, pushed buttons for extra cream and extra sugar, and awaited the spluttering drip of coffee. As if she had time for this.

Some women were chattering in the hallway. Whatever they were discussing was clearly unrelated to business. Jannie tuned in and made out Joelle's voice, among others.

"Thanks awfully for the fantastic gifts. Ben and I are so lucky to have friends like you."

It was a sucker punch to the gut. There'd clearly been a social function Jannie had known nothing about.

Joelle entered the kitchenette, carrying an empty cup. When she saw Jannie, the smile on her face froze. Her eyes faded from lit-up sparkly to spud-skin dull.

"Good morning," she said. Her voice rang with all the enthusiasm of Donald Trump greeting his old pal, Hillary.

"Hi, Joelle. What was that all about?"

"What?"

"You know, the gift thing."

"Oh, nothing. Listen, I'm a bit late for a meeting. Could I use the machine?"

She walked forward, but Jannie stood her ground in front of the coffee maker, feet planted and arms crossed.

"'scuse me," Joelle said.

"Not 'til you tell me." Jannie didn't budge.

Joelle gave one of her long-suffering sighs. "Okay, if you must know, I was saying thanks for the shower gifts."

Jannie's heart plummeted into her designer boots. Yes, the two of them were separated by rank. But they'd been desk-mates for a long time. Jannie had lived through the rollercoaster ups and downs of the Joelle and Ben dating days. She felt gutted she hadn't been invited to the shower.

"Oh," she said in a small voice. She moved away from the machine to let Joelle use it. "I'm glad it was a success."

"Thanks." Joelle's attention seemed to be riveted on adding nondairy cream to her coffee and giving it a stir.

Jannie gave herself a mental shake. A good leader must rise above petty personal issues. The junior staff members had thrown Joelle a shower, and she hadn't been invited. So what? They'd probably not been comfortable with the idea of having their boss at a girly party, where people decorated paper plate hats and played idiotic games. Jannie could grasp that. Kind of.

"Well, have a nice day. A profitable one! And don't worry about the shower oversight. I'll look forward all the more to the wedding!" Jannie motored past Joelle without glancing at her again.

There. She'd made it clear. Joelle had better deliver.

Suze had slept for eighteen hours. Nightmares had plagued her, though, and she felt more tired than ever. Her eyes were crusty around the edges from all that crying. Her throat was dry, and her tongue felt too big for her mouth. She badly needed a shower. If only she had enough energy.

In the end, what propelled her out of bed was an urgent need to pee. Then, refusing to allow herself to dive back under the covers, she turned on the water and spent the next ten minutes scrubbing away the negativity of the previous day and night. With her hair still wet, she dressed herself in a pair of Jannie's old boyfriend-style jeans and a long-sleeved, dusky pink t-shirt.

There. Fresh, clean. No artifice. Suze wiped mist off the bathroom mirror and stared at her reflection. Not bad for her age. With makeup on and hair styled, she'd be even better. Definitely a woman who should be hired. By someone, somewhere.

Maybe she'd call Jannie. A talk with her daughter would give her the boost she needed.

"'lo?" Jannie answered in a distracted manner.

"Hi, sweetie. How are you? Things better at work?"

"Yeah, I guess." Jannie's voice didn't convey conviction.

"That's encouraging." Suze waited a beat, but Jannie didn't elaborate. "And how's Earl?"

Dead silence. Then, "Oh, he's fine. Haven't really seen much of him lately. Too busy at the office."

"You're busy, or do you mean Earl is?"

"Me. He's *dying* to get together, but it's so crazy here. Still working out how to inspire and lead. It's not easy."

"Just be true to your inner compass. You've got a warm heart. Listen to it."

"Yeah, well, I'll continue to read the books I bought. I

haven't come across anything yet about management by warm heart, but I'll give it some thought."

"Good. Well, I'll let you go. Chin up, sweetie!"

"Thanks, Mom. And—it's really good to hear your voice."

"Same to you, kiddo. Talk soon."

Suze hung up. Jannie sounded like she was coping. Maybe not thriving, but much less frantic than she'd been the last time they'd talked. Perhaps the worst of her adjustment period was over.

Typical, though. Jannie hadn't even asked how she was doing. But Suze was the mom, not the daughter. She was the one who needed to be strong and set a good example. And what if Jannie *had* asked? The poor kid had enough on her plate without learning her mother was totally broke and about to be evicted.

Suze's phone buzzed. She looked at the display. Aram! The man was persistent. It was flattering to be pursued, if that was what he was doing.

"Hi." Suze tried her best not to sound breathy and excited.

"Hello, Suze. I'm in the Bathurst and Bloor area this morning on business. Care to get together for coffee? Say, 10:30?"

Yes, she cared. Very much. But she didn't want to sound too enthusiastic.

"Hmm, well, I think I could do that. Where do you want to meet?"

"Why don't I swing by and pick you up?"

"Really? You don't mind?"

"Of course not. My pleasure."

"How kind of you, Aram. I'll wait for you in the lobby."

In the last month, Suze had seen him a few times over

coffee or tea, usually on a last-minute basis. In the beginning, they'd told each other tales about their pasts— Aram's move as a child from Lebanon to Paris, his Oxford education, and finally his emigration to Canada as a young adult. Suze's much less peripatetic life in Toronto was mundane to her, but Aram seemed fascinated to hear about her childhood, and what growing up in Riverdale had been like.

Eventually, after they'd covered the basics, they moved on and discussed things that concerned them now. She almost always talked about her two greatest priorities— Jannie and job-hunting—and Aram was unfailingly patient and supportive. He gave her updates on Jannie sightings and listened to Suze's stories about her interviewing progress. She never revealed how desperate she was. Nevertheless, on each visit, he offered her help in securing a position, which she always refused. She wanted his respect, and maybe much more than that, but not his charity.

Suze walked back over to the mirror and studied herself. Should she do her hair and makeup? But why bother? This had to be their sixth coffee get-together. If he had motives other than being a Good Samaritan he'd have been more forthright a while ago. And she was at least a decade older than he was. In fact, how ridiculously vain to think Aram had ever felt the least bit attracted to her. It was so obvious he was just being kind, as he would with any pathetic case.

She grabbed a comb, yanked it through her damp hair, applied pale pink lipstick but shunned the much-needed under-eye concealer, and put on an old quilted jacket. There. Good enough for a coffee with a platonic friend.

As she crossed the lobby, making her way to the exit, she saw Gleb. Creepy, slimy Gleb, wearing a leather belt laden with clunky tools, and wafting a hammer in one hand.

"'Morning," Suze said in a low voice. She kept her eyes trained on the exit, searching for Aram.

"Hallo. Is end of month. You pay now?" Gleb's voice oiled its way down Suze's body.

"Soon. Although there might be a further delay. I'm still looking for work."

"No good. I need rent now."

"I'll get it. Soon."

"You better. Or, it's Form N4 for you. Unless . . ." He studied her, from top to bottom, and then in reverse.

"Unless what?" She wasn't sure she wanted an answer.

"You and me. Maybe make deal. Work for Gleb."

"Really? What kind of work?" She was halfway interested. Possibly it could lead to something else. And, she could list it as recent experience on her resume.

"I show you. Free preview."

Gleb slotted his hammer into his leather tool belt. With the speed of a striking cobra, he grabbed one of her arms and, using his empty hand, chucked her chin up. Suze saw puckered lips closing in on hers, and froze in horror. She shut her eyes, twisted her head away and opened her mouth to scream. Somehow, though, her throat constricted. She couldn't utter a peep and hated herself for being so timid. She writhed away from Gleb's protruding tongue, but his rancid breath still assaulted her.

She tried again to call out for help. Her voice failed her. The man's hands were everywhere. And then they weren't.

Suze's eyelids popped open. There was Gleb, against the opposite wall, clutching his head with both hands. And there was Aram, standing in a protective stance beside Suze, fists up in a classic boxing pose. Aram, dark hair disheveled, breathing hard, with fury in his eyes. He scowled at the super as if daring him to get back on his feet and take it like a man.

"You pay for this," Gleb muttered. He didn't get up.

"No, my friend. But you will, and dearly, if you ever touch this woman again."

"Aram . . ." Suze whispered.

"Are you all right?" Aram dropped his clenched hands and turned to her. "I'm sorry I didn't arrive a minute earlier."

"I'm fine. Let's go."

With a toss of her head, Suze turned her back on Gleb, who was still slouched against the wall. Aram put his well-muscled arm around her shoulder. She hoped with all her heart his touch conveyed more than kindness. Surely, a mere friend would never hold her with such tenderness.

The time had come. She was going to find out just what Aram's intentions were. This would be the most interesting coffee date ever.

TWO ON ONE

*a*s they approached Aram's silver Audi A4, Suze surprised herself by slipping her arm around his waist. She felt her feminine curves meld to his masculine angles. A wave of pure heat coursed through her body as she pressed herself against his side.

He looked down at her and smiled, and at that moment the first snowflakes of winter began to fall, floating in fluffy cascades from the sky. They landed on Aram's hair, latching onto his eyelashes. It was as if everything else disappeared—no financial woes, no concerns about Jannie, no evil archvillain Gleb—just Aram in the dancing snow.

But as he handed her into the car, reality returned, striking with the impact of a cue stick connecting with a billiard ball. Aram was a kind man. A kind, *younger* man. Who was being thoughtful to an elderly, penniless widow. Because he was an ex-neighbor. Because she was needy. And because he was a do-gooder.

Not because he was attracted to her. Never that.

She looked down at her hands, raw from the cold. One

bore a circular brown mark—her first age spot, there as a cruel reminder she was so much older. He would be horrified if he suspected the depth of her feelings toward him.

They sat side by side. Suze fastened her seatbelt. Aram started the car but made no attempt to pull away from the curb. She had to say something. She couldn't bear any more of these café dates; she yearned for something more intimate. She wanted his hands on her body, his lips on her mouth, and his skin against hers.

She'd thank him for being a friend but tell him that after today they should stop seeing each other. She'd make something up—maybe that she was dating an older gentleman who didn't approve of her having coffee with another man.

She turned toward Aram at the same instant he turned to her.

"I can't see you again," she said, just as Aram said, "I can't go on like this." They both recoiled as if burned by flying sparks.

Aram was the first to speak. "*What* did you say?"

Suze squeezed her knees with shaking hands. "I can't see you again. I appreciate everything you've done, helping me find work. I'll use all your tips. But my new boyfriend—"

"Stop right there." Aram's face was carved from stone, every feature hard and cold.

"No, I need to—"

"But *I* need to do something I should have done weeks ago." Aram leaned toward Suze with intent.

As first kisses went, it wasn't the most elegant. They were sitting beside each other, and Suze was hampered by the shoulder strap of her seat belt. The car radio was blatting out some kind of business report, and the temperature was freezing because the heater hadn't kicked in yet.

But, to Suze, Aram's lips felt like velvet bliss, and although she tried to make herself pull away after the first contact, she found her body had a completely different plan. The kiss was light and tender—a promise of more kisses to come and true passion to follow. She loved the slight brush of his moustache and beard on her sensitive skin, and leaned against her shoulder harness, hoping for more, but Aram sat back.

"What's this about a boyfriend?"

"I made him up. I thought you were just being kind to me. I couldn't continue like this."

Aram hit the steering wheel with both hands. "That's what I get for being overly reserved." In his agitation, his accent was more pronounced. "I've wanted to tell you from the minute I met you, Suze, how attracted I am to you."

"I'm older, you know," she said in a small voice.

"Are you? Immaterial. You are everything I admire and want. I promise to show you I'm worthy. But, no other boyfriends ever again, not even made-up ones!"

Coffee with Aram that day was different from their other dates. This one was wrapped in gauzy romance and tied up with a vivid bow of desire. They held hands. They pressed foreheads together. Few words were spoken, but Suze had never understood any conversation more fully.

It was another long night at the office. Jannie struggled all alone in the weltering mess of paperwork. And then, yet another restaurant-bought dinner. Healthy sushi, plus a side order of those tempura vegetables—a tasty way of getting her greens.

For weeks on end, she'd subsisted on takeout. Her skin had lost its bloom and her clothes were getting tight. If she didn't reverse the trend, she'd have to up-size her wardrobe or risk ripping out the seat of her pants the next time she bent over. That wouldn't be in keeping with her new theory of management, which combined dressing for success and controlling the staff via implanted suggestions.

Like, "Chandran, it's so great you're following up today on the Printz and Popper business. You know how much Grant Popper loves chocolate chip cookies, right?"

And then Chandran, who probably didn't know anything of the kind, would have a giant lightbulb flash in his brain, and he'd rush out to the bakery and take care of this task. He'd think it was his very own idea. Brilliant!

Reflecting on her Machiavellian strategy, Jannie boarded the condo elevator and hit the button for the fifth floor, just as she saw gorgeous Aram walk through the building's front entrance. With a total disregard for her spiffy Stuart Weitzman suede boots, she kicked out a foot to stop the elevator doors from closing. She hid the sushi takeout behind her back and finger-twiddled a coy hello at the adorable Mr. Krikorian with the twinkly eyes and the fantastic head of hair and the to-die-for beard and the long, lanky frame. He was so delicious Jannie almost forgot she was famished for real food.

"Is that tempura I smell?"

Damn. He'd caught her with takeout. Again.

She thought quickly. "Yes, and the finest sushi in this part of town. I've got plenty. Care to share?"

He looked at her, those straight brows of his slightly raised. Jannie couldn't decipher his expression. He was full of sexy mystique—which she bet he was using on her deliberately, knowing she was a luscious catch, if ever there was one.

"I'd love to have dinner with you," he said, the hint of a smile warming his features. "Your place or mine?"

Jannie almost dropped the bag of food. Maybe she really *was* irresistible. But there was no way Aram could come to her place. It was a rat's nest, piled high with old cartons and bags in the kitchen, and designer clothes strewn all over the bedroom and living room. Although making love on her new, faux-furry Mango coat might be the ultimate in sensuous sublimity, she wanted to clean the place up before entertaining a gentleman caller.

"How about your place?" She used her purring cat voice, projected from the back of her throat, like ujjayi breathing in yoga. It created a very sexy effect, but tickled. She coughed and Aram patted her on the back.

Jannie thanked him and handed him the bag of sushi as they exited the elevator. "Be with you in a mo'."

She dashed toward her own door, intending to drop off her snow-sodden coat and exchange her boots for some sexy heels. Plus, she needed a couple of minutes to freshen up: brush teeth, re-apply makeup, spritz cologne onto the essential pulse points. And put on better-quality lingerie: the matching set with black French lace that pushed up, in, and out in all the right places.

Less than five minutes later, she knocked on Aram's door. He opened it wide and ushered her in. As she passed by, she made a point of brushing her body against his, but he didn't seem to notice. Perhaps she was being too subtle. Or, maybe he was just hungry. No worries, she'd try again post-sushi. Fish was high in protein—excellent for the libido—and she had no doubt she'd succeed in her plan for tonight's seduction.

At last. The time was now. He *would* be hers.

In the minutes it had taken to spruce herself up, Aram had debagged the collection of sushi. He'd arranged the cartons on the coffee table in front of his leather couch and laid out white, porcelain plates. Wooden chopsticks, courtesy of the restaurant, were the only implements. Jannie squinted at them uncertainly but said nothing.

"Drink?" Aram stood in the entrance to his kitchen, holding a bottle of white wine. "I've got a fresh, light Chablis from the Loire Valley that will go well with sushi, I believe."

"Yes. I would love a glass of Chablis." As if Jannie knew her Chablis from her Dr. Pepper, but she wanted to appear sophisticated. As well as voluptuous and ravishable.

"Here you are, then." He approached, a glass of wine in each hand, and gave her one. They sat side by side on the leather couch and clinked their crystal together. Jannie took a cautious sip. Not bad, but it was hard to concentrate on the wine when their knees were almost touching. She felt the heat radiating between their bodies and wondered if he did, too.

They took plates and served themselves, Jannie barely suppressing a curse as she fumbled with her chopsticks. Somehow she managed to capture a little sashimi, a bit of maki, and heaps of those healthy, tempura veggies. Plus, she dolloped out plenty of soy sauce into a dainty bowl, threw in some wasabi, and gave it a good stir. She looked up to see Aram regarding her with his inscrutable hazels and wondered if he thought she'd done something gauche. She hoped it hadn't been a turnoff.

They ate in silence. Aram seemed calm, but Jannie was getting increasingly edgy, unable to control the pincer action of her chopsticks and get any food to her lips. Whenever he looked down at his plate, she grabbed a piece of sushi with her fingers, gave it a saucy swirl, and stuffed it into her mouth. If she didn't seize these opportunities, she'd starve.

She was concentrating on conveying a morsel to her mouth when Aram finally spoke. "How's work going?"

Innocuous, but he'd startled Jannie, making her jump at a delicate moment. A piece of sashimi fell from her chopsticks, plummeting straight down her jacked up cleavage. She smiled widely, hoping he hadn't noticed. Or if he had, that this was a turn-on. She felt a trickle of soy sauce pointing toward the tidbit between her breasts. Perhaps he'd like to lick his way down the path to the promised land?

Apparently not. He sat perfectly still, regarding Jannie with his expression jammed firmly in neutral, waiting for her to answer. What was it he'd asked? How's work, perhaps, or something similarly yawny.

"Sales are going through the roof," she said.

It was true. Ever since she'd taken over as boss, BB&M's revenues had been astonishing. Not that anyone had given her credit or anything. The CEO in New York hadn't said boo about it, but Jannie still had the top job, which was a good sign.

She wiggled her torso to settle the invading sashimi. It seemed to have made itself a snug home in her lacy bra. She'd have to try to ignore it for now and evict it later when Aram wasn't looking.

"And your workload?"

"Pretty crazy. Way too much overtime. Still covering for our missing receptionist, too."

"Why not hire?"

"Corporate won't approve any new permanent staff members." Jannie sighed.

"What about a temp? You might be able to slide it through as an expense instead of a new headcount."

She stared at Aram. He'd just said something effing brilliant and yet so obvious she couldn't believe she'd never thought of it before. Yes, of course she should hire a temp and stop spending her spare hours cleaning up reception. What a great idea!

His eyes were trained on a piece of avocado roll that was pinioned perfectly between his chopsticks. Without looking up, he said, "You must know someone who's searching for work? Maybe a lady of a certain age who can take charge and lighten your own load?"

Jannie tried to give this serious thought, but she was entranced by the way his lips opened when he slipped the sushi into his mouth. The flash of his square white teeth was dazzling.

She recollected herself and shook her head. "Nope. Don't know anyone like that."

Unfortunately, with this movement, she'd sent Sashimi-san a bit farther down the pleasure chute. The damn fish was starting to itch. And, within the warmth of her bosom, it would likely start to smell soon, too. *Eau de poisson* probably wasn't Aram's perfume of choice.

But he was looking at her as if he expected a better answer. She wrinkled her forehead, trying to come up with something semi-intelligent. "I do know of some temp agencies."

"Agencies tend to charge hefty fees. A wise boss looks for efficiencies. Think about it. Surely you must know someone who would be perfectly suited. And available."

Again she shook her head. With her chopsticks, she reached for some more maki and was successful in dipping a piece in her soy-wasabi concoction. As she prepared to lever it from bowl to mouth, though, she lost control. The maki, dripping sauce everywhere, seemed to freeze in midair before landing—plop!—right on Aram's (how could she even silently say this delicately?) crotch.

For an instant, she was at a loss for what to do. She

hovered, wondering if she should grab it with her fingers or attempt to ply her wooden sticks with breezy élan and snatch it from Aram's hillock of delight.

She leaned forward with her sticks, snapping them in and out with the determination worthy of an enraged lobster, but Aram reached out and held her wrist. He seemed unperturbed. Maybe he was actually kind of stimulated.

Or maybe not. He just said, "An inevitable consequence of eating takeout Japanese. No worries. I'll get that," and he did, and added, "Perhaps we should call it a night."

He got up from the couch, collected the plates and started to pack up the leftovers. He was still über-sexy, even with a soy-stained man-mound. In fact, now Jannie couldn't take her eyes off it.

While she obsessed about this, he said, "Give my idea some thought. There must be a mature, capable person out there who would excel in a temporary receptionist job. Just until you get the go-ahead to hire someone permanent."

"All right. I'll think about it," she said, doubt twanging her voice. The minute he started to carry dishes to the kitchen, she reached into her cleavage to retrieve the pesky, elusive pisces. She froze as she heard him coming back into the living room, then quickly stuffed it back down her bra. It prickled like hell but it'd be embarrassing to be caught with it, now that he'd cleaned everything up.

Later that night Jannie mulled over their dinner together, thinking about how much Aram must like her. Otherwise, he wouldn't have asked her over to his place. Maybe she needed to make the first move. And she should eat before visiting. She seemed to have problems juggling portions with passion.

13

GAINFUL EMPLOYMENT

*I*t was the morning after their storybook first kiss and Suze was still feeling euphoric. Yesterday, when Aram had taken her home, he'd escorted her right to her apartment door to protect her from possible stalkers or lecherous supers. Before leaving, he'd given her one last kiss.

Thinking of it now, she had no words to describe it. Soft? Yes, it had been feathery light and filled with tenderness. But soft didn't begin to capture its aching sweetness, its patient eagerness. Gentle? Yes, but beneath the restraint she'd sensed Aram's longing, deep and insistent. It was a kiss that evoked a whole new world, bursting with promise. Suze savored the sensation, touching her fingertips to her lips, trying to replicate the whispering touch of his mouth on hers.

When she finally came back down to earth she noticed a white envelope lying on the mat inside her door. She opened it.

True to his word, Gleb had served her with the dreaded N4 form. As of tomorrow she had fourteen days before building management could force her to move. Unless Suze's fairy godmother appeared, twangling a spangled wand and magicking up rent money, Suze was on her way out the door. Evicted.

Yesterday, if she'd received the N4, it would have destroyed her. She'd have been a compacted mass of shame and nerves, unable to function.

Today, buoyed by romance and newfound hope, Suze felt capable of dealing with the threat of homelessness in a calm, methodical fashion. Surely, it wouldn't be that easy to force her to move. She'd do some research. The internet likely had lots of good advice for people like her.

Yeah, deadbeats. Who stiffed their landlords.

Being unreliable wasn't like her. It had been her late husband, Desmond, who'd been the irresponsible partner. During their marriage, Suze always managed to hold onto enough household money to keep the family unit warm and fed, with a roof over their heads. But then Des died, after gambling away almost every penny. Suze swore she'd never get that close to disaster again.

Now, here she was. Right on the brink.

This pattern of thinking was not in keeping with the positive tone of the morning. Pushing all negative thoughts aside, Suze sat down at her computer. She'd consult the experts and get a reprieve. Somehow. And, she'd renew her efforts to find a job. So what if she'd sent dozens of applications that had ended up being ignored or rejected? With every rejection she was that much closer to an acceptance.

She worked deep into the night. Later, when she slept, her dreams were adventurous and upbeat. And ever so racy.

Jannie arrived at the office well before nine o'clock. Already, sales reps were dashing around, frantic looks on their faces, trying to pull together presentations and get to their first appointments on time. The gang was working pretty hard these days, even if most of them left each evening at five o'clock on the dot. Maybe the heightened energy was the product of Jannie's new motivational strategy of pointing out who the lowest performers were and hinting that those who didn't pull their weight might be in jeopardy. Of course, she was always subtle about saying this, as the nuanced senior manager she was.

The phone lines were blinking up a storm in reception. Before she'd sushi-bombed Aram's crotch last night she had cleared most of the paperwork, but the first mail delivery of the day was already teetering perilously on Bonnie's old desk.

As Jannie entered her office, her phone beeped. It was Mom, which was handy, because maybe this would be a good time to seek advice about dating Aram. No, Earl.

"Hiya, Mom. How are you?"

"Doing great. You?"

Her voice sounded like it had been injected with tiny bubbles of excitement. Mom was so cute.

"I'm okay. Still swamped at work."

"Well, better to be busy than out of a job entirely." A few of her happiness bubbles seemed to have popped.

"Oh, that's right. I keep forgetting you're still looking for work. You are, right?"

A pause. Then Mom said, "Yes, sweetie," in a soft voice. No bubbles whatsoever.

"Well, I'm sure things will pick up for you soon. Hey, I need to talk to you about my latest date with, uh, Earl."

"I'm all ears."

"We had dinner together last night, and I thought he

was enjoying being with me, but I spilled food on him, and it was like he completely lost interest."

Mom was making little squeaking noises. Why wasn't she taking this seriously?

"Stop laughing at me!"

"Yes, all right." But she made a lady-like snort, quickly corked, before continuing, "I hope it wasn't hot soup. And you didn't drop it on anything delicate."

"Well, it wasn't soup. But, the delicate part? I hit a bullseye, unfortunately."

Again, Mom chuckled. "I'm sure Earl is still interested. He was probably concerned about his dry cleaning bill, that's all."

"I hope you're right."

"Sure I am. You'll see."

"Great. Well, Mom, if there's nothing else . . ." Jannie looked at the message light flashing on her desk phone. No more time to dilly-dally.

But Mom interjected before Jannie could disconnect. "Actually, there is. I know I haven't asked you this before. I've been trying hard to find a job without bothering you. But I want to put a little bug in your ear. If you hear of anything that might be suitable for me, anything at all, I'm extremely interested in applying for it. Can you keep a lookout?"

And that's when it hit Jannie. Lightbulbs flashed pure incandescence behind her eyeballs. Her brain sizzled like a Gordon Ramsay groundnut-seared sirloin. It was all so obvious.

"Mom, I may be able to help," she said, slowly. "But you'll have to pretend not to know me. Can you do that?"

"Sounds strange." Mom's words weren't enthusiastic, but Jannie could hear a lilt of optimism in her voice.

"You have to trust me. I think I have the answer to a problem that's been bugging me, and it'll help you, too."

"Tell me all about it."

"Not now. But can you come to my office at noon today? Bring a resume, and dress like you're going to an official interview. And whatever you do, don't tell anyone you've ever met me before, okay?"

"All right, Secret Agent Jannie Morris. I'm intrigued, and will see you at noon."

Jannie hung up. Her hands quivered, in the most joyful kind of way possible. Was it really going to be this simple? Could she hire her mom as a temp and keep it a secret from the troops?

Mom had kept her maiden name when she'd married, so she was a Foster to Jannie's Morris. And the two of them looked completely different, her mom being all angelic beauty and Jannie being a sassy, female version of her father. She winced, never liking to dwell on the bad old days, but at least he'd been a good-looking fella.

The point was, it might actually work. Jannie sat down and began to plan.

Suze removed her shabby winter coat and bundled it in her arms. When she stepped off the elevator, clad in her interview clothes, there was no one to greet her at the curved reception desk. Piles of paper were stacked in precarious Leaning Tower arrangements. The phone was ringing nonstop. It was a strange way to run a business.

A youngish man of South Asian descent appeared, clutching a sheaf of printouts and looking as though the hounds of hell were on his heels.

"Hello," Suze said. "Could you please tell me how I can get in touch with Ms. Jannie Morris?"

He stopped in mid-gallop. "You have an appointment with Jannie?" The way he said "Jannie" was interesting. It sounded as if he wanted to spit out a mouthful of arsenic.

"Yes. My name is Suze Foster."

"Well, Ms. Foster, I'll call her for you. Are you sure, though?"

"Why wouldn't I be?" Suze was genuinely curious.

"No reason." But the man looked at her with concern in his eyes. Was that pity she saw there?

"Thanks so much . . ."

"Chandran. And it's my pleasure." He put his stack of paper on the reception desk and punched in some numbers on the phone. "I'm sorry to disturb you, Jannie. It's Chandran. There's a woman named Ms. Suze Foster in reception to see you." He listened a moment and then hung up.

"She's on her way. And I'm definitely on mine. Good luck. I mean it." With that, he gave Suze's right hand a two-pump shake, grabbed his printouts, and hightailed it out of there.

Within sixty seconds, Jannie appeared. She was dressed Lois Lane-style, with a sharkskin gray skirt and matching jacket over a clinging raspberry knit top featuring a just-this-side-of acceptable décolleté. Her dark hair curled around her head in a jubilant riot, her brown eyes danced, and her grin stretched from ear to ear.

"Why, hello, Ms., uh, Foster! Welcome to BB&M!"

"Thank you for agreeing to meet me, Ms. Morris."

"Do call me Jannie."

"And you must call me, well, I guess you can call me Ms. Foster." Suze drew the line at having her daughter call her by her first name. It was too weird.

"Right, then, Ms. Foster, please follow me. Could I get you anything? Water? Coffee?"

"No, thanks. I'm fine."

The two women walked through the open area, past several flurried sales people who didn't look up, to Jannie's impressively furnished executive office. In a twinkling, Jannie closed the door and jumped about in a mad caper of exultation.

"Hallelujah! I've had a bolt of genius! I'm going to hire you as our temporary receptionist."

"*You're* going to hire me?" Suze heard her voice slide up an octave. "Really? You can do that?"

"Yes! Just for a short time, of course. Until Head Office approves someone permanent, but that could take weeks. Do you want the job?"

"Of course I do. I really need it. And I'm sure I can handle it. But won't you get into trouble? I mean, I'm your mom."

"Shhh!" Jannie hissed. She looked to the right and left, as if the office were bugged.

"Okay, I get it. We can't let anyone know, right?"

Jannie bopped her head up and down with great energy. "Nobody, Mom. I'd get into huge trouble for that. So, can you keep it a secret?"

"Absolutely. And from this moment onward, even when we're alone, make sure you call me Ms. Foster, not Mom. Oh, hell, if you have to, call me Suze."

"You know what, I think I'll stick to Ms. Foster. Calling you by your first name feels wrong. Besides, we could use a little class around this joint."

Suze smiled, and went on to ask about the responsibilities of the position, the hours, and the salary, which she thought was more than generous. She would start the next day, and be paid on a biweekly basis, although Jannie warned her she'd likely be there for only a month, or at most, two. By then, Head Office would in all probability have approved a permanent hire, and there was no way it could be Suze. This masquerade couldn't be sustained forever.

Suze hugged Jannie like this was their last embrace of all time. Which, in their new pretend world of not knowing each other, was apt.

As she left BB&M, she felt the lingering squeeze of Jannie's arms and the warmth of her daughter's love surrounding her. Life was grand, just grand.

14

NIPPED IN THE BUD

*H*iring Mom was a stroke of brilliance. From now on, Jannie wouldn't have to spend hours each night cleaning up administrative headaches. She'd get home at a reasonable hour. Maybe have time to clean up her neglected condo. Possibly even learn to cook so she could invite Aram over for dinner. Delectable after-dinner activities, too.

But first, she needed to start going to the gym again. Between the takeout food and the lack of exercise, Jannie was feeling uncomfortably flabby. She'd like to fix that before her upcoming nakedness with Aram. He might like a jiggly woman, but her wobbles were turning into rolls. With all the lust she felt, she might squash him in a frenzy of uncontrolled passion.

She grabbed her neglected exercise bag and checked her watch. Six o'clock. There were still a couple of people at their desks. For the first time since Jannie had been promoted, she was not going to be the last one there. She cast a carefree look at the messy desk in the foyer and left. First thing tomorrow, Mom would arrive and start setting things in order. Jannie gave herself an imaginary pat on the back for the inspired flash she'd had in hiring her.

Ignoring the rumbling in her stomach, Jannie cranked up the Mini. She drove directly to the gym, eyes resolutely on the road, not even glancing at the fast-food joints she passed.

It had been so long since she'd packed her workout clothes, she couldn't even remember what they looked like. In the changing room, she sorted out her supplies. Pristine gym shoes, socks. A high-tech aerobics outfit with a cool-looking bra top and ultra-fitting pants. She was good to go.

Or almost. The shoes fit. But the supposedly stretchy two-piecer was a trifle on the tight side. Actually, a whole lot on the tight side. Jannie stuck an index finger between the waistband and her belly and felt all circulation to that digit immediately cease.

She must have gained more weight than she'd thought. Rogue formations of fat were trying to escape the bra, like turbulent ocean waves crashing against a cleverly engineered Dutch dam. Jannie shook her head in dismay.

No one would notice the overstretched fabric if she put on a chic headband and applied lots of mascara. She admired the effect in the mirror, then sashayed into the slick-looking gym with the impossible to figure out techno-machines. Immediately, she felt more daunted than desirable.

She took a deep breath. Better to take the first step in a journey than stay mired in the past. Now *that* was quotable! She'd have to remember to use it in her next inspirational email.

First, the treadmill. A nice, brisk five-minute warm-up. But so many buttons. She pushed a few at random.

Within two minutes, Jannie wondered if she was on the brink of cardiac arrest. She hadn't moved this vigorously in ages. Her heart was trying to beat its way out of her chest. And speaking of which, her breasts were making best efforts to escape the confines of her too-tight outfit. Thank God they were forcibly restrained by the miracle fabric, which was carving huge red tracks into her flesh. Could boobs blister?

Three minutes in. At this point she was supposed to raise the pace to level six. She didn't. She loped along like a graceless wildebeest, toggling between levels four and five. Occasionally she tugged at her designer bra straps to relieve the soreness where they were etching perma-grooves into her shoulders.

In her misery, she didn't at first notice the young man who'd commandeered the adjacent machine. Between gasps for air, Jannie stole a peek. No way, it was Kirk!

He had no right to look so fit and attractive in his modest shorts and t-shirt combo. And how could he afford membership here? He must be doing better on his computer fix-it salary than she'd thought. She flicked sweat out of her eyes, hoping her mascara truly was waterproof, glad she was dressed in the hottest new fabric and style, and wondered if she looked as attractive to him as he did to her. Not that they needed to appeal to each other. They were buds, nothing more. Supportive, equally scarred comrades who'd survived high school remedial classes and gone on to successful futures.

Kirk hadn't recognized her yet. Jannie upped the pace of her treadmill so she'd appear more athletic. As she pitched herself forward into cheetah-like velocity, she gathered up what breath she had left, and engaged.

"Hiya, Kirkie!"

He stopped fiddling with the controls on his machine and looked over at her. His dark green eyes widened. "Jannie! You're the last person I thought I'd see tonight!"

"Really? I'm a bit of a workout queen, you know." Gasp, pant, heave. She pulled at the athletic bra. Instead of lifting and displaying her assets to best advantage, it was trying to hack her to pieces.

"I'm here about four times a week," he said, slowly. "Haven't bumped into you before."

"Well, I've been working late. But you may see me more often from now on." She tried to say this in a calm, collected way. But it came out in a series of nasty grunts and huffs. She was struggling to get air into her lungs. When the machine finished its five-minute program, she felt over-the-moon grateful.

Chest heaving, Jannie turned toward Kirk, who hadn't yet fired up his treadmill. She started to tell him something about how committed she was to a healthy lifestyle, combining local, farm-sourced produce with a fanatical dedication to a well-tuned body, when she noticed him staring at her. Which would be fine if he were drowning in the velour-plush depths of her chocolate eyes. Or gazing at her curvaceous body in an appreciative way.

But, he was googly-eyed staring at Jannie's breasts as if they were suddenly able to whistle Dixie. Strange. They were ample and definitely two of her best features, but the last time she'd checked, they hadn't really been the performer types.

She looked down. Miss Left Breast was doing a splendid job of allowing the athletic bra to control her natural exuberance. Miss Rightie, though, had figured out how to beat the system, and had popped up and out of her harness, like a runaway horse fleeing a burning barn.

OMG, she'd *nipped* poor Kirkie. Here, under the fluorescent lights in this high-tech gym. Without even having been plied with a glass of lemon gin, which would have given her some kind of excuse.

There was only one thing to do. Distract Kirk with chitchat.

"What's the setting on your treadmill?" An inane question from someone who was flashing boobage at a platonic friend. But she needed him to look elsewhere—anywhere but at her escape artist breast.

As in a trance, he turned and checked the dial. While his eyes were focused on the machine, Jannie grabbed Rightie and pushed her with mega-strength back into her restraints. There was an ominous creaking sound, but at least now decency had been restored. Everything had happened so quickly that Kirk would think it had just been a dream.

"I start at a five and work my way . . ." He looked up at empty air and swiveled his head back and forth.

Jannie was already heading for the changing room. Now that her breasts had tasted freedom, they might make another break for it if she did any more exercising.

"Great seeing you, Kirkie," she called over her shoulder.

Fortunately, he'd already switched on his machine and was lolloping like a shy puppy, arms flopping and feet slapping away at the moving belt. He'd always been a trifle awkward. Jannie smiled; it was endearing. She slipped through the door and cast one last look at him, watching as he picked up speed, his spiky brown hair hardly moving, but his well-muscled legs starting to blur.

How wonderful it was to have a routine and to be surrounded by friendly, helpful people. Suze couldn't believe how lucky she was to have this job. Temporary or not, it was the best thing that had happened to her in years.

Well, maybe the second-best thing. The wonderful, caring, sexy *very* best thing now called her each evening. She'd been too concerned about her new job to see him midweek, but today was Friday, and she was looking forward to having dinner with the man she was beginning to think she loved.

Her cell phone buzzed. Suze frowned. She was at work. Aram knew he shouldn't call her during business hours.

"Hello?"

"Suze, darling. I have to cancel tonight's date. I'm leaving town right away. My mother's ill."

"I'm so sorry to hear this." Of course she was concerned his mother was sick. She was also very sad she wouldn't be seeing the man of her dreams this weekend. She pinched herself. "Don't worry about our date. You need to be with your mom. Where does she live?"

"Outside of Montreal. Small town called Hudson."

Suze wasn't familiar with Montreal. All she knew was it was too far away.

"She's been taken to Lakeshore General on the West Island. She has a tricky heart that sometimes acts up, but fortunately this time her condition doesn't sound too serious. Still, I must go."

"Of course. And I wish your mom a speedy recovery. When you have time, though, please call me," she said in a low voice.

"Without fail. And we'll see each other soon."

Suze slid her cell phone back into her handbag, which she kept under her desk. Her neatly organized, almost paper-free desk. She took pride in keeping it in spick-and-span condition.

The main phone line sounded. Suze answered it after one ring.

"Good morning, BB&M. How may I direct your call?"

"To the fucker who sold me a shitty ad campaign."

Suze paused. This was a new one. But she was resourceful and had growing confidence in her receptionist's skills. She'd learned quickly that while technology may have changed, charm and intelligence never went out of style.

"Yes, sir. May I have your name and company, please?"

"Yeah. George McFurious at Going-Out-Of-Fucking-Business, Incorporated. All due to BB&M's sloppy approach to my account."

"Oh, sir. Please let me help. I need your name and company. I'm sure we can set things straight."

One beat. Two. Then, "Listen, lady, you seem nice. I'm sorry to be such a jerk. My name's George Rogers and my rep's name is, let's see, Gord. He's ignored all my emails. I'm bleeding money here. Can you get hold of him for me?"

"I can do better than that, Mr. Rogers. I'll put you through to the Branch Manager, Jannie Morris. She'll move mountains for you. I guarantee it."

"Thanks. You're the first person at your crazy, mixed-up company who hasn't given me the runaround."

"It's my pleasure, Mr. Rogers." Suze transferred him to Jannie.

Later that day, Gord headed past Suze's station. He had his coat on, and he carried a box. Suze shrugged. Mr. George Rogers had truly been fed up. Jannie wouldn't have fired Gord on a whim. It wasn't anyone's fault but his own.

A few minutes later, Joelle, the pretty young blonde who was wrapped up in wedding plans when she wasn't hard at work, slipped out to the front desk. She had developed the habit of consulting Suze on details about her upcoming reception, and Suze had grown fond of her.

"Hi. Has Gord gone?" Joelle talked in a conspiratorial undertone. She looked to the left and right.

"Yes. I saw him get on the elevator. Carrying a box."

"Good. He was costing us all money. I guess Janna the Hutt cut him loose. She's brutal, but it serves him right."

"Sorry. Janna the what?"

"You know. *Star Wars*. Jabba. The great big slime monster that has ultimate control and strikes randomly."

"And you see Jannie as—?"

"Not just me. We all know it. Jannie's a Hutt, through and through. She's controlling. Manipulative. Just plain scary. And, worst of all, she's totally unpredictable. We live in fear."

While Joelle had been talking, Chandran had wandered into reception. He bent his gleaming head toward the two women, and leaned on Suze's desk.

"Don't worry. Gord was an idiot. Too bad for him he ran afoul of Janzilla." Chandran started monster-stomping around, his elbows tight to his sides and his forearms outstretched in a passable imitation of a T-Rex on a rampage.

Joelle laughed, her hand covering her mouth. Suze tried to maintain a bland expression, but she felt her eyes widen with shock. She wanted to defend Jannie. She wanted to ask questions. But how could she, without giving away their mother-daughter relationship?

"I'm sorry, you two. I've got to get back to work." Suze turned her face to the computer screen and began typing something on her keyboard.

"Yes, or Janzilla will attack you, too. She looks hungry today," Chandran said.

"Janna the Hutt is always hungry. And angry." Joelle

tossed her head. "The monster doesn't remember that she was once a lowly sales rep, too."

"At least she's had her blood sacrifice today. Rest in pieces, Gord."

"And God save the rest of us. Keep your head down, Suze, and your nose to the grindstone. And never, ever look the monster in her eyes."

Chandran and Joelle returned to the bullpen, nudging each other and chortling. Suze stopped typing and stared at her screen. It was a jumble of nonsense words, without order or meaning.

If Jannie wasn't careful, her life would end up in a similar state of chaos. And, for the first time ever, Suze didn't have the faintest idea of how to help.

15

TEMPORARY INSANITY

*H*iring Mom as a temp had been a stupendously inspired move. Freed from administrative burdens, Jannie was able to roll up her sleeves and really manage, instead of just firing off zillions of emails. Her staff was super-lucky to have her full attention. Everyone was working smarter, and sales were pouring in.

Mom was so cute, too, sitting at reception, staying on top of the paperwork and keeping communications flowing. She'd only been there a few weeks, but she'd turned the place around. Everyone loved her.

But today was Mom's last day. And Jannie had to be the one to tell her.

In a way, it was good news. Shivani in HR had finally agreed to allow a permanent replacement. And Mom had always known the job was short-term. Still, she'd be missed —by Jannie, and everyone else, too.

"Ms. Foster, may I see you in my office?" Jannie tossed the words over her shoulder as she passed by the tidy reception desk.

"Of course. I'll be right there." Mom was always so positive. A great role model for the rest of the staff.

Jannie closed the door and waited for Mom to sit, then joined her, not behind the huge-ass corporate desk but on an adjacent visitor's chair. She took her mom's cool hands and gave them a squeeze.

"Oh, oh. I think I know what's coming." Mom smiled reassuringly. "Don't worry, Jannie. We both knew it couldn't last."

Jannie sighed. Mom was so sweet. And this wasn't easy.

"Yes. I've had approval from New York to hire a permanent receptionist. HR's told me to sever your contract. I'm so sorry."

"It's perfectly all right. I've enjoyed this job tremendously. And I've learned a lot."

Jannie swallowed with difficulty. "Of course I'll give you a great reference. It'll be kind of weird doing that for my mom, but nobody will ever know."

"Thanks, sweetie." Mom sat rock still, gazing thoughtfully at Jannie. Then she added, with a slight quaver, "One more thing?"

"Yes?"

"All the people in this company are aware of how hard you work. They're grateful for your dedication. Sales are going so well, right? But . . ." Mom seemed to be picking her words with care.

Jannie prompted her with another, "Yes?"

Words began to pour out of Mom's mouth. "I think you may need to soften your approach. Learn more about each person and what makes them tick. Remember their names. Relate to them as individuals, not cogs in a machine."

By the end of this speech Jannie was looking at her mom in disbelief. Was she *criticizing* her? Mom, who was a lovely woman but had no work history to speak of, was telling Jannie, the top executive in BB&M's Canadian office, that she wasn't connecting with her staff? Was she kidding?

"I don't see what you're getting at." Jannie wiped her face of all expression.

She was wounded to the core. Her mom, who was supposed to cherish and bolster her, had scolded her —*Jannie*, her beloved only child. The person who'd helped Mom out when things had been tough.

Jannie rose from the modest visitor's chair and walked with long strides to her execu-chair, behind the impressive desk. The position of power. Not to be questioned. By anyone, no matter how closely related.

Hint delivered. And so, she couldn't quite believe it when Mom tried again.

"I wouldn't be a good parent if I didn't tell you that you've got some budding problems here. If you try being more observant, you'll see what I'm getting at. I think you still have time to patch things up before it's too late."

"Too late?" Icicles dripped from Jannie's tone.

"Before you have a mass revolt, you've got to fix things."

Jannie had had enough. Dearly as she loved her, Mom had no right—and no expertise whatsoever—to give business advice. Pride in tatters, Jannie gave her the coldest glance she was capable of, more frigid than any look she'd shot her mom in her entire lifetime.

"Thanks for your advice, Ms. Foster. You may leave. Please close the door on your way out." This was harsh, but Mom had been much meaner.

Without another word, Mom got up from her chair. Her posture was erect as she exited. It was the stiff-shouldered stance of a woman doing her best not to cry. She closed the door with exaggerated gentleness.

Jannie felt awful. But Mom had crossed a very sensitive line and pitched her into a bleak world of self-doubt and anxiety.

Jannie laid her head on her execu-desk and had a good bawl.

Suze fled down the hall to the ladies' room. She checked underneath the doors of the cubicles. Thank heavens. Nobody there.

The wail that broke from her was primal. It echoed off the tile walls with a shrillness that shocked her. She couldn't stop herself. Another deep-seated sob tore its way up out of her belly and through her lungs, wracking her body with brutal force. And another.

She had to control herself. She was at work. Someone could walk through the door at any moment. And the last thing Suze wanted to be was the cause of new rumors about Jannie's cruelty to staff members.

Janna the Hutt. Janzilla. Well, Suze had tried to help. In the gentlest possible way. But, she'd failed.

She turned on the cold water tap. Shoulders still heaving from the strength of her crying, she splashed her eyes. She told herself she'd be fine. She'd pull herself together and get back to reception. It would be business as usual on her last day, and she wouldn't let the company down. Especially not Jannie.

Had she been wrong to criticize? Maybe, but Suze couldn't stand the way everyone mocked Jannie behind her back. And they seemed to have a point. Now that Suze had seen her in action, she couldn't help but agree that Jannie had an inconsistent approach to management. In fact, a downright scary one.

If Aram were in town, she'd consult him. He'd be the perfect person to counsel Jannie. But he was far away, and he had other priorities. Suze and her annoying daughter would be way, way down his list at a time in his life like this.

No, she'd have to carry on as if nothing was wrong. She'd said what she needed to say. Now, either Jannie would digest the information and do something about it, or she'd continue on her path to self-destruction.

Once her eyes had lost their cherry-red hue, Suze made her way back to her desk. She was checking phone messages when a casually dressed young man carrying a battered briefcase got off the elevator and approached. She glanced up at him and froze. It was Kirk Molenaar, Jannie's old school chum. Perhaps, though, he wouldn't recognize her.

"Ms. Foster!"

Apparently, yes, he would.

"Shhh, Kirk." Suze made tamping motions with her hands.

"Okay," Kirk whispered back. "But what are *you* doing here?"

"I'm temping. Today's my last day. Jannie and I are pretending we're not related, so please, please, please don't blow our cover."

Kirk looked right and left, and then leaned toward Suze. "You got it. I would never do anything to hurt either of you." He tried to wink but seemed to have difficulty coordinating the eye movement. Instead, he ended up giving Suze a bizarre, green-eyed squint that made her laugh.

"Oh, Kirk, it's good to see you again!"

"Same here. It's been ages."

Kirk had been a regular visitor to the family home when he and Jannie had been in high school together. It had been a safe haven for them, and Suze had done what she could to make it as cozy as possible. They'd both been atypical students, and high school had not been easy for either of them, academically or socially.

"What are you up to these days?" Suze asked. As a sales rep rushed by with briefcase in hand, Suze said more loudly, "How may I help you, Mr. Molenaar?"

Kirk waited until the rep boarded the elevator. "I'm co-owner of a computer servicing firm. Spectrum Computing. BB&M is one of our clients."

"I'm delighted for you! How wonderful that you're doing so well."

"Thanks; we got lucky. We struggled for a long time, but then one of my partners, Tyler, found an investor who helped us get a start. You may know the guy—Aram Krikorian? Neighbor of Jannie's. Tyler's, too."

Suze nodded, feeling dazed. Small world. And thank you, Aram Krikorian, for funding a deserving guy who needed a break.

Kirk didn't seem to notice Suze's expression, but kept talking. "I'd better get to work. Jannie can be demanding." He smiled as he said these words, but looked beyond Suze as if impatient to start moving.

"All right. And remember, mum's the word! Oh, I didn't put that well. I mean, don't say anything about me being Jannie's mom, okay?"

"Sure, Ms. F."

"And, if you hear of any work for a receptionist or clerk, please let me know. My contract here is up today. I need to find something new."

"Seriously?"

Suze looked at him. Of course she was serious. She waited for him to explain himself.

"Well, my partners and I are desperate. We're three dudes who know just about everything there is to know about computers, but we're hopeless on the organizational front. Can you come in on Monday morning and meet the other two guys? We might have something for you." He handed Suze his card.

"You may just be the answer to my prayers."

"And, Ms. F, you could be the answer to ours, too."

Suze felt a flicker of hope as she turned back to answer phone messages and forward calls. One career door had closed—well, basically slammed shut, given this afternoon's altercation with Jannie—but another might be opening.

"Suze? Is it true?"

She glanced up and froze. Joelle stood in front of her, looking concerned. Had Kirk already blown Suze's cover?

"It depends. Is what true?"

"That you're leaving us?"

"Oh. That. Yes, I'm afraid I am. Today's my last day."

"No! That can't be right! We all love you. You're the best thing that's happened to our group in ages, and we won't let you go!"

Joelle spun around and tore out of reception. Evidently, she rallied the entire sales force. Reps and assistants began streaming to Suze's desk, proclaiming their distress over her upcoming departure.

"I'm flattered you all care—" Suze began.

"Did the Hutt fire you?" Joelle's eyes snapped with fury.

"No, no—"

"Did she pull a Janzilla move and force you to quit?"

Chandran interjected, waving his forearms about madly and making two of the young assistants giggle.

"No! It's just that my contract has come to an end. You'll be getting a permanent replacement soon. It's been approved. I'm very grateful to Jannie, and to all of you, for treating me so kindly, but it's my time to go."

The dozen or so people who were clustered around Suze's desk made sounds of commiseration. Some of them hugged her. None of them made a move to leave.

"I guess what we want to say," Joelle said, "is that we've really enjoyed working with you. You've only been here for a short time, but you've made our dysfunctional office feel functional. We're going to be lost without you."

"Aye, aye!" A general shout went up.

"I can't tell you how much I appreciate this," Suze said. Tears began to form in her eyes, but she couldn't let herself lose control. She got up from her desk and shooed everyone into the bullpen area, then sat down, turning to her keyboard again.

"One more thing." It was Joelle, who had snuck back.

She held out a large white card. It was printed in a formal and elegant script. Suze accepted it and looked at up at Joelle in wonder.

"My wedding's coming up in January. In Niagara-on-the-Lake. It'll be gorgeous that time of year. We're having a family-only Jewish ceremony, but the reception's going to be a bash. A carnival theme with masks and all. Almost everyone from here is invited, and I'd be honored if you'd come, too."

"Oh, Joelle." Suze held the invitation to her heart.

"Bring a guest, of course. You've saved my sanity, and I want you there on my special night."

"That's so sweet of you. Of course I'll come." She'd

invite Aram, who would look striking in formal clothes. And Suze would buy something new. Something sophisticated but slinky.

Surely by then she would have settled her debt. And made peace with Jannie.

THE START OF A BUSY WEEKEND

First things first. Suze needed to pay at least part of the rent she owed. She wouldn't be able to relax for the weekend until she confronted her despicable super and forked over as much as she could scrabble together.

She knocked on Gleb's office door.

"Enter." There was no welcome note in his voice.

"I'm here to pay my rent." She opened the door and went in.

Gleb sat sprawled in his padded chair behind his shabby manager's desk. Suze tried a smile. He stared back at her balefully.

She knew she wasn't in a moral position of strength. She'd defaulted on her rent and she was fortunate Gleb had never followed up on the N4 threat to evict her. He'd have been within his rights.

On the other hand, with Aram as her witness, she could have pressed charges for assault.

Finally, he spoke. "Good. Give here." He stretched out

work-stained fingers and grasped her check. He looked at the figure written on it. His mouth curled downward.

"I know," Suze said, quietly. "It doesn't cover everything. But I'll keep paying you until we're caught up."

"Bet your ass you will, lady. And this better not bounce."

"It won't."

Gleb tossed the slip of paper onto his desk. Suze turned to leave.

"Wait."

She froze in place. He had risen from his chair but hadn't yet moved out from behind his desk. The last thing she wanted was for him to approach her. She felt vulnerable, alone in this basement office, and with Aram so many miles away.

"Lady, relax. I not touch you. But I need money you owe. I got problems of my own. I give you one more month, yes?"

"Gleb, I'll do everything I can to pay you."

"That not promise."

"No. But it's not a lie, either. And you know I'll do my best."

"Lady, I know nothing." Gleb sighed and sat back down.

Suze seized the opportunity to escape, out of the dark office and up many floors to her apartment in the sky. Even though she doubted Gleb would ever come right to her door she somehow felt safer once she closed it and applied the lock, bolt, and chain.

She poured herself a glass of white wine, a splurge purchase she'd allowed herself when she'd received her first paycheck. Then she sat down and dialed Aram.

"Suze, darling." His voice held the warmth of a

summer's day. Immediately, she felt her clenched jaw relax into a smile.

"Oh, I'm so glad I reached you."

"It's Friday night. We should be having dinner with candlelight and champagne." He gave the word "champagne" its French pronunciation. Suze's smile widened.

"Aram, we will have that in our future. I know it."

"We shall, certainly."

"Most importantly, how's your mom?"

"Mother is working her way through a bad patch. She suffers from a sluggish heart valve. We're considering surgery. I think what disturbs her most is the doctor's suggestion that pig tissue may need to be implanted."

"Can't say I blame her!"

"No, but it just may save her life. And she's a feisty soul. I'd like to keep her with us as long as possible."

"Of course. As a mom, I approve of your sentiment and totally understand. Oh, and this is likely a bad time to ask, but I've been invited to a fancy wedding reception in January. In Niagara-on-the-Lake." Suze paused, feeling equal parts sassy and shy. "Would you be willing to be my date?"

"I'd be honored." He was quiet for a moment, offering Suze a chance to give herself a tiny hug of self-congratulation. Then, he continued, "I miss you. Give me a few more days. I'll be home by next weekend. We'll have our dinner with candlelight and champagne then."

They went on to talk about nothing and everything. Suze could hear the sincerity and commitment in his voice. Aram wanted to be with her. She wanted to be with him, too. There wasn't a shred of doubt in her mind.

A week would go by quickly. And then they'd be together. *Together*, together, body and soul.

The next morning at sunrise, Suze sat bolt upright in her sofa bed and swore, which wasn't like her at all. She'd been having such a racy dream, packed with full body contact and interesting positions. As a fantasy, it had been entertaining, not to mention extremely stimulating.

But a real, live, red-blooded Aram was coming home in a week. They were both adults, even if Suze, at fifty-eight, was a bit more of a full-fledged grown-up than he, a whole decade younger. And, they'd progressed beyond the flirtation stage. They wanted each other, fully and passionately.

Therein lay the rub. Suze walked over to the mirror. She flattened her nightgown against her body and checked herself from various angles. On the surface, she looked pretty good. Still too thin, although she'd been eating better-quality food lately and had regained a few pounds. Other than that, she was in excellent physical shape, especially for her age.

But it was precisely that age of hers, obvious or not, that might be a problem. She hadn't been intimate with a man for a long, long time. Her husband had been so lost to his vices that sex had stopped being part of their married lives when Jannie had still been small. And Suze was a lot older now. Her body had altered. Her hormones had plummeted.

Oh dear God. What if things had changed down there? What if she couldn't consummate the relationship?

The bags under Jannie's eyes were purplish gray—the color of guilt. She'd been mean to her mother. But Mom had been hateful, too, telling Jannie people at the office didn't like her. Of course she'd wildly exaggerated how bad things were. But Jannie had thought about it all night long, and she had a horrible feeling Mom might be right, in a limited kind of way.

It was true sometimes Jannie didn't remember names. And, yes, she'd been switching management styles on a regular basis. She'd just been trying to find the method that worked best. She'd never realized all those changes might make her seem psycho.

Mind you, she was still mad at Mom. She'd been judgy. Harsh, too. But she probably meant well, and it might be almost time to forgive her. Not today, but soon.

Deep, cleansing breath. Good stuff in. Poisons out. That was better.

Even though it was Saturday, Jannie headed to the office. She had some important catching-up to do. First on her list, she intended to memorize names. She'd study the staff list and the ID photos and make sure she knew every single one by Monday.

Jannie was at it for one hour. Then two. This was such a drag. She'd never been good at putting names to faces, and she had over forty to lock away in her brain. On Monday she'd astonish everyone with her friendliness and approachability. If she could just keep them straight.

She'd try that memory trick, the one where you connect the name of the person to one of their prominent features. Like, Lilith Smith in Accounting was the one with the lisp. Okay, that was one. Next, William Butterick. This was easy. He was the guy with the ginormous butt. So, she could handle Butterick, but what would she do about the William part? Maybe if he had a big butt, he also had a big, well, willie. It was possible. And definitely memorable.

By the end of three hours, she was confident she knew the first and last names of every employee at BB&M.

Unless they all went out and bought toupees and fake moustaches, she'd keep them straight from now on.

She hoped they'd like her better now. She was trying so hard.

Next on her Saturday agenda: off to the gym. She'd packed different clothes this time. They weren't the latest in glam, high-tech fabric, but they were comfy. She'd set up a meeting with a new trainer/nutritionist. The temple of her body was going to be treated with the respect it deserved.

"Hey, you're back for another workout." Kirk stood there, dripping gallons of sweat. The boy pushed himself hard.

"Yes, Kirk Molenaar. Indeed I am."

Kirk flicked some free-flowing perspiration from his brow, but not in Jannie's direction, for which she was grateful.

"What's up with calling me by both my names?" For some reason he seemed pissed off.

"Why, Kirk Molenaar? Does it bug you?"

"Yeah. It's weird, and I don't like it."

Well, that was useful information to file away. She'd thought on Monday she'd start using everyone's full name so they'd be doubly impressed she actually knew both parts. To go by Kirk's reaction, she'd have to conclude that this might not be the best way to inspire love and devotion.

"Oh, sorry, Kirkie. I've been trying to learn people's names at work. First and last. My mom told me I should. I was just practicing on you."

"Well, don't. Hey, remember all those charts they used to make us look at and identify the emotions? You know, in Special Ed? The ones that had the frowny faces and the smiley ones?"

"Oh, yeah. And the one that had a big 'O' for the

mouth, and I always said it was because the person had just sat on a pin and was screaming, and you'd say it was because the guy was burping, and then the teacher would get mad at both of us."

"Yeah, that's right. Well, you gotta keep expressions in mind, too, when you deal with people at the office. I've been around there enough to know sometimes they're giving you visual cues you don't always pick up on."

Jannie's jaw dropped. Kirk, the man who was at least somewhere on the Aspie scale, was giving her, the person who was definitely more of a neurotypical, advice on how to read facial cues.

"Have you been hanging out with my mom lately? Are the two of you trying to destroy my feelings altogether?"

Kirk looked at his sneakers. Sweat beaded up and sluiced down his nose. With all that running moisture, Jannie couldn't tell if there was a tear or two mixed in. She'd forgotten how sensitive he was, and immediately felt remorseful.

"It's all right, Kirkie. I know you're trying to be helpful. Yes, I'll pay more attention to people's faces next week."

"And their body language." He looked up and did that crazy winking thing that never quite worked for him.

"Don't push it or I'll 'Kirk Molenaar' you from now on."

He grinned and held out a sweaty fist. She bumped it with hers, and he took off to the men's changing room, while Jannie went in search of salvation in the form of her new trainer.

Suze sat in the waiting room of her doctor's office. She'd called early that morning and was relieved when the pleasant woman on switchboard said she'd squeeze her in. Unfortunately, it wouldn't be with Dr. Whitehouse, a kindly woman who looked very much like Mrs. Santa Claus and always made Suze feel about ten years old, but at least someone would see her.

She looked at the ceiling-mounted television. It was playing silly animal videos, interspersed with tips about health. There was a tattered sign on the wall saying magazines were no longer available because of germ transmission concerns, and since Suze hadn't thought to bring a novel, she stared at the screen, watching promos aimed at very young and very old women. It seemed females went right from breastfeeding babies to breaking osteoarthritic bones with very little fun or excitement in between.

"Suze Foster? Dr. Purvis will see you now."

Suze stopped looking at a video on incontinence and jumped to her feet, clasping her handbag tightly to her chest. She followed the nurse's impressive Afro into the corridor and patiently went through the routine weight and blood pressure check.

"You've lost five pounds since your last check-up. Any reason for this?" The nurse studied her closely.

Suze reflected. Yes, a few. Poverty. Anxiety. Gleb, the leering super.

But she said, "No, none," and privately rejoiced that at least she wasn't as thin as she'd been a few weeks earlier.

"Please remove all your clothes. Put the jacket on backward and cover your lower body with this sheet." The nurse handed over sickly blue paper cover-ups and exited.

Suze changed, and then tried to find a dignified way of sitting on the bench while she waited for the doctor to appear. In spite of her near nudity, she was sweating. Her clammy hands trembled.

Dr. Purvis knocked on the door, waited a nanosecond, and let himself into the examination room. Suze gazed at his well-lined, patrician face and his precision-parted, thin gray hair. He looked so reserved. So proper. She wished her own physician, sympathetic Dr. Whitehouse, worked Saturdays.

"Well, well, well. Suze Foster, is it? Female, fifty-eight years old, slightly underweight. What seems to be the issue?" He talked in a clipped, disinterested way.

Suze felt like a thing. An elderly thing.

She shrank back, clutching her papery cover-ups. She opened her mouth to explain but couldn't force any words to trip off the end of her tongue.

"Ma'am. Shall we try again? Why are we here?" Dr. Purvis held a manila file folder with Suze's name on it, and he started flipping through the pages. Maybe he was looking for mental health issues.

"Well, I'm here because … that is to say, I need to know if …No, let me start again. I'm wondering if you can tell me . . ."

Dr. Purvis closed the file with a snap and put it on the metal desk behind him. He crossed his arms and peered at Suze over the top of his wire-rimmed reading glasses, like Clint Eastwood staring down a lunatic.

"Other patients are waiting. Please get on with it."

Suze took a deep breath and expelled it. "Okay, fine, I'm sorry to be incoherent. It's just that . . ."

Dr. Purvis said nothing. He continued to radiate negativity. To Suze, it felt like he was serving her a heaping helping of disdain.

"I apologize for being such an idiot." Closing her eyes and clenching her fists, she began to talk rapidly. "The thing is, I want to be physical with someone I think I love but I haven't done it in so long, and I'm past menopause, and I'm so nervous about it, and I'm afraid things won't work. And that my private parts may have all shriveled up like a prune. You know. Down there."

Suze opened one eye and peeked at the doctor. He was standing in exactly the same position as before. He wasn't laughing. He wasn't exactly scoffing, either, but he still seemed to be looking down his nose at her. He waited until she opened both eyes before he spoke.

"Ms. Foster, I assume that when you say you *haven't done it* you are referring to sexual intercourse."

Well, of course she was. Why did he have to make her feel dirty about it? And like she was a randy teenager going behind her mother's back?

She swallowed her resentment and said, "Yes. I'm talking about sexual intercourse."

"Thank you. Now, let's try to have an adult conversation about this, please, Ms. Foster. With proper terminology. We are not in a high school gymnasium; we are in a place of medicine. Science. What you seem to be worried about is vulvovaginal atrophy. Is that correct?"

Suze stared blankly at the doctor. Her mouth was open, but once again she was unable to form words.

"That's right, Ms. Foster. Vulvovaginal atrophy. Sometimes called Vaginal atrophy. Atrophy indicating the wasting away of tissue. In this case, tissue related to the vulva and vagina of a postmenopausal woman. Is this what you suspect your problem to be?"

"I really have no idea. I haven't done it—I mean had sexual intercourse—in years. I'm worried things have changed."

"Apparently. And so they likely have. Shall we take a look?" He patted the examination table and indicated she should swing around and insert her heels into the metal stirrups. Suze complied, and scooched her lower body down the bench until her knees flopped open in an ungainly, froglike position. The paper cover-up over her lower body felt like a silly affectation. From where he stood at the base of the table, Dr. Purvis could see almost all the way to her tonsils.

"I shall do a pelvic examination and a Pap smear," he announced and commenced poking and prodding. "Hmmmm."

"Hmmmm? What do you mean by that?" Suze asked with a squeaky voice.

"Nothing. Yet. Please relax. Now on to the Pap smear. This may pinch."

It did more than pinch. The cold metal speculum burned against Suze's delicate tissues. The scrape of the stick felt like he had taken a rusty knife to her insides. She couldn't help emitting a gasp of pain.

"No dramatics, if you please."

Hateful man. Suze levered her head up and gave him a look of disapproval. He returned it full force.

"That's that, then," he said. "Why don't you get dressed? When I come back we can have a quick discussion about your concerns, such as they are." He left the office, closing the door with the percussive thump of a man who didn't have time to put up with Suze and her nonsense.

After five minutes, Dr. Purvis returned. Suze was fully clothed and sitting on the visitor's chair. She'd lost all shyness on the examination table and was now determined to get answers from this physician, whether or not he approved of her.

"Do I have, what did you call it, Vulvus Vagina Atrophy?"

"Vulvovaginal. And the answer is a definitive maybe."

"What? Can't you tell?"

"Ms. Foster, everything down there, as you would say,

looks completely normal. Your tissues are pink. There's no bleeding. But you are a physically mature, postmenopausal woman. The walls of your vagina may have thinned somewhat. And, according to you, you haven't been sexually active."

"What's that got to do with it?" Suze couldn't help herself. She felt her pulse throbbing in her temples. This doctor was behaving in such a holier-than-thou way, when all she wanted was important information about her health.

"My dear Ms. Foster, the vagina is a place where, to put it in layman's terms—ha ha, good one, I must say— using it helps keep you from losing it. I'm putting this colloquially so that it makes it easier for you to comprehend."

"Doctor, I just need some good advice. Please don't talk down to me."

"Ah, a little testy are we? That may be understandable, given your situation. All right, I'll try to make this as straightforward for you as possible. I propose to offer you a choice."

"A choice?"

"Yes, Ms. Foster. Either choose to go on as you were, without *doing it* as you so eloquently put it. That way, you will continue to enjoy good health, without the fear of dyspareunia."

"Dyspar-what?"

"Really. A little research before your visit might have been a wise first step. Point made? Well, then, dyspareunia is pain or bleeding during sex. Another symptom is urinary tract infections, which I gather you've never suffered from."

"No, that's one thing I've been free of. So, option

number one is to avoid sex. That's a lousy choice. What's the alternative?"

"Proceed with caution. Give sexual intercourse a try. Protect yourself from possible STD's by making your partner use a condom. And see what happens. But I warn you, you may feel sensations ranging from mild discomfort to excruciating pain."

"Oh, God, it sounds awful," Suze said, braiding her fingers together in her lap. "Isn't there anything I can do to, well, ease things along?"

"A good, water-based lubricant may lessen unpleasant friction." Dr. Purvis rifled in a desk drawer and found a sample of K-Y Jelly, which he handed over. "What nature takes away, science may cure." He smiled thinly at his aphorism. "Our time is up. The office will contact you if there's any problem with your Pap. I'm not anticipating one."

"That's good, at least."

"Yes, well, all the best with your Lothario." He snickered.

"I object to your sarcasm. And I must say, I feel throughout this whole appointment you've treated me in a disparaging way. I wanted knowledge and help, not put-downs. I've shown you respect, which I would have expected you to reciprocate."

"Dear Ms. Foster—"

"See? That's exactly what I mean, *dear* Dr. Purvis. You're talking to me as if I'm stupid. And I'm not. Also, whether or not I *do* have slightly rusty lady parts—yes, sir, I'm using the *colloquial*—I'm going to figure this situation out. On my own. Because I'm in love. Not with a Lothario, but with a wonderful, intelligent man who loves me back. And guess what? We're going to *do it* and *do it* until we get it right. With or without your approval."

She shot a triumphant look at Dr. Purvis, in an at-least-*I*-have-a-life kind of way. Satisfied by the stunned expression on his face, Suze rose from her chair, reached into the drawer of the desk and grabbed four more samples of K-Y Jelly. Waving them at him in a jolly farewell gesture, she left the office, laughing as she walked away from a place of clinical judgment and, hopefully, toward passion and love.

PREPARING FOR PLEASURE

*I*t was great to have an eager new trainer. Jannie loved Beverly Checkeris (Beaver Cheeks!), who smiled constantly and was such a cheerleader. Beverly was ever so fit in a slightly chubby way, which worked for Jannie, who'd never aspired to be reed thin but wanted to get back to cute roundness layered over muscle. Like a size eight or ten, not Mom's severe four. Cuddly, not statuesque. A nice, squeezy armful for Aram.

Ah, Aram. Who'd been out of town for some reason but had texted once or twice to see how Jannie was doing. Nice of him, but kind of impersonal, texting. Jannie craved hearing his baritone voice, with its teeny tiny accent that drove her wild. She wanted to get up close to his incredible body and inhale bergamot spiciness. And, at some point soon, she intended to run her hands through his glorious, gray-sprinkled hair. And that was just for starters.

After her workout, the next thing on Jannie's weekend agenda was housecleaning. It'd been a few months since her condo had been scrub-a-dubbed. She planned to have the place so attractive it would be the perfect bower of seduction for when Aram returned from his trip. He'd enter the sparklingly fresh foyer, tip her brunette head back, and give her the smoochiest kiss ever. Then, he'd lead Jannie into her spotless living room and strip off her —by then much looser—clothes, piece by piece. Finally, he'd carry her over the threshold of her immaculate bedroom, not huffing or puffing at all because she'd have lost so much weight, and fling her onto her neat as a pin bed. At which point, they'd make it gloriously messy in a ravishy kind of way.

But cleaning solo was lonely work. Tyler and his lovebug dream bunny Frodo might be home. Maybe they'd help a girl do a bit of tidying.

"Knockety-knock, Tyler. You there?"

No response for a minute or two. Then, "That you, Jannie?"

"Yup. Open up."

"Why?"

Jannie sighed. Tyler was a cutie, but sometimes he was overly suspicious. As if Jannie ever had anything less than the purest of motives.

"Because I want you to." There. If he had a heart, he'd open up.

"Negative."

Apparently, he lacked ventricles.

"Come on. Let me in."

"It's okay, the moment's passed," Frodo said in the background, and Jannie blessed his little hobbit soul.

The door swung open, revealing Tyler in gray sweats. He'd evidently thrown them on in a hurry because the pants were inside out. The lenses of his black-framed glasses were foggy.

"Really? D'you ever think to call ahead?" He scowled.

"I'm a busy businesswoman. Not interrupting anything important, am I?"

He stared at her with that "O" look on his face. What was it? Oh, yes. He hadn't sat on a pin. He was showing astonishment.

"Why so surprised?" She tilted her head to one side, studying him.

"I just can't believe how dense you are. But come on in. What do you want?"

Frodo in all his white-fleshed skinniness sauntered up. He wore navy sweats, but his were right-side-out. He stood behind Tyler and put his scrawny arms around his lover's neck. Tyler's whole being lit up.

"Oh. I get it. I'm sorry," She felt her face turn crimson and started to back toward the door.

"Where you goin'?" Frodo asked. He looked genuinely curious, but Jannie was so ass-bad at reading expressions lately, this could have been wishful thinking on her part. Maybe he really wanted her to jump out their fourth-floor window, and she was just not getting it.

"Home. Upstairs. Gotta clean my place."

"And you dropped by, why?" Tyler asked. He took off his glasses and polished the lenses on the tail of his sweatshirt.

"Uh, I thought you guys might like to help." As soon as these words came out of her mouth, she realized how ridiculous they sounded. When was the last time she'd wanted someone to come over on a Saturday afternoon and ask her to clean their apartment? Like, never.

Tyler put his glasses back on and looked at Frodo. They were good at this inaudible communication thing. They both nodded at precisely the same moment.

"We're coming," Tyler said.

"Give us five minutes. We're bringing supplies," Frodo added.

She gawked at them, hardly daring to believe they were actually willing to help. What great guys!

"We're only ever going to do this once," Tyler said. "And only because you've been our fairy godmother."

It was so touching to hear this. Jannie's eyes began to well.

"And because the hallway outside your condo is starting to smell, well, frickin' raunchy," Frodo said. Jannie stopped welling, as he continued, "What the hell do you have rotting in there, anyway? Ancient food from an Egyptian tomb?"

Humiliating. Still, they were going to help. Jannie smiled, waved adieu for now, and trotted off, intending to pitch as much garbage and old takeout cartons as she possibly could before they arrived. She had her pride to maintain.

And a love nest to prepare for the man of her ultimate fantasies.

Once Suze reached the sidewalk, she stopped laughing. Dr. Purvis had been such a supercilious jerk. He'd given her almost no useful advice. However, the Pap smear had been overdue, and he'd told her he wasn't anticipating a problem with the results, so at least that gave her some comfort. And thank goodness the whole procedure was over with.

She began to walk along the busy street, wondering what she should do next. How could a few tubes of K-Y Jelly get her to her desired objective: a committed, passionate relationship with Aram? The yucky mechanical details eluded her. She didn't have the first clue how to use lubricant. Would she need some kind of applicator? Or would she apply it to herself or to him? On top of a condom? Oh heavens, this was confusing and so very unsexy! Here she was almost sixty years old and as nervous about having sex as if it were for the very first time.

Which, she concluded after a minute's reflection, it kind of *was*. This body of hers was a completely different model than it had been, pre-menopause. She was driving a brand-new vehicle, and she hadn't even earned her learner's permit yet.

There were a variety of fascinating stores on Queen Street West. Small, trendy boutiques were squashed cheek by jowl with tattoo shops. Tiny bistros cozied up to hodgepodge antique shops. And, lo and behold, there was even the occasional emporium dedicated entirely to sex.

Suze stopped dead in her tracks in front of a store called sucCUM that she'd walked by many times. Until now, she'd always averted her eyes from the hypersexual window display. Today she raised her glance and boldly studied the products that were exhibited for all passersby to see.

A bubble gum pink sign announced, "Wrap yourself in ecstasy." It was Condom Month at sucCUM. There were condoms in packages, condoms pegged on clotheslines, condoms attached to surprised-looking plastic piggies. The condoms came in a mind-blowing variety of colors, shapes, and textures. And, the sign promised that visitors to the store would find much more variety and a huge line of other sexually stimulating products inside.

Suze pushed the door handle and entered the long, narrow room. As the door swung shut behind her she heard bells tinkle out a tune. *You Can Ring My Bell.* Cute.

The store was well-lit and lined with product bins,

neatly arranged in rows. The condom zone took up at least half of the floor. In the Games and Gifts section, two young females giggled and waved giant, inflated penis toys in each other's face. There was a For His Pleasure and a For Her Pleasure area. Suze started to make her way toward the latter before she noticed a For Couples display. That seemed like a good place to start.

"Do my eyes deceive me? Is it you, Susanna?"

Oh, dear Lord. Who had spotted her? In a sex shop, no less?

Suze spun on the spot, searching for the owner of the voice. It wasn't the bored-looking counter clerk. It wasn't either of the two girls, who were still getting a kick out of bopping each other on the head with fake penises. No, it was a larger-than-life, burgundy-haired person who was walking toward Suze, holding out both arms in a welcoming gesture.

"Darling Susanna! What a pleasure it is to see you again."

Suze was swept into a heavily perfumed embrace and crushed between what had to be the most enormous fake breasts ever. She looked up and smiled into the meticulously made-up face of Lola Devine, the first person ever to interview her.

"Ms. Devine," Suze said.

"Lola."

"Yes, Lola. How nice to see you!"

"My sweet, did you ever find a job that suited you?"

"Yes, well, it was temporary, but I'm off to a great start."

"That's wonderful, my pet. Although I think you could still have a fantastic future at C.S. Adventures." Lola winked, sending her furry fake eyelashes fluttering.

"You're too kind, but thanks." Suze laughed. "You know, you're a very interesting woman."

"Aren't I just? And a knowledgeable one, too, Susanna. You, on the other hand, look like a little lamb who has lost her way and has somehow stumbled into the pen of the horniest ram in the flock. Can I give you any advice?"

Suze thought about this. Dr. Purvis had been next to useless. The young guy behind the counter wouldn't be much help. Maybe Lola Devine held the keys to sexual paradise.

"I'd love your help." She felt her skin grow warm but didn't pause. "I'll try to tell you my problem in as few words as possible. Here goes. I want to make love to a man. I haven't had sex in years. I'm afraid things won't, well, work properly anymore."

"Sweetheart, say no more." Lola Devine held up a purple-taloned hand in Suze's face. The effect was somewhat marred by the fact that she had a knobbly-looking plastic circle dangling from her index finger. "Ah, first I'll just put the cock ring back where I found it, shall I?"

That done, Lola led Suze to the For Her Pleasure section.

"The problem as I see it, dearie, is that you haven't been practicing solo. Am I right?"

"Yes," Suze said. "At least, I don't own any special equipment." There. Might as well be frank.

"Don't despair. We shall set things straight. What you need is a boot camp approach to rev up your sex life. And the thing you need most is . . . no, not a dildo, although check out how realistic this one is." She waved a particularly bulbous and hideous ten-incher at Suze. "Not a G-spot vibrator, not those crazy stimulating balls, unless you want to buy them now and save them for your post-graduate enjoyment."

"No, that's fine. No balls today, thanks." Suze wondered what the heck they were for.

"Here's what we want. Dilators!" Lola held up two streamlined objects made of silicone, one pink and the other neon blue. "They come in different sizes, see?"

"Yes, Lola. But, ahem, I'm not sure what size . . ."

"Ha! No worries. They also come in handy sets. Look. Start at Size 2 and gradually work your way up to Size 6, and enjoy the stimulating vibrating action as you move along on your adventure."

"It's kind of expensive," Suze said, looking at the sticker and thinking about her overdue rent.

"You can't put a price on great sex, dearie," Lola said. "And, if you don't mind me saying so, you look like a woman who could use some really great sex."

"You're right." Suze sighed. "What else do you think I'll need?"

"Lube. There's nothing like lube to get the party rocking."

"Oh, the doctor gave me some. Look." Suze opened her purse and showed Lola the sample tubes of jelly. She leaned closer and whispered, "But I'm not sure how to use it."

"Sweet girl, there's no right way, as long as you're open and caring." Suddenly, Lola's voice lost its bantering quality. She put her muscular arm around Suze's shoulder and said, "You both need to play a part in the experience. Touch each other. That's all there is to it. Share the love and the lube! And cherish your relationship."

Suze was grateful to Lola for demystifying things. And the mechanics seemed easy enough. But what about the product? Suze held up a free sample of K-Y and raised an eyebrow at Lola.

"Sure. That'll do. But why not experiment with some of the more stimulating lubes?" Lola led Suze over to the couples section. "I can personally recommend this one. Comes in two delicious flavors. Chocolate strawberry is my fave. Oh, and grab yourself this one, too. It's tingly. Hubba hubba. Just make sure that anything you wet your downtown whistle with is water-based and water-soluble. Then, try out a few, and see if they lead you straight up the stairway to heaven."

"I think we need a shopping basket." Suze was struggling not to drop the products that Lola kept handing to her.

"Damn-tootin' we do. Oh, Susanna, this is such fun. And here I was just shopping for a little old cock ring. And maybe a butt plug. Then along you came and made my day!"

At the check-out, the bored clerk rang up the purchases. Suze's eyes bulged, but she reached for her one non-maxxed-out card and handed it over, just as Lola added to her haul by throwing in a large package of batteries and a rainbow selection of condoms.

Suze paid and turned to thank Lola, who was smiling kindly down at her, evidently proud of her star pupil's progress.

"Don't even open your mouth. It was my pleasure," Lola said.

"But . . ."

"No. Absolutely it was. And now, you must go home and start your boot camp exercises. Don't overdo it! Although you may be tempted to; I know *I* would be. Size up gradually! And be liberal on the lubing!"

Suze threw her arms around Lola Devine. "I am very, very grateful."

"Well, you know where you can reach me. Call if you need me. I'll be rooting for you! I look forward to hearing all about your romantic and carnal progress." Lola's face beamed sincerity tinged with lust.

"I will. Promise."

Lola made her way back to the For His Pleasure display of cock rings, as Suze picked up her heavy bag and left the store. It was Saturday evening, but there was another whole day left in the weekend. Tomorrow, after she tidied her apartment, Suze intended to start day one of Sexual Boot Camp.

It was never too late. All would be well. She didn't need to learn Dr. Purvis's depressing-sounding medical terms. She just needed the right attitude. Oh, and some high-tech, battery-operated, vibrating dilation.

With lube. Lots and lots of lube.

CHANGES IN THE WORKPLACE

*S*tarting today, Jannie intended to turn things around. She strode into the office at top speed, but faltered when she saw the empty reception desk. How sad not to see Mom's cheerful face.

Before too much more time passed, Jannie planned to apologize. Perhaps pay Mom a surprise visit. Christmas was just days away, and now that Jannie had a clean kitchen maybe Mom could come over and cook the turkey and all the fixings. It'd be like old times. Plus Jannie could use a little advice from her on how to snare Aram. Mom was always good with romantic tips, even if she was old, and low on the lustiness scale.

A chrome-haired, string bean of a woman walked by. "Good morning," she tossed over her shoulder.

"Hello, Lilith," Jannie replied, without hesitating.

Lilith almost dropped the load of accounting files she was carrying. Jannie had never called her anything but *hey, you* and *Yo, Accounting Person* before. Now Lilith was bound to love her.

At the weekly meeting for the sales reps, Jannie

circumnavigated the boardroom table and called each person by the correct name. She could tell they were impressed because their eyes were big and round and they leaned forward in their chairs. What a pro she was, reading expressions *and* body language!

"Team, we're ahead of budget," she announced, "and we're going to hit a new record if we all keep up our efforts."

Everyone in the room was paid on commission, and it didn't take an Einstein to know they were all going to make a whack of dough. They seemed moderately pleased, although it was hard to tell because their eyes tracked every which way but at her.

"Let's knock ourselves out and see if we can get to twenty percent overachievement. I have faith in all of you. Let's do it."

She pumped a fist in the air, hoping a raucous team cheer would accompany her rousing words. But they just looked at each other, nodded vaguely at her, and trudged out of the room, heads down. Had she done something wrong?

"Wait. Joelle?"

Joelle stopped mid-shuffle and turned around. Her eyes were calm, and her mouth formed a straight line. Damn, that one was hard to read.

"Yes?"

"Why isn't anyone excited? We're kicking ass this quarter."

"Oh, we're aware of that. And we're looking forward to the payout. But . . ."

"Tell me."

Joelle pushed back a lock of her dark blond hair and met Jannie's gaze. "Well, we're all nervous about how secure our jobs are. None of us are sure we'll be around to collect commissions. You've been, well, hard on us. Not one of us feels safe."

"That's ridiculous! Is this because I fired Gord? He was dragging us down. He screwed up constantly. You know that! But if people are doing their jobs properly, they have no need to worry." Jannie reached out a hand, but Joelle backed away.

"Good to hear. Now, I should get back to work. I want to do *my* job well."

Dang it, Joelle was being sarcastic. At least *maybe* that was the effect she was going for.

Perhaps this leading by example thing couldn't be achieved in a single day. Jannie would just have to keep trying to be consistent. Which was not just hard, but boring, too.

Joelle was almost through the boardroom door, when Jannie stopped her again.

"Hey, your big wedding bash must be coming up soon. It's in January, right?"

"Um, that's right."

"Shouldn't you be thinking about sending out invitations soon?

Silence. No eye contact.

Oh. No. This couldn't be happening.

But it was.

"We've already sent the invitations. We were limited to how many people we could ask. I hope you understand. You know, Ben has such a large family to begin with—"

"But we're best work friends, Joelle. You, me—out in the bullpen, always the top two sales reps, doing our part to show that women can do at least as well as men in this business. In our case, much, much better."

"We were work associates. Now, you're my boss. I respect that. But I'm afraid you're not invited."

"No," Jannie said, giving the short word about five syllables, each one rising in pitch. She couldn't quash the expanding bubble of hysteria. Joelle had deliberately left her off her invitation list. And, whether or not she considered Jannie friend-worthy, she was the closest woman in Jannie's life, other than Mom. The closest in her *entire* life.

Jannie's body began to fold in on itself. She waved Joelle out of the room with one hand and covered her eyes with the other. Joelle motored off down the hall and didn't look back. As Jannie collapsed in a heap on the carpet, she somehow managed to kick the door closed. Then, she lay there and sobbed.

Time passed. Eventually, she rose. She blew her nose as noisily as a Whoville Who blowing a floofloover. Emerging from the boardroom, she walked through the bullpen, which hummed in a quiet, industrious way. Phones rang. Reps click-clacked their keyboards, cranking out new sales proposals. Business as usual.

Someone knocked on her door. Just Kirk, toting the tools of his trade.

"Jannie? I'm doing an upgrade to the sales system. Is now a good time?" He looked flushed. Maybe he was remembering their semi-naked encounter at the gym. Damn, as soon as Jannie thought of it, she felt herself blush, too.

"Sure, Kirkie. Come on in. I'll clear out."

"You don't have to. I just need a couple of minutes."

Jannie moved away from her desk to give him room to manoeuver. As he started doing his techie thing she grabbed a revenue management report and sat down in a visitor's chair to study it. Every now and then she glanced over the top and caught his cute butt poking out from under her desk, where he was trying to untangle the mass of wire spaghetti.

"Hey, Kirkie," she said to his butt. For some reason, she found it easier to talk to it than to his face right now.

"Yeah?" he said in a muffled voice.

"What would you do if you weren't asked to an event you really, really wanted to go to? Would you beg for an invitation?"

"No way."

"Why not?"

"First of all, I hate social functions. Would rather stay home and code. Second, I don't beg."

"Never? Not even if it's something you want with all your heart?"

Kirk didn't answer right away. His butt wiggled its way backward until his head emerged. He sat up on his heels. His spiky hair was askew and his forest green eyes were solemn. "There's only one thing in the world I want with all my heart."

Oh boy. She'd hit a sensitive spot. Kirkie had gone all sentimental. Jannie wondered what on earth he could hanker after so badly. Maybe a new supersonic computer with more bells and whistles than a one-man band. Or tickets to some nerdy concert where the Toronto Symphony played themes from *Star Wars* and extras ran around the audience in plastic Stormtrooper outfits.

But she wanted to talk about *herself* right now. So she said in a small, tight voice, "Can you believe Joelle didn't ask me to her wedding reception?"

"*That's* why you're so upset?" Kirk pursed his kissy mouth so that it stuck out in a perfect bow shape. It was adorbs, in a nerdy kind of way.

"Well, of course I am! I thought we were friends! I feel

awful. I bet everyone out there was invited. Everyone but me!"

For some reason, Kirk started to fidget. He looked around the office, then made a dive back under the desk. Once again, all Jannie could see was cute man-butt in nicely fitting jeans.

But wait a minute. Maybe she couldn't always read faces, but she knew an evasive tactic when she saw one.

"Kirkie, get out from under that desk."

He wriggled back to the surface, like an otter coming up for air. He didn't meet her gaze.

"Tell me the truth, Kirk Molenaar. You got an invitation to Joelle's party, didn't you?"

No answer.

"Speak up. I can't hear you," Jannie said in her most authoritative boss voice. She got up from her chair and towered over him as he crouched on the floor. He seemed to be getting ready to do another deep dive back to safety, so she leaned over and grabbed him by his spiky-otter hair.

"Ouch. Stop that!"

"Fess up. Now. Did you get an invitation?"

"Well, okay. So what if I did?"

"So what you'll do is take me. As your guest! There's a plus-one on the invite, isn't there?"

"Maybe." He looked ill, and started rubbing his hands together in that way he used to do at school when he was anxious. Normally Jannie would try to calm him down but emergencies like this called for drastic measures. She continued to pull his hair.

"And have you RSVP'd yet?"

"No." Rub, rub, rub. If he kept that up his hands would ignite from all the friction.

"Then do so. At once. Kirk Molenaar plus guest will be happy to attend. Oh, Kirkie, this will be so much fun!" She let go of his hair, and he massaged the top of his head with red hands.

She felt a glow inside her breast. Yes, it hurt like hell that she hadn't actually been specifically invited, but Joelle would be pleased to see Jannie as Kirk's date. Of course she would be. And Kirk would be much more comfortable being there with his old pal, Jannie, than going on his own or with some girl he hardly knew.

She threw her most sunshiny smile at him. He shot her a trembly one in return, before disappearing under the desk. A few minutes later, when Jannie left the room for her next meeting, he was still down there in the murky wire jungle.

You'd almost think he was avoiding her. But that was impossible. Kirkie was her pal. And they were going to attend Joelle's reception together!

"Good morning. Spectrum Computing. How may I help you?" Suze's voice had a new lightness and sparkle to it.

There were a number of reasons for her happiness. She had a great new job with three wonderful young bosses. The man of her fantasies, Aram, was coming home any day now. And she'd had time to start exploring her sucCUM purchases. Bit by luscious bit. She was making progress of the most deliciously sexy kind.

Now, if only her spat with Jannie could be resolved. Suze sighed, but brightened when her thoughts turned once again to her upcoming reunion with Aram. She couldn't wait to see him. She knew she loved him, and she was no longer panic-stricken about the idea of physical closeness. *Thank you, Lola Devine, and God bless you.*

It hadn't taken more than a day or two for Suze to get

comfortable in her new workplace—a high-ceilinged, brick-walled space in a modernized early twentieth-century factory. Kirk had hired her on the spot as Office Manager, with duties ranging from reception to accounting, when she'd come in on Monday morning.

Tyler, who remembered her vaguely from when she'd lived in the same condo building, was gracious, welcoming her in his ungainly style.

"Greetings, Jannie's mom. Hope you can tolerate us," he said.

"Likewise," Suze replied, thinking that she couldn't be luckier in her new, relaxed office. These guys were beyond cute in their awkward ways.

"And this here's Bruno." Kirk pointed to a dark-haired, olive-skinned young man.

Bruno sat at a metallic desk facing a rough, yellow brick wall. Tiers of computer screens were mounted in front of him. He didn't look up from his work, but when Kirk slapped his head from behind, he waved a hand.

"We range here from Aspie light, which would be me, to full-fledged autistic, a lofty category which Bruno proudly represents," Kirk said.

Suze gasped at this, but Kirk continued, "That's basically why we named ourselves Spectrum Computing, ha ha. Bruno's the genius on the team, by the way. Can solve backend issues of the most snarly kind. Don't be fooled by how quiet he is—he's a software beast."

By the end of her first day, Suze had straightened up the mess on the antique oak desk that served as reception in the one-room office. By the end of the week, she'd made herself indispensable, updating the payables and receivables and re-arranging schedules to maximize revenue potential. Kirk, Tyler, and Bruno were freed up to do what they loved best: deal with technology.

She was buoyed by their obvious affection for her. Bruno even broke out of his cone of silence to say hello and good-bye to her every day, and Tyler glowed whenever she admired his framed wrestling posters. Only Kirk, who'd known her for half his life, seemed strangely distant.

"Tell me, Kirk. What's bothering you?" Suze asked one morning when the two of them were alone in the office. "I know there's something."

Uncertainty and sadness filled his eyes. He blinked owlishly at her but said nothing.

"Come on. Spill it. You know you can trust me."

"I trust you, Ms. Foster. But I don't think I can tell you."

"Call me Suze. You're my boss now! And of course you can. So spill."

"Well . . ."

Suze waited. When he eventually began to talk, he burbled nonstop, as if she'd hit a verbal artery.

"It's Jannie. I can't help it. She's everything to me. Always has been. But I didn't run into her for years, and now BB&M's a client, and I have to see her almost every day, and it makes me crazy, absolutely crazy, to have to pretend to just be friends. And she'll never be interested in me. She's gorgeous and a big exec. and I'm still as clumsy as I was in high school, and I don't think I can go on like this, and I don't know what to do."

Suze looked away discreetly to allow Kirk to grab a tissue and wipe his eyes. She was touched by the depth of his feelings for Jannie. She was also surprised by his profession of love, but, truth be told, she wasn't shocked by it. Way back when Kirk had been a regular after-school visitor to their home, she'd known he was head over heels for her daughter. Nobody made those velvety cow eyes like that at a girl, except for someone who was madly in love.

Now Kirk wanted help. And Suze had no idea what to do.

Jannie was dating an older man. But Suze liked Kirk. She thought he'd be good for Jannie. And she'd never been comfortable hearing vague stories about the mysterious father-figure Jannie had fallen for.

"Your secret is safe with me," Suze said. "I'm not sure what advice I can give you, but I do know Jannie loves romantic surprises. Christmas is coming. What about sending her one or two small gifts—perhaps in Secret Santa style—and eventually letting her know they're from you? I could help with some suggestions, if you like."

Kirk brushed a hand across his face. He sat up straighter and looked Suze squarely in the eyes. Suze could tell it took great effort to do this.

"I'll take whatever advice you give me, Ms. Foster, I mean Suze. I should have come to you years ago. I've just never been good at this kind of thing."

"None of us are," Suze said, sadly. "We're all on the spectrum when it comes to looking for love. Just don't let your whole life go by before you take a chance. You're worth it, and so is she."

IN FLAGRANTE DELICTO

*W*hat a week it had been! Not one, but two romantic gifts had arrived for Jannie. From a secret admirer! It was as if whoever had sent them knew her deep down, right to her soul. First, a huge bouquet of white freesias—Jannie's very favorite, delicate and fragrant. Pure beauty. And then, the book of poetry by Emily Dickinson. Simple, yet so filled with longing.

It had to be Aram. He was the only man she knew who would show this kind of insight into her heart. He'd been away for at least a couple of weeks now and must miss their hallway encounters and Jannie's subtle flirting. With absence, he must have realized the depth of his passion.

She needed to talk this over with her mom. Maybe drop by to see her tonight. It was about time they put aside their petty hurts and moved on. Besides, Christmas was almost here, and Jannie couldn't bear to be spatting when they should be 'tis the seasoning together.

It was Friday evening. The week had been busy but fulfilling. Suze was thrilled with her new, jack-of-all-trades job at Spectrum Computing, and fonder of her three bosses than she'd ever thought possible. They were some of the smartest people she'd ever worked with. And in many ways, the most vulnerable. She intended to do everything she could to make their business thrive and their lives happier.

Especially Kirk's.

She'd given him the soundest advice she could think of about how to woo Jannie. To the best of her knowledge, he'd followed through. For Kirk, the next step would be the hardest, fessing up to Jannie that he was the sender of the thoughtful gifts. He told Suze he planned to do this within the next week. Suze hoped he wouldn't chicken out.

She had just stripped off her work clothes and put on jeans and a t-shirt when there was a knock on her door. Strange. Visitors to the building were supposed to buzz in from downstairs. She hoped it wasn't Gleb, coming up to harass her about overdue rent. Or worse, to try to cop a feel.

"Who's there?" She unbolted the latch but left the heavy-duty chain attached, then inched the door open a crack.

"An uninvited guest. May I come in?"

Immediately, Suze pushed back the chain, threw the door open, and pulled a weary-looking Aram inside. He was travel-rumpled and his eyes looked strained, but he smiled broadly down at her. Feeling as if Santa had come early, Suze smiled back, unable to tear her gaze away from his. She beckoned him inside, carelessly kicking the door closed behind them, and helped him remove and hang up his winter coat.

Then, as if in a trance, she took his hand and led him

farther inside her modest apartment. It could have been the royal suite at the Ritz, for all she cared. Without a word, they sat down on the sofa, holding hands and savoring each other with hungry eyes. Suze breathed him in. Delicious traces of spiciness—manly bergamot mixed with the smoky overtones of air travel. She wanted to get closer, to bask in his essence, to feel his arms around her.

This was their moment. It might be in a tiny studio apartment, and they might eventually have to take care of ungainly details such as removing clothing and unfolding the sofa bed. But passion was in the air. Romance would trump any mundane logistics they'd have to face.

Aram leaned forward and tipped up her chin with one hand. "I've been waiting too long for this." His eyes telegraphed want, desire, urgency.

She was speechless. Her body tilted into his. And when Aram's mouth closed on hers, Suze surrendered herself to him completely.

There was no time like right this minute to make things up with Mom. It was Friday evening, and Jannie had finally managed to hire a decent, full-time receptionist. His name was Bill Parson, and yes, he looked a bit like a duck-billed minister—Jannie would do her best to remember *that* on Monday. She felt almost light-hearted as she left work at a reasonable hour and headed for her mom's building.

Passing through the first set of doors, she studied the ranks of buzzers, hunting for the correct one. There were so many buttons to choose from. The complex was huge and Mom was way up on the twenty-second story.

"Intercom is broken." A nondescript man with a strong Russian accent stared Jannie down.

"Then how are guests supposed to get in?"

"Two choices. You call on phone. Or you ask Gleb." He pointed to his chest, which he puffed out in an important manner.

"I take it you're Gleb. Okay, I'll bite. I want to visit Suze Foster in Apartment 2206."

He glared at Jannie. What she'd thought might be lust in his eye just a second ago had turned to something cold and evaluating.

"Who are you to Suze Foster?" he finally asked.

"Daughter. Jannie Morris."

"Daughter not look like mother."

"True. But she's my mom and I'd like to go in."

"One moment. You are aware mother not pay rent?"

"Say what?"

"She is terrible tenant. Owes two thousand dollars."

"*My* mother? Suze Foster?"

"Correct. She tell me always, 'Gleb, I look for job,' 'Gleb, I try my best,' 'Gleb, I do everything I can.'" His voice was a shrill mockery. "She pay some. But still not all."

Jannie clutched her stomach. Mom had been looking for a job this autumn, yes, but Jannie had thought she'd had plenty of savings. Had she been struggling while Jannie was buying designer boots? Did Mom have to fend off this sleazy jerk to keep a roof over her head? Where had Jannie been when all this drama was happening?

What a terrible daughter she'd been!

She made an on-the-spot decision. She was going to fix this.

"Gleb, I'll pay you whatever's owing. Where's your office? I want to clear this up right away."

He was only too willing, and buzzed both of them through the inner security doors. She went to his dodgy basement lair, wrote a check, flashed all kinds of ID to prove she was good for the money, and grabbed a handwritten receipt before beating it out of there.

Jannie took the elevator to the twenty-second floor and started to plan what she'd say to Mom. First and foremost: *please forgive me.* Jannie had been an awful daughter, incredibly rude when her mom had just been looking out for her. She'd ask if they could spend the holiday together. Just like old times—the two of them in the condo on Christmas Eve with Mom sleeping over. They could cook, or at least, maybe Mom could, and teach her a few things about preparing Christmas dinner. Jannie would pitch in and help. And they could hang out in their pajamas and drink cocoa and talk and talk and talk.

By now, Jannie had stepped off the elevator and was walking toward Apartment 2206. She touched the handle, expecting resistance, but the door swung open. She went in.

And that's when she got the shock of a lifetime.

More like infinite lifetimes.

There were two people on her mom's little couch, although they were so entwined that Jannie had to look closely to be sure. They were on Planet Passion, apparently, and didn't even notice her, so she took an open-mouthed moment to stare at them. She spotted a silver head that she was pretty confident was her mom's. And another, a manly one, dark hair with gray threads. Both bodies were fully clothed, thank God, but it was still a grotesquely horrid experience to catch her own mother making out with anyone, no matter who they might have been. She should be tatting doilies or baking cookies or doing anything more mom-like. Definitely not getting physical with a man friend. That kind of thing was behind her, wasn't it?

Jannie wanted to make like a Harry Potter character

and disapparate, but she was mesmerized by this scenario. The conjoined couch duo was making moany noises now, like Jannie did when confronted with molten lava cake.

She either had to sneak out the door or interrupt them. Both options sucked. Backing out meant she wouldn't get to see the guy Mom had the hots for. Jannie's brain would explode from unsatisfied curiosity. Also, leaving now meant she'd have to further delay the apologies she was aching to make. Plus, she wouldn't be able to tell Mom she'd saved her from her nasty landlord. So there were lots of good reasons to hold her ground.

But staying put meant everyone in this room was going to be red with embarrassment for the rest of their days on earth.

Yes, it was best to sneak out. Jannie could quiz Mom later about her new boyfriend. She didn't need to meet him under the present, tongues-down-throats circumstances.

But that's when the creep started to put his hands on Mom in a way that Jannie just couldn't sanction. He actually slid one paw under that ratty old t-shirt she was wearing. And, instead of clocking him across the head with a righteous slap, she made another of those moany sounds, but this one was long, protracted, and downright disgusting.

Not in front of the kids, folks. Jannie simply had to put a stop to this behavior right away.

She faked re-entering the apartment, banging the door behind her, and tootled out, "Mom? You home?"

That did the trick. The two supposed adults on the couch snapped to attention. Mom adjusted her t-shirt. Her skin was flushed, her eyes starry. Her silver hair fanned out around her face as if she were a mermaid, swimming in a sea of lust. She gasped when she saw Jannie, and put a hand to her swollen lips. Still, she tried to smile, apparently not mad that her make-out session had been interrupted.

Jannie attempted to send an answering beam, but she felt like she had lockjaw. In fact, the rest of her muscles were frozen, too, and she stood statue still in the entranceway. She had no idea what to do or say in this awkward moment. A casual hello wouldn't cut it.

Mom's swain shifted his body and displayed a partial profile. Jannie was no longer staring directly at his back, which, she had to admit, was muscularly attractive for an old fart. He took a moment, probably to psychically command certain body parts to relax, if they were able to at all after being blue pill-stimulated. Then he turned toward her.

Jannie felt like a cartoon character with eyes that goggled right out their sockets like bobbly Slinky toys. A horrible tableau lay before her. Her mom had just been making out with—and she choked just thinking this name, oh God, it really couldn't be. But it was.

Aram. *Jannie's* boyfriend in the making. *Her* love of loves to be. Mom was the other woman! In a sordid triangle Jannie hadn't even known existed.

Oh, God, it was so confusing.

"What are you doing with . . ." Jannie stuttered, trying to force the words out. "I mean, that's Aram. You know, the older guy I told you about. Earl. Earl Grey. He's supposed to be *my* boyfriend."

Mom's eyes changed from starry to stupefied, but Jannie didn't pause for a cheery family catch-up chat. She turned on her heels, threw open the apartment door, and sprinted. Down the staircase she clattered, all twenty-two floors, as if chased by a swarm of zika-infected mosquitoes, mascara running unheeded in streams down her cheeks. She galloped past a startled, smarmy Gleb, straight to her Mini, and took off in a squeal of injured indignation.

"Suze." Aram put his hands on Suze's shoulders.

"Don't." Suze involuntarily gave her whole torso a convulsive twitch. When that failed to dislodge Aram's grip, she reached up and removed his hands, one at a time. She focused on his chest, unable to look him in the eye.

"Please, Suze," Aram began.

"No. I can't. Hear. This." Suze couldn't string together coherent words. It was as if they were flying around in her brain like rabid bats, and she was unable to trap them and force them out.

"Suze, I love you."

"No!"

"I love you with my mind, my heart and my body. You are everything to me."

"Stop. Now. And leave. Please." Suze gasped each word out as if coughing up something poisonously loathsome. In her head, the bats kept swirling and colliding, swirling and colliding.

Aram took Suze's shaky hands in his strong, warm ones. She flinched, and her trembling intensified. She opened her mouth to say something, then closed it, and shook her head helplessly.

"Suze, I can't leave you like this."

"Yes! You must! I can't. Be with you." Suze gave up trying to harness her words and burst out crying.

"You know Jannie was just shocked by seeing us together."

"Jannie. Oh God. Earl Grey." Suze shook her head back and forth, eyes streaming. She made no move to wipe

them, and rivulets of tears coursed down her cheeks
unheeded.

"Who? Never mind that. For the record, I have never
been anything but fatherly toward her. I swear."

Suze held up a quivery hand. Aram fell silent. The
studio apartment was filled with the sound of her sobs,
jagged and inelegant.

"Go," she finally managed, when she was able to catch
her breath. "Just go."

"If you're sure . . ."

"Go." Suze closed her eyes and slumped back against
an upholstered couch cushion. She waved in the direction
of the door. If only Aram would leave, she could have a
good bawl in private. And try to figure out what the hell
had just happened.

A few minutes later, Suze heard the squeak of a jostled
hanger in her closet, and then her door open and shut with
a click that sounded as final as a coffin lid closing. She
peeked to verify that she was alone, before flinging her
body lengthwise on the couch to cry her eyes out.

20

A VERY DIFFERENT CHRISTMAS

Spectrum Computing was closed for the holidays. Even though Kirk and his partners had given Suze a nice bonus payment in recognition of the contributions she was making to their business, she wasn't in the mood for celebrating.

Yesterday, on Christmas Eve, she'd sat in her apartment and worked through her expenses. She was finally in the black. She wrote a check, and went downstairs to pay Gleb the back rent she owed him.

"What is this?" Gleb asked, as she tried to hand it to him.

"All the money I owe. From now on, I promise to be on time."

"As if." Gleb snorted. He made no move to take the slip of paper she was wafting at him.

"Why aren't you taking my money? It's not going to bounce. Really."

"No need. Daughter already paid. You owe nothing."

Suze's jaw dropped. *Jannie* had paid her rent?

"Are you sure? When?"

"Yes, sure. It was day when buzzers did not work. Daughter paid, and then I let her up in elevator to see you. Nice kid."

Suze felt sick. Jannie had made a generous gesture, just before walking in on the scene that had torn them apart.

And what kind of mother was she, to be dependent on her child? She was supposed to be the nurturer.

Worse, what kind of mother stole her daughter's would-be boyfriend?

Suze's head throbbed. She gave Gleb a vague wave and left his office. This was the rottenest holiday ever. The loneliest, the saddest, and the most guilt-ridden.

On Christmas Day, alone in her apartment, Suze got out her old photographs. There she was as a young mom, baby Jannie cradled in her arms, the two of them looking at each other in a state of post-feeding shared bliss. And there was a laughing Jannie as a feisty toddler on a swing, curly hair corkscrewing as a gust of wind caught her on a downward swoop. Photo after photo was of Jannie, occasionally with Suze. Only a few showed Jannie with Desmond, her erratic dad, who had missed most of the important moments of his daughter's life.

Suze picked up a random picture, taken when Jannie was eleven years old. She remembered the day well. It was Christmas, and Jannie wore a special red velvet dress, belted with a green tartan sash. She sat beside her father, looking up at him with adoring eyes and clinging to his hand as if willing him to stay. Desmond was bundled in an overcoat and stared at the camera with haunted eyes.

Suze recalled she'd begged him to pose for just one photo before he took off. With Christmas dinner not yet out of the oven. To play poker with some buddies. To try to reverse a bad streak of fortune.

To break his daughter's heart, again. And again. And again.

Viewed sequentially, Jannie's official high school photos were poignant milestones. In grade nine, she grinned at the camera, appearing confident and optimistic. By grade ten, she stared at the lens with defiance and anger. She'd been identified with a number of learning and social deficits. Many fellow students and even some of the teachers had started treating Jannie with disdain.

The grade eleven photo portrayed a girl with hollow eyes and a blank expression—a teenager on the edge. Jannie had survived it, barely. By grade twelve, the anger was back, but Suze also spotted something else. It was determination. Grit.

The system hadn't broken Jannie, but she'd had to show remarkable stamina in order to succeed. And Suze had been with her every step of the way. Desmond, in the grip of his addictions and never in touch with his family's needs, had floated in and out of their lives like dandelion fluff, but their mother-daughter relationship had never weakened.

Now, alone on Christmas Day for the first time in her life, Suze realized the link had snapped. Jannie was refusing to speak to her. Suze had lost her precious daughter. And all because of a man.

But what a man.

Try as she might, Suze couldn't get Aram out of her mind. At night, she dreamed about him, waking up in despair when he wasn't by her side. During the day, she refused his calls and tried to soldier on. She had to accept he had no place in her life. Jannie had made it plain that he was *her* object of affection. And, although Suze felt soul deep that Aram's heart was hers and would never be

Jannie's, she couldn't be with him, knowing it would shatter the mother-daughter bond forever.

It had been two weeks since the blow-up, but things weren't getting any easier for Suze. No Jannie. No Aram. Just solitude, and memories, and unfulfilled yearning.

It was frigging Christmas and Jannie was trying to make the best of the shittiest situation ever known to mother and child. In the spirit of the season, she'd spent most of the day sleeping in heavenly peace. Ignoring the whole scenario. Shunning Mom's calls. Because, even if she hadn't meant to, she'd stolen Jannie's man.

Wasn't it against the laws of nature for someone's mom to get the guy? Why buy the beautifully packaged but somewhat dusty box at the back of the shelf when the fresh-out-of-the-oven product was available?

Jannie wished someone would explain this to Aram. Because the man seemed positively distraught. Bereft, battered, and bewildered. Maybe those weren't the right lyrics, but they fit.

Jannie didn't see him that often, but when she did, he walked past her in the hallway, shading his eyes with one hand as if the sight of her brought him physical agony. This morning, for example, he carried a suitcase, perhaps off to visit his family in Montreal.

"Merry Christmas, Aram," she said.

By now she knew enough not to swish her eyelashes and try to flirt, since apparently he thought her about as appealing as a codfish at the end of a long market day.

"Same to you, Jannie," was his monotone response. He sounded like a wind-up toy that was as wound-down as it could get before going totally dead.

Then, he continued down the hall to the elevator, pushed the button, and, after the briefest of waits, went inside without a backward glance. Jannie made a face—a really scary, twisty one—hoping if he actually glanced at her it might snap him out of his lethargy. It wasn't like he could be any less attracted to her. For now, anyway.

Time was what was needed. It was good he was leaving town for the holiday. Once he got over his misplaced interest in Mom …

Jannie's eyes misted over, taking her by surprise. Even though she felt wounded, she missed her mom. Very much. Their rift wouldn't last forever. Just for the time being, until things worked out properly on the romance front.

In the late afternoon, after a solitary Christmas morning, Jannie headed down to good old Condo 4B. Tyler and Frodo had invited her to dinner, and Kirk and Bruno would be there, too. It would be as festive a holiday feast as it possibly could be without Mom. And there'd be wine!

Jannie's contribution was a plate of diverse cheeses from Holland, France and Canada. She'd tried to make sugar cookies, using Mom's traditional recipe, but they'd turned out like the coals Santa put in bad kids' stockings. Cheese wasn't a bad back-up, and Jannie had asked the counter lady to put little paper flags attached to toothpicks to indicate which cube was from which country. Very classy. And nobody had ever gone wrong with cheese.

"Knock, knock. Santa's here," Jannie called out as she arrived at Condo 4B.

"Enter the realm," Frodo's reedy voice responded.

Yes, the realm of total nerddom. Which, for some reason, made her feel right at home.

She handed her platter of assorted cheeses to Tyler, and there were fist bumps all around. The four guys looked like clones in their red plaid shirts and jeans, and Jannie blended in with her red hoody and upscale black stretchy pants that would accommodate lots and lots of caloric Christmas intake. There was some kind of a demented, electronic mash-up of carols playing, and Tyler's three cats had jingle bells on their collars and strolled in and out of legs, doing their best to bring someone tumbling down. Somehow all the humans remained upright, as they took the action into the kitchen, where the best parties always happened.

Apparently, Frodo and Tyler had spent all day cooking. Mouth-watering smells of turkey gusted forth, and the three guests squashed into the small space to watch the hosts put the final touches on the meal.

Bruno, a guy Jannie had only met once or twice, was in charge of the wine. He was as silent as the night, but he gave her a generous pour so she told him they'd be keeping him on wine duty throughout dinner. He chuckled and nodded, and everyone toasted each other's good health.

By the time the food was served, they were all a bit tiddly thanks to Bruno's lavish sommelier act. Jannie enjoyed each morsel of her meal and washed everything down with glugs of wine. They feasted and feasted.

"Here'sh to your ex'shellent health," she toasted at dinner's end, holding up her wineglass, and nearly slopping Pinot Noir onto Kirk's head. Jannie felt witty even if her tongue was thick and her words came out jumbled.

"Here's to yours, Jannie." They clinked glasses all around. Everyone was jolly, but Kirk looked at her with an odd expression in his foresty eyes.

"What'sh up wish you, Kirkie, old boy?" she asked, and guffawed for no particular reason. She'd been collecting tiny cheese flags, and she threaded a Canadian one into Kirk's spiky hair. He caught her hand and lowered it to the table, but the flag was still where she'd placed it. She chortled again.

"Jannie, maybe you've had enough." Kirk was solemn, but the rest of them were splitting their guts because he was acting all responsible, with a flag sticking out of his hair.

"Leave her alone. She doesn't have to drive," Frodo said.

"Yeah, give her a break. It's Christmas. Time to be merry," Tyler said.

Bruno said nothing. He tried to pour more wine but Kirk put his hand over Jannie's glass. Nervy.

She took the opportunity, while he was distracted, to put another flag in his hair. This one was Dutch, in honor of his Molenaar heritage. It looked crazy silly, and Jannie laughed some more.

"I'm taking you home." Kirk rose from the table, flags flying.

Jannie scanned from Bruno to Tyler to Frodo. They were yucking it up, sticking flags into each other's clothing and hair and being just as juvenile as she'd been acting. Everyone was tipsy, and Jannie grinned, feeling goodwill toward all these men.

"Thanksh for ashking me to dinner." What great guys they were. She would have been lost all alone up in her sad, Mom-less condo.

"You're welcome. Give poor Kirk a big smooch before he leaves your place," Tyler said, and Frodo started making slurpy, kissy sounds in the air.

"Ah, Kirkie'sh jusht my bud," Jannie said. "Right, Kirkie?"

Kirk was fully occupied trying to keep her from falling down, and he didn't respond. In fact, they didn't talk at all on the elevator ride or the off-balance walk down the hall to her place. And when he turned to leave, after making sure Jannie was safely inside, with a glass of water and some ibuprofen by her bedside, he made no attempt to kiss her.

Oh, what the hell.

"Here'sh one for the road!" She grabbed him by his plaid collar, pulled him toward her, and laid a messy, wet one on him. It was just for fun, Kirkie being like family, and all.

So why, even through her drunken haze, did it seem like this one sodden kiss changed everything?

Jannie didn't have time to consult with Kirk or to apologize for her behavior. He was cantering down the hallway like one of Santa's reindeers, desperately late for his appointment with the next rooftop.

Why did men run away from her, she pondered, as she dutifully swallowed her ibuprofen and flopped into bed. She hiccupped, giggled, and settled down for a night filled with visions of sugarplums and kissy lips.

In her dreams, she galloped faster than any old reindeer. She caught all the men.

21

A TANGLED MESS

*I*t was a relief to get back to work in the New Year. Christmas had been so lonely. Between mourning her lost love and missing her absent daughter, Suze had barely been able to survive what had been her worst holiday ever.

"Good morning, Spectrum Computing." Suze's phone voice was steady and professional.

She'd never been more thankful to have a job. Her gratitude had surprisingly little to do with receiving a paycheck. It was all about taking her mind off her personal life. The bustling pace of the office kept Suze too busy to do anything but focus on business. Usually. But not always.

"Happy New Year, Ms. Foster—damn it, I mean Suze. How are you?" Kirk slouched past her on the way to his desk.

She swiveled her head, watching him. It wasn't like him not to chat for a few minutes before getting down to work.

"I'm fine, thanks," she said, but Kirk was already bent over his computer. Strange that he was being so aloof.

Her personal line rang. She looked at the display. Oh no. It was Aram. Again.

She couldn't avoid him forever. She held the phone to her ear and took a deep breath, before whispering, "Hi."

"Hello, Suze." That's all he said. Two words. Nothing profound. Not poetic or meaningful or memorable.

But Aram's deep voice was filled with love so genuine that Suze could feel its tender touch. On her skin, which grew immediately warmer. In her heart, which began to beat more quickly.

She gave her head a severe shake. She needed to be tough. She couldn't allow him to keep calling. He mustn't break through her steely resolve.

"I'm at work."

"I know. But I tried calling you many times over the holiday, and you never picked up. I'm at my wits' end." Aram, in his evident agitation, spoke with a stronger accent than usual.

Suze looked left and right, then behind her. Kirk, Tyler, and Bruno all had their heads lowered over their laptops and were busily tapping away, lost in their intricate coding worlds and paying her no attention.

"I'm sorry," she said, keeping her voice low. She tried to say more, but the words caught in her throat.

No! She wouldn't let herself cry. Too many tears had been spilled already. And she was at the office and could not—would not—allow herself to lose control.

"I can't go on like this." He paused a moment, then rushed on. "You are everything to me. And, unless I read the situation completely wrong, you love me, too."

"We can't have this discussion now!"

"When else, then? You've been avoiding me. For what feels to be an eternity. It's destroying me." His breathing was ragged.

"Avoiding you?" She needed to discourage him, even though the hurt penetrated right to her soul. "You're right. And I'm afraid it's not temporary."

"Why? Because your deluded young daughter fancies herself in love with me? If this weren't so terrible a situation it would be laughable."

"I'm not laughing." In fact, Suze was almost in tears. She was clinging to the last vestiges of her tattered self-control, as if grasping a slippery lifeline.

"Nor am I! You must trust me. I never behaved inappropriately with Jannie."

Suze had given her daughter's relationship with Aram much thought over Christmas. The truth was, Suze believed Aram. Jannie had never been a good reader of character or motives. And Suze knew the love that shone from Aram's eyes when he looked into her own couldn't be faked.

It was pure. A once-in-a-lifetime, heartfelt passion.

Nevertheless.

How could she continue to see him when Jannie felt Suze was betraying her? It would permanently sever their mother/daughter bond. Much as Suze loved Aram, she had to put her daughter's feelings first. As she had all of Jannie's turbulent life. It was her motherly duty. No man could step between them, no matter how desirable. No matter how *good*.

And so, she did what she had hoped never to do. She said the words that would break Aram's heart. As she did, she broke her own.

"I believe you. And I'm sorry. But Jannie is my daughter. She's all the family I have. I won't abandon her for you."

"It's not abandonment!"

"To Jannie it is. In fact, it's worse: it's betrayal. She thinks she loves you. I can't get in her way."

"But, you are the only woman—"

Suze cut him off. "And you *were* the only man. But I've made up my mind. We can't see each other. Not now, not in the future. And that means I have to take back my invitation to Joelle's wedding, too. I'm so, so sorry. Good-bye." Before he could interpolate, she hung up, then softly added the words, *my love* to the empty air.

She sat at her desk, going through the mail and trying to breathe, blinking rapidly to keep tears from forming. When the office phone rang, this time from a Spectrum client, Suze was able to answer it calmly.

By evening she was exhausted. She took the subway home, went up to her apartment and poured herself a tall glass of Pinot Grigio. She drank half of it quickly, tasting nothing.

Then she picked up her phone and called Jannie. She got voicemail and hung up. Tonight she'd drink wine and nurse her broken heart. Tomorrow she'd try again. At some point she'd say the words she dreaded. *I've broken up with Aram. He's all yours.* But not tonight.

This New Year was going to be sensational! Over the holidays, Jannie had given her life a lot of thought and made three resolutions:

1. Get the man!
2. Make up with Mom
3. Kick ass at work

She'd tackle these one at a time. After all, she was a

senior executive, and CEO types like her were always logical, determined, and ever so organized.

So, when she wrote *get the man*, she meant it. Aram was her destiny. The drunken Christmas kiss she'd laid on Kirkie had merely been a displacement of her passion. That had to explain why it had tingled southward, all the way from the crown of her head through her girly bits, right down to her baby toes.

Kirk was her buddy, but Aram was her obsession, and now that he understood she was interested in him, he'd reach out and touch, for sure. When he came home from his trip, Jannie planned to keep an eye out and grab him when he least expected it. Then, bingo, bongo—bells would chime, angels would dance, and firecrackers would pop. They'd have the most epic sex ever. And true romance, too, naturally.

Next up, resolution number two. Time to make up with Mom. It hadn't been her fault that she'd fallen for Aram. He was so dreamy; anyone would, even an older lady like her. And Jannie should never have lied and called him Earl Grey instead of his real name. Mom hadn't known she was trespassing. Jannie would be gracious and forgive her.

Her phone rang. What a coincidence—Mom. Time to stop giving her the cold shoulder.

"Sweetie?"

Aww, Mom was so cute. No one else called Jannie *sweetie*. It made her feel all toasty warm inside.

"Hi." Jannie hesitated, not knowing where to steer the conversation next.

"I miss you so much. And I want you to know that *you* are the most important person in my life. If I'd been aware you were interested in Aram, I never would have dated him."

Jannie's thoughts immediately leapt to those terrible

make-out images that were branded on the folds of her brain. She blinked them away.

"I totally understand," she said, magnanimously. "You had no idea. I don't blame you. But it just about broke my heart." Jannie tactfully refrained from adding that seeing them together had also made her want to self-combust. Really. Her mom in sexual cahoots with the man *she* fancied!

"Listen, we need to get together soon. Put all this behind us," Mom said, a catch in her voice. "I've told Aram I won't see him. Ever. He's out of my life completely."

"Really?" Jannie felt a fleeting pang of pity for her. This couldn't be easy. He was a babe.

"Yes. I've canceled all future dates. Including Joelle's wedding. We're officially finished."

"That must have been so hard. I'm sorry this ever happened."

Jannie's words were sincere. But, as she hung up, she also felt a zap of excitement. Joelle's wedding! The one she'd forced Kirk to invite her to. Maybe now she could go with Aram, and let Kirkie off the hook. God knows he hadn't seemed thrilled when he'd agreed to take her. It wouldn't even mess up Joelle's numbers. Mom and Kirk could go as singles and Aram could escort Jannie. So what if Joelle hadn't officially invited either of them? Four people were still four people.

Meanwhile, poor Mom. She'd thought she had a new boyfriend. If Jannie didn't feel so strongly about Aram she'd back off. But he was too young for Mom. Jannie was perfect, and she knew he liked her; he'd spent lots of time giving her advice and chatting her up and pouring her glasses of wine. And he hadn't yelled at her for spilling soy sauce on his crotch. If that wasn't a strong like, maybe even love, she didn't know what was.

As for her third resolution about her work life, she was determined it would be her most successful season yet. She and her staff were going to burst through this year's record sales and go on to new glory. Head Office would applaud her and give her a huge bonus, and maybe by year's end she'd use it for a down payment on a house to share with Aram. Their love bower! The nookie nest! A place where all their dreams would come true.

But for now, she needed to face reality. And today was her first day back at work. Bound to be a busy one.

"Jannie, you're needed urgently in the conference room," the new receptionist said.

She looked at him, struggling to remember his name. Duck-shaped mouth. Aha!

"Thanks, Bill. I'll be there momentarily." She swept to her office to dump her winter coat. She took two seconds to text Kirk, telling him she couldn't go to Joelle's wedding with him, and that he needed to go alone so he didn't mess up the numbers. Then she grabbed her laptop and headed to the boardroom to handle whatever emergency was happening.

This was what she did best. Crisis control. If only the rest of her life could be as easy.

22

WEDDING PREPARATIONS

"*K*irk, you're avoiding me," Suze said, as he walked past her without saying hello.

It had been a few days since their return to work after the Christmas break. Kirk had been reclusive to the point of antisocial, barely mumbling a greeting in the morning, and responding in monosyllabic grunts to any questions she asked.

She knew he was upset. She suspected the cause might be Jannie, and Kirk wouldn't be anxious to share his concerns. But Suze wanted to cut the tension in the office. She was having a hard enough time dealing with her own sadness, and Kirk's poutiness wasn't making things easier. Maybe she could help.

He sat at his computer and picked up his headphones, but Suze walked over to his desk and stood in front of him, arms crossed. After a slight hesitation, he rested the headphones on his desk and looked at her. His face was pale and drawn. Even his hair had lost some of its spikiness; it seemed less enthusiastically bristly than usual.

"Talk to me. You're unhappy." Well, that was an

understatement. And presumptuous, too, maybe. She hoped Kirk wouldn't take offence.

He didn't seem to. He just nodded.

"And maybe it has something to do with Jannie?"

He nodded again.

"I'm guessing you never told her that it was you who sent the gifts?"

He took a breath. "I was going to. At Christmas. But she drank too much wine. The moment wasn't right. And now she's head over heels for Aram."

"I know." Suze tried to keep her features neutral, but it was hard to conceal the hurt that radiated throughout her body.

"And what am I supposed to do? Tell a girl who thinks of me like a brother that I'm in love with her? She'd be horrified."

"Maybe not horrified. But taken aback, for sure."

"Argghh!" The sound seemed torn from Kirk's chest, emanating straight from his broken heart. It was so loud, Bruno and Tyler pulled off their earphones and wandered over to find out was wrong.

"'s up?" Tyler asked.

Bruno put his head on one side, inquisitively. Suze waited for Kirk to answer, not wanting to betray his confidence.

"It's Jannie, of course." Kirk smacked his brow with the heel of one hand, as if to propel the pent-up frustration out of his brain.

Tyler and Bruno nodded. Evidently, they knew all about Kirk's obsession.

"Has anything specific happened, to make you so upset?" Suze asked.

"She canceled our date for next weekend. By *text*! Didn't even take the time to give me a call."

"Brutal," Tyler said, and Bruno reached out and patted Kirk on the shoulder.

"I'm sorry," Suze said. "Jannie isn't always the best when it comes to being sensitive."

At this, Tyler and Bruno started to laugh, and Suze had to smile. Here she was, with a group of Aspies, saying that someone *else* had social skills problems.

"Not only that," Kirk continued, ignoring the stifled laugher of the other two men. "She dumped me for *Aram*. He's like twice as old as she is. It's gross! And, she told me I have to go on my own."

Suze froze. Aram had agreed to go on a date with Jannie? Before the embers of their own relationship had even grown cold? And what kind of a date could Kirk be talking about if Jannie'd told him to go solo?

"What do you mean?" she managed to stutter.

"You know. Joelle's reception in Niagara-on-the-Lake. Jannie says she's going to take Aram. But that I still have to go to keep the numbers even. And I can't possibly do that. How could I stand to see them together?"

"I'll go with you." The words were out of Suze's mouth before she knew it.

"*You?*"

"Not as a date. As a friend. A much older friend. We'll go together to support Joelle, who is expecting us to attend. And we'll coach each other through what's going to be a very rough evening."

"And I'll come, too," Tyler said. "I'll bring Frodo. For a sexy weekend! Not to the actual wedding, of course, but in the background as your support group."

"Me, also," Bruno piped in. The others paused for a moment. It was always a rare moment to savor when Bruno spoke.

"What do you say, Kirk?" Suze asked.

He shrugged. "Let's do it."

The three young men earnestly exchanged fist bumps, before returning to their computers and picking up where they'd left off earlier. Suze sat at her desk, too, but had difficulty focusing on her screen. Aram had agreed to go to the wedding with Jannie? Had Suze been wrong about him all along? Was he actually interested in Jannie, not herself? And, why, if she'd told Jannie that she wouldn't get in the way, did Suze feel so hurt? And betrayed by Aram, the love of her life, even if she *had* told him she couldn't see him ever again?

Maybe attending the wedding would give her the answers she needed. It would be a gut-wrenching experience, but it might provide closure. A definitive end to any remnants of her shredded romantic dreams, too.

Jannie had spent a long day, industriously making everyone at BB&M richer and more esteemed in the business community. It was time to go home.

Normally she'd head to the gym. She'd been working out at least four times a week, and her trainer, Beverly Beaver Cheeks, was super proud of her. And so she should be. Jannie was a weightlifting prodigy.

This evening, though, she had a bigger priority. Tonight she'd ask Aram to Joelle's wedding. It had occurred to her she may have been a tad premature in dumping Kirk before confirming Aram as her date. But she had almost zero worries. Of course the man would want to go. His strong like for her was turning to love; she just knew it.

They'd spend a sexy weekend together. Jannie had booked separate rooms at an inn for Kirk and herself. But now she had a feeling there might be some sneaking down the hall in store. And if Aram didn't take the sneak initiative, she might just do it herself.

Mom would be at the reception, of course. Joelle had had the nerve to invite *her*, but that was okay. Now that Mom had given Jannie the blessing to push things along with Aram, the light was green, the path was clear, and it was all systems go for love.

"Good evening." Ernie held the door open, as Jannie bustled in with a bag-load of groceries.

"Hi, Ernie. Going up to make another healthy dinner." She basked in the beam of his approving look.

Jannie was no longer the patron saint of Toronto's fast-food joints. Instead, she routinely cooked protein-rich, low-carb meals for herself. She'd learned to use her appliances! And, she'd dropped eight pounds. Ten more and she'd be perfect. Her body was a temple, and soon it would be more church tower-like and a whole lot less onion-domed in dimensions.

Plus, her apartment was spick and span. Ever since Tyler and Frodo had helped her clean it from top to bottom, she'd maintained its state of tidiness. Maybe it wasn't as dust-free as when Mom had lived there, but it was pretty damn orderly. All spiffed up and ready for lovemaking.

She was well prepared. She had a sleeker body and an enticing booty lair. Now, all she needed to do was invite Mr. Sexy from Condo 5D for a cocktail and they'd seal the deal.

Hearing footsteps in the hall, she snuck a look through a crack in her door. Bingo! It was the man of her fantasies.

She opened the door wider and popped out. "Hi, Aram."

She'd caught him just as he was trying to get his key

into his lock. He seemed to be in a hurry. Jannie wondered why.

"Hello." His face didn't light up with joy. But it was dinnertime. Maybe he was starving.

"I'm roasting a chicken. Can I tempt you?" She waved a heavy-duty, two-pronged fork at him as proof. Cooking chicken was one of her new domestic accomplishments, and the way to a man's heart, and all.

"No, thank you. Now, if you'll excuse me …" He turned his back on her.

"Before you go," she said, wanting to get the wedding situation straightened out and trying to ignore her disappointment that he didn't pine for her poultry. "I need to ask you something. It's important."

At that, he stopped fiddling with his keys. He turned toward her with a hard-to-interpret look on his face. It wasn't the "O" of surprise. It wasn't the clenched jaw of anger. And Jannie didn't see lowered eyebrows, so it wasn't —well, whatever *that* was supposed to tell her.

It was like his eyes had more of a light in them. But she wasn't exactly sure why.

"Yes? What is it?" By golly, his manly baritone rang with some kind of curiosity, maybe even hope. She wondered what it was he wanted to hear.

"I'd like to ask you to go to Joelle's wedding with me. I know you were going to go with my mom," Jannie said, trying not to choke on these words.

"Oh. That." The small twinkle that she'd spotted a second ago evaporated.

"Well, I'd like it if you'll go with me."

"Jannie, I'm afraid—"

"Joelle invited Kirk and Mom plus their escorts. So, now that they're on their own, there's room for the two of us. I'm sure Joelle is dying for me to be there, and you can be my date. It's formal wear. Plus masks. I'll provide those, if that makes things easier for you."

Aram stared at her for what felt like several minutes. There was still no sparkle in his eyes, but he seemed to be doing some kind of internal calculation, like his brain was rattling out a series of complicated equations. He evidently came to a conclusion, because he nodded.

"Right. Well, if Joelle is counting on you, then I'd be happy to attend. Niagara-on-the-Lake, yes?"

"Yes. And I've booked a room." Aram's face did a peculiar twisty thing, so she clarified. "Actually, two."

"Fine, then. I'll drive. We'll leave just after lunch on Saturday."

"And if you want to get together before then—"

"Thanks, but I'm up to my ears in business issues. And still dealing with my mother's doctors in Montreal. Incredibly busy, but I'll see you Saturday."

He started to go inside his condo, but she added, "And, thanks for the thoughtful Christmas gifts. I knew all along it was you."

It was a gamble. She wasn't one hundred percent sure he'd been the person who had sent the lovely presents. But who else could it have been?

"I have no idea what you're talking about."

"Of course you don't." She winked, but his door was already closing.

Staring at the shut door, she frowned. But what the heck. Maybe he did send them, and he was trying to pull her well-shaped leg. And, anyway, OMG, it was happening. Jannie and Aram were going on an official date. An overnight one! She had time to lose at least two more pounds by Saturday. Things couldn't be any better!

Just a few more days were left until Joelle's wedding. Kirk had done the research and booked rooms for them at a small inn in the middle of town. Four in total: the grandest one for Tyler and Frodo, and, far away from *that* action, one each for Suze, Bruno, and himself.

He'd also arranged to rent a van that would easily accommodate their party. He named himself primary driver and Suze, who hadn't been behind a steering wheel in years, was more than happy to comply. All she had to do now was buy a new dress and a mask.

All she had to do? It seemed like an enormous, arduous task. One that, in her heartbroken state, she didn't feel up to. But she had to wear something fancy, and she had nothing appropriate in her wardrobe. And now that her credit cards were back in a relatively healthy state, she could afford it.

But, God, she was so lonely. She'd lost Aram. She wasn't comfortable talking to Jannie these days. The young men from work were wonderful, but they'd never understand how she felt. She needed help from a friend. Someone with an eye for fashion.

Suddenly, it struck her. She searched in her purse for a certain business card, then picked up the phone and punched in some numbers.

"Good evening. C.S. Adventures. May you rise to the occasion each and every time," a sultry voice said.

"Hi, Lola. It's Suze. Suze Foster."

"Darling girl! Such a pleasure to hear from you. I've had it up to here with deviants for today. And apropos of nothing, how are you nethering these days?"

"That part of my life isn't going so great."

"Devastated to hear this, my sweet. I'm all ears. Talk."

"Actually, I'm wondering if you can help me. I have to buy clothes for a wedding reception."

"Is Mr. Lube going to be there?"

Suze sighed and paused. Then, she said, "Yes, but not as my date."

"Well, be that as it may, our hero will appear in the room. And it sounds like you want to look pretty."

"Not for him. He's dating my daughter."

"Ooh. Kinky."

"You have no idea."

"No, but I'm open-minded. And what I'm picking up is that you want to look good for the occasion."

"Yes. I need a formal dress and, believe it or not, a carnival mask. And advice in general. I hope I'm not being too bold."

"Not at all! Consider me tickled pink with a feather from stem to stern. Give me your address. I'm coming over. We're going shopping!"

As outrageous in appearance as Lola was with her burgundy hair, vivid makeup and preposterous proportions, she had an excellent eye for fashion and a very kind heart. She dropped her more outré mannerisms, and gave Suze sincere and tasteful advice on selecting the perfect, almost-within-budget dress. By evening's end, after trying on many options, Suze found herself in possession of a long, silvery gown, cut across the top of the breasts in a straight line that culminated in off-the-shoulder, gauzy sleevelets. The bodice was fitted tightly to just above her natural waistline. From there, it dropped in river goddess streams of diaphanous fabric, sewn with swaths of sparkles that caught the light as she moved.

And that wasn't all. Lola was adamant that Suze needed accessories.

"Shoes. Evening bag. Maybe gloves?" Lola caught Suze's eye. "No, maybe not. Too drag queen. As if I'd know, right?"

"You're a godsend. I'm willing to believe you're an expert in everything. And I'm blessed to have you in my life."

Lola blushed an extroverted shade of pink. She gave Suze a brilliant smile, before pulling her by the arm toward the shoe department.

At the end of the evening, parcels in hand, Suze turned and thanked Lola.

"You're welcome, darling. We've checked off everything on our list. Except, of course, the mask."

"Oh, no worries. I'll buy one of those cheap ones at the dollar store."

"That you most certainly will not do, my pet. I shall craft you one that's perfect for the occasion." Suze's expression must have been a giveaway, because Lola continued, "Rest assured, in the most tasteful possible way."

"You're the best friend I've ever had, I think," Suze said, meaning it.

"And you can repay me."

"How? Name it."

"I have a hankering to go to Niagara-on-the-Lake with you. To be your personal dresser on the night of the wedding. I'll take care of your hair and makeup. And have a little R&R while you're off at the big event. I know a certain sommelier who might want to uncork some fine vintage Lola."

Suze gave a tentative laugh, her first in what seemed like ages. "Really? Well, there are enough seats in our van. As long as you let me pay for your room at our inn, I accept."

"Done!" Lola hugged Suze with such vigor that she gasped.

She was sure Kirk and the others wouldn't mind. The

more, the merrier. And Lola's over-the-top affability would lighten the mood in what would otherwise be a very solemn journey.

Suze might be taking a trip toward certain heartbreak, but at least she'd have Lola's broad shoulder to cry on after she allowed the two people in the world she loved most to inflict their mortal emotional blow. And as painful as this weekend was going to be, she might as well face it looking drop-dead gorgeous.

23

SURPRISE AT WORK

*O*nly two more sleeps left until the grand Niagara-on-the-Lake love-a-thon! Jannie had bought a crazy-expensive Naeem Khan extravaganza of a gown. It was in two pieces: a sleeveless, floaty, coral overdress, swirled in ferny patterns, layered above a body-hugging, nude sheath. The front was high-necked, but the back opened dramatically to display her va-va-voom vertebrae. She'd decided to go for the less-breast-being-more look this time, to avoid possible spillage issues.

Anyway, with her dark eyes and curls, she'd look divine. Aram would be smitten.

She walked into the office, imagining how his hazel eyes would pleat at the corners in his delight at seeing her. He'd stretch out a large, manly hand to take her tiny, well-manicured one, and—

Bam! Receptionist Bill grabbed her arm and piped up to announce yet another emergency. Jannie was needed in the conference room *tout de suite*. Like she was the only person in this whole organization who could fix things. She was getting sick and tired of pulling magic business solutions out of her ass.

She entered the imposing boardroom. There, in front of her, sat three of her most senior sales execs—Chandran, William, and Joelle, who was looking anxiously at her watch. Last-minute wedding details to take care of, likely. So, good; Joelle was not going to want a protracted meeting, whatever the issue may be.

Nobody said a word. Jannie swept to the head of the grand table, took a seat and waited. One minute, then two went by. It was eerily quiet. She raised an eyebrow to indicate her readiness to listen. Empathetic, that's what she was. Still, not a peep.

The silence was only broken when Shivani, BB&M's Human Resources contact from New York, glided through the door in billows of saffron silk. Her black hair was coiled stylishly at the neck. Jannie wondered if she'd be able to replicate that look for the wedding.

"Good morning," Shivani said, gazing at each of the attendees in turn.

They all nodded back. Jannie glanced sideways at Joelle, noting her neutral expression. She did her best to mimic it.

Shivani continued, "It is indeed a pleasure to be back in Toronto. BB&M is impressed with your top-ranked revenue status, internationally."

At that Jannie smiled modestly, and lowered her eyes. When she raised them again, everyone was staring at her. Jannie's grin widened. *She* was the reason they were all about to be handed the big checks Shivani likely had tucked away somewhere in all that wavy, translucent silk she had on.

But Shivani hadn't finished talking. "Everyone at

BB&M acknowledges your hard work, Jannie. You have certainly driven the business forward."

Jannie inclined her head. It was true. She was the best.

"And there's much to be said for your determined and aggressive approach to sales."

Also true. But Jannie began to wonder what Shivani was getting at. Where were those checks?

Then Shivani dropped the bomb. "This brings me to a rather delicate issue. There have been a number of complaints from your people. Not all of them are willing to come forward in person. But these three senior execs have bravely offered to meet with you, face to face, to describe their concerns, which, they've assured me, are shared by the rest of the team. And I am here as moderator, to make sure we keep this discussion professional and positive."

Jannie goggled, struggling to prevent her jaw from hitting the hard surface of the boardroom table. Shivani couldn't be serious. These people, all much lower on the food chain, had the audacity to criticize *her*? The one who put money in their pockets?

She sealed her mouth and gritted her teeth. There was no way she'd lose one jot of poise by talking to these jerks. Ungrateful traitors that they were.

Shivani seemed to realize that Jannie's lips were not about to start flapping any time soon. With furrowed brow, she looked around the room. "One by one, please share your top concerns."

For God's sake. This was an intervention.

Still, no one spoke. Shivani clicked her pen open and shut several times. "Joelle, why don't you lead off?"

Joelle shrank in her chair, as if fearing the hand of God might smite her. She cleared her throat. "Well, people have complained about Jannie's inconsistent management style."

Shivani lifted a cautionary hand. "We've discussed this. You must use actual examples. Generalizations won't help Jannie at all. And please address her directly."

"Well, all right." Joelle sighed and appeared to consult her inner rolodex of Jannie's sins. "There was one week when you went around imitating us whenever we said or did anything. That was really weird."

No fair! Joelle was recounting ancient history. Internally, Jannie fumed. But she kept her feelings corked and stared, sphinxlike, at her accusers.

"Yes," piped up Chandran. "And there was another week when you kept telling us to solve our own problems, and then you'd get mad at us when we messed things up."

Jannie bit the inside of her cheek. Their cruel words could not cause her to explode.

William Big-Butt Butterick just sat there staring down at his hands, which, Jannie noted, were of regular size. She shot him a look of fiery disdain. He glanced at her for a second, but then telescoped further into himself without speaking.

"And there were all those incidents when you called us by the wrong names," Chandran ventured.

All right. That did it. Could these people not give her one iota of credit? Those mistakes had happened weeks and weeks ago. After that, Jannie had memorized the personnel list. She knew all of their names, first and last. She hadn't slipped up in ages.

The three of them were being totally unjust. And Jannie knew she should protest, fight back. But the words caught in her throat. They were all picking on her, like the playground bullies who'd never let her in on their games. She wanted to run away and hide. Or clobber someone, using her new, pumped-up muscles.

Instead, she took the high road. Mustering the shreds

of her dignity, she said, "Thank you for your input." She rose to leave.

"Not just yet," Shivani said. "We need to have lasting take-aways from this meeting. Joelle, Chandran, and William: please tell Jannie what you would most appreciate from her, in terms of changes in her approach."

Dear God. This wasn't really happening.

"Show more empathy," Joelle said, after thinking for a moment.

"Try to be consistent," Chandran said.

Jannie glared at William, who eventually came out with a shaky, "Be less scary."

This couldn't possibly have been any more painful. Or ridiculous. They were a bunch of whiny babies, not a team of pro sales reps who had just had the most successful quarter ever. All, thank you very much, due to Jannie's efforts.

Hers. Not theirs.

Shivani graced the group with a dazzling, uncomplicated smile like the most splendid sunrise after a storm. "Thank you, everyone. It has taken courage to come forward. I know Jannie will put these important insights to good use. She is one of our most promising executives, worldwide, and I hope she can count on your support, going forward. And now, you'll all be happy to receive these extraordinarily healthy commission checks." She conjured up a small stack of envelopes and handed them out.

"Jannie, do you have anything to say before we part?"

Jannie surprised herself by saying, "I do, indeed."

She had no idea what words were about to flow from her own lips. All she knew was how steamed she felt. Shivani could yackety-yack as much as she liked about Jannie being so promising, but the woman had just humiliated her in front of the staff. Like back in high school when Jannie had been told she was special and definitely not stupid, but the kids in the regular classes had laughed at her. That kind of shame was a terrible feeling. One you never forgot or totally recovered from.

"Go ahead, Jannie." Shivani folded her hands on the table, in a pose eloquent of patience.

"Thanks for the check," Jannie said.

Shivani bowed her head in a queenly manner.

Jannie wanted to say something else. But did she, really? She paused.

Yes, as a matter of fact, she did. She opened her mouth and added, "Also, I quit."

Whoa, she hadn't known she would ever utter those words. They'd come out of nowhere. She had no idea why she'd said them.

But as she bolted from the room, stopping only to grab her coat and purse before plunging down the elevator and out onto the street, she realized she *did* know why.

The words had come from years of being ridiculed. They'd come from a deep hurt inside that had been there all her life. And they'd come from that awful place of shame—shame that she'd never been good enough, that she was crap socially, that she just couldn't learn or retain information the way everyone else could.

In business, this one sacred part of her life, she'd thought she was a star. But now she saw herself for what she must be. A sociopathic, forgetful jerk. Horrible with people. Hated by all.

She headed home. But first she stopped at the liquor store. Before today was over, she had some serious drinking to do.

24

ROAD TRIP

"*H*ave you packed your sexiest underwear, my darling?"

"Yes, Lola."

The magnificent presence of Lola Devine made Suze's compact apartment look particularly tiny. Kirk had already buzzed to say they were waiting in the turnaround in front of the building, but Lola seemed to be in no hurry to leave.

As for packing the fancy bra and panties, it wasn't that Suze expected anyone to appreciate their lacy prettiness. It was just that she thought that an important, glamorous event warranted extra effort; that she'd feel more confident dressed in beautiful garments, right down to her skin.

"Good. And your sexual aids?"

"Lola!"

"Don't *Lola* me. A girl needs to pack for all contingencies. Where's that tingling lubricant we purchased?"

"In that table, where it's going to stay."

"No, and no again, my sweet." In one stride, Lola was in front of the bedside table. She pulled out the drawer, rooted through the contents, and removed an item or two of a personal nature.

Suze didn't bother to protest. She opened a compartment on her overnight case, yanked out a half-empty plastic bag and allowed Lola to fill it to the top, before zipping and re-packing it. It was easier than arguing.

"So you've got everything, then?" Lola asked.

"Were you able to get a carnival mask for me?"

"Never fear. I have it safely stowed in my luggage." Lola pointed to the huge chest on wheels that earlier she'd maneuvered through Suze's narrow entranceway. It looked large enough to contain an entire wardrobe.

"Thanks."

If the mask Lola had bought featured an excess of plumes or sparkles, Suze would do some judicious plucking and pruning before the reception. At the moment, she was too tired to care.

"Traffic reports are saying we can expect lots of delays." Kirk stepped forward to help Lola and Suze bump their suitcases down the front steps of the building. "What have you two been doing up there for so long, anyway?"

"Private girl stuff." Lola gave Kirk an extravagant wink and a nudge that sent him staggering across the pavement.

As he recovered his balance, Lola started stacking the luggage into the vehicle. She hoisted her own, gigantic trunk into the back as if it were as light as a carton of feathers. Then she laid Suze's much more modest case on top with the tenderness of a mother for her baby. Giving it a final pat, she signaled Suze to hop on board, joining Tyler, Frodo and Bruno. Kirk waited for Lola to climb in and then jumped into the driver's seat.

"Greetings, ladies," Frodo said. "We've planned a soundtrack for our trip."

"Featuring wrestling themes, of course," Tyler said, starting up his connected iPhone. Japanese electronica poured forth, filling the van with noise. Frodo and Bruno grinned and nodded their heads vigorously to the beat, while Kirk began driving, seemingly untroubled by the racket.

Suze looked across at Lola. They shrugged at each other, before sitting back and closing their eyes. There was no escaping the wall of sound, but Suze found, during most of the two-hour-plus trip, that she was able to attain a state of half-consciousness, buoyed by the friendly presence of the others and lulled by motion and rhythm.

Whatever lay in her future, she would not be entirely alone. But where was the fairy-tale ending that she craved? Sadly, nowhere in sight, no matter what might occur over the next twenty-four hours.

And so, an occasional tear stole down Suze's cheek as they wheeled closer and closer to their destination, and she made no effort to wipe it away. There was no point.

Crash, thud, boom. Jannie's brain felt bludgeoned after a night of drinking way too much. For way, way too long. She'd sobered up in time to pack for the wedding reception, but it was going to be a rough trip.

She'd actually toyed with the idea of not going at all. Blushing bride Joelle had made it clear she disliked Jannie. Strongly. Along with all those other haters from the office. Damn them to hell.

The only reason to attend was Aram. The man who'd told her he'd be happy to be there with her—Jannie, the person everyone else in the world detested. Except for Mom, of course. And Kirkie and the boys. But that was a different kind of affection altogether. Motherly and brotherly, not hot and passionate. Like it would be with Aram.

He was her destiny, her dream come true. And if they came together at this wedding reception, then nothing would ever rend them asunder, or whatever the correct language was for this type of unbreakable union.

Still, thank God it was a Venetian carnival theme and they'd be wearing masks. Jannie wouldn't be able to look her ex-co-workers in the eyes any time soon. Plus, her own glorious brown orbs were more than a tad bloodshot from all the booze. There'd be plenty of Visine in her near future.

And ibuprofen. Lots and lots of ibuprofen.

Someone knocked on her door. "Jannie? Are you ready?"

"One moment, Aram."

Before she opened up for him, she took a breath spray atomizer out of her purse and blasted it into her mouth to dispel any lingering reek of alcohol. She knew this was overly optimistic on her part. Vodka was misting right out of her pores.

But when Aram entered the condo, she was momentarily transported by his own heavenly scent. Bergamot, manliness, leather. He looked down at her, his straight brows knitted together in concern.

"Are you feeling okay?" He leaned toward her and sniffed. It wasn't very subtle.

"I'm staving off a cold, that's all. Taking some naturopathic pharmaceuticals. Quite pungent."

Aram's nose wrinkled, but all he said was, "We'd better get moving. Traffic is going to be heavy."

Jannie fetched her stuff and began to trundle everything toward the door, but Aram kindly took the handle of her overnight bag from her and rolled it into the hall. She held on to her gown, which was in a hanging garment bag, plus her handbag. She locked the door behind them. There. All set.

She should have been filled with happy anticipation, but all she felt was nausea. And a touch of self-loathing that all the alcohol imbibed last night had not managed to dispel.

"Allow me," Aram said, as they reached his Audi in the underground parking. He opened the passenger door and handed her in. What a gentleman. No wonder she adored him.

While he sorted out the luggage arrangements in the trunk, Jannie scrabbled through her purse, looking for the plastic bag she was sure she'd stuffed in there earlier. Indeed, it was a barf sack, and she might need it once this car was in motion. She'd hold it on her lap just in case.

Aram got in. He looked over at Jannie, who gave him a shaky thumbs-up, totally unable to talk for fear of retching.

Without a word, they set out on their journey. Within five minutes, Jannie was fast asleep. Or passed out. It didn't really matter. At least the barf bag remained unused.

The Hathaway Inn was a sprawling, red brick building that had once been the home of a prominent Niagara-on-the-Lake family in the late nineteenth century. By the time Suze and her friends arrived, it was early evening, and welcoming lights glowed in the leaded windows. Suze, Lola and the four young men spilled higgledy-piggledy out of the car and stretched, inhaling the frigid air that seemed so much cleaner than Toronto's. Their breath puffed out in frosted gusts in the subzero temperature, and they began to gather their luggage quickly so they could escape the bitter cold.

"Sorry, folks; we're running late. We'll have to rush. Meet me back here in sixty minutes, tops," Kirk said, after they had all been given keys to their rooms by a wholesome-looking, middle-aged lady behind the quaint Edwardian reception desk.

"Not us," Frodo said, pulling Tyler close to his side. "We'll be otherwise engaged." The two launched into an unembarrassed and prolonged smooch. The receptionist beamed at them and clasped her hands to her heart.

"Yeah, yeah. Get a room. Oh, that's right. You've got one." Bruno laughed at his own joke. Tyler and Frodo paid him no attention, but Suze and Kirk stared at Bruno in wonder, never having heard him say so much at one time before.

"I'll be ready in an hour," Suze said. "It's just the two of us going, right?"

"Right. Sorry. I'm a bit muddled. Long drive." Kirk rubbed his eyes and lumbered off down the corridor, wheeling his bag behind him. Frodo and Tyler were still mid-kiss, but Bruno and Suze checked their keys and began to gather up their luggage.

"Hold up a mo', boyos," Lola said, placing one hand on Frodo's shoulder and reaching out with the other to stop Bruno from leaving.

"Sure; but why?" Frodo's voice had a thickened, dreamy quality to it, filled with passion and yearning and love.

"You'll see. And, Suze, off you go. Don't worry: I'll be right with you, my precious chickadee." Lola blew an air kiss and flapped her hands, shooing Suze away.

Suze hovered. "Everything okay?"

"Everything's divine. Just give me a few minutes, my

love." With that, Lola gathered the coterie of young men to her bosom, leaving Suze to navigate the narrow halls of the historic inn on her own.

She had booked two rooms on the ground floor for Lola and herself, with a connecting door between them. The mirror-image accommodations were spotless, and the furnishings featured some charming antiques, including plush four-poster beds. White terry robes hung in the closets. Suze wasn't sure which of the twinned rooms to claim and wandered back and forth between the two areas indecisively. Finally, Lola burst in and took the initiative, tossing her huge case effortlessly onto one of the beds. Suze was relieved that the venerable piece of furniture didn't crash to the ground from the impact.

Room assignments accomplished, Lola clapped her hands and said, "We can have girlfriend chatter when you get back tonight. I may leave the door open in case you're in the mood to talk. But feel free to lock it from your side if you bring a special someone home with you. Don't worry about me—I brought my earplugs. Industrial strength. And, who knows, maybe I'll lock the door from my side if I find my long-lost sexy sommelier."

Suze reached up to pat Lola's strong shoulder. "I hope you do, Lola. You deserve some fun out of this trip. But I'm sure I'll be alone."

"Never say never, my dear. I'm going to make you so beautiful that every heart in the reception hall will melt when you walk in. Even the groom's. Now into the shower with you. Scrub a dub, head to feet. And especially in between."

Lola wasn't speaking idly about the planned transformation. By the time Suze emerged from the steamy hot shower, skin scrubbed and rubbed to pinkness and hair lofted up into a towel, Lola was ready for her. She had been busy, and the capacious trunk was open on the bed, with bottles, vials, puffs, and palettes of makeup spilling out.

"Suze, my dear. We're about to get real close. Think of me as the professional I am. Now drop the towels."

With anyone else, Suze would have refused. But she had complete faith in Lola. She did what she was told and stood naked in the middle of her room.

Lola went to town. First, she applied a tightening body lotion that smelled like vanilla and blackberry and made Suze's skin feel supple and youthful. Then a deodorant underarm cream that Lola said was not only extremely effective and natural, but nontoxic. Just in case. At that point Suze insisted on putting a robe on, claiming she was freezing. Lola nodded, handed Suze a special balm, and told her to go into the bathroom and apply it liberally to the delicate places that might need extra moisture.

"Lola, it's not like I need it. Tonight I'm here to support Joelle. That's all."

"A girl can dream," Lola replied, steering Suze into the bathroom and closing the door to allow her a private moment. "Feeling twenty-five years old again? Then, out you come. It's time for hair."

"Please, not too big," Suze pleaded.

Lola snorted. "Child, not everyone can carry off my awe-inspiring look." She sat Suze on a wooden chair and made sure no mirror was in sight. "Relax and let me be the judge of what's right for you. I've got serious work to do."

Suze gave herself up to Lola's stronger will. Obediently, she submitted to having her hair blown dry, and twisted, strand by strand, onto a large-barrel curling iron. Lola didn't use a comb, arranging each shining tress with her oversized but surprisingly dexterous fingers. That accomplished, she stared at Suze critically and gave a sharp nod, before going to fetch her vast collection of cosmetics. Suze sensed sponges and powder puffs and brushes making magical passes across her face, neck and décolleté. She kept her eyes closed and listened to Lola whistling tunelessly under her breath as she worked. Suze felt like a wall being spackled and hoped like heck that the end result would be more glam than goop.

"There. All done." Lola stepped back to make a final examination of the made-up and coiffed Suze.

"May I look?"

"Not until you're dressed. Put on your hot mama lingerie while I fetch your frock."

Suze complied, donning the wispy, silvery undergarments with care. Lola unveiled and brought over the dress, draped over both arms as reverently as if it were a priceless designer gown, not the pretty but mass-market garment Suze had purchased.

"Hands high in the air," Lola said, lowering it over Suze's head without disturbing a single gleaming hair. "Yes, that's right; hold still and I'll zip you up. Good. Now, the sandals. Exquisite. Are you ready? Turn around and prepare to be amazed."

Suze rotated slowly, not knowing what to expect. She'd never had so much help getting ready for anything before and, while she had enormous respect and affection for Lola, she wasn't entirely sure her new image would suit her own, much less flamboyant taste. But when she regarded herself in the full-length pedestal mirror, she was astonished.

"Is that really me?"

"Ninety-nine percent gorgeous you. One percent Lola artistry." Lola gave Suze a smug smile.

Suze stared at herself in wonder. The beautiful, slim woman she saw reflected in the antique glass stood tall in her perfectly fitted silver gown. Her hair fell in natural-looking waves to just below her chin, and shone in synchronicity with the color of her dress. Her makeup was subtle perfection, emphasizing Suze's gray-blue eyes and accentuating her lips, which were tinted a deep rose.

"I don't know how you did this, Lola. But I don't think I've ever looked better. Thank you." Suze tried to give Lola a hug, but the bigger woman held her off with one hand.

"Don't you dare wrinkle your gown or smear your lipstick. Stand back. And, dearie, you're so welcome."

"Now, all I need is my clutch and my mask," Suze said, looking inquisitively at Lola.

"Ah, of course. Here's your bag." Lola presented the delicate, spangled accessory to Suze, who held it easily in one hand. "And, compliments of C.S. Adventures, an evening wrap to protect you from the cold night air."

With a magician's flourish, Lola produced a silver-and-cream wool shawl that had luminous, paler silver threads running through it. She wrapped it around Suze's shoulders and stood back to take a look.

"It's not the most practical thing in this weather. But you're only steps away from the big party. Don't stay outside in the cold air for long!"

Suze fingered the soft fabric. "It's perfect. Lola, you shouldn't have, but I really appreciate it."

"And, finally, the *pièce de résistance*. Ta-da! My lady's disguise." Lola held out a mask. "Don't put it on yet. Give your makeup time to set."

Suze took it, surprised at how light it felt in her hands, and held it under a Tiffany desk lamp in order to appreciate it fully. Like her dress, the mask was made of silver fabric, iridescent with tone-on-tone sparkles and star-shaped symbols. It was asymmetrical, with two curving wing-like swoops that would follow the outline of the right side of her upper face and curve inward just above her forehead. When she tied the silver ribbons behind her head, the bottom half of her face would be visible, but the upper half, apart from her eyes, would be covered.

"I love it."

"And I love that you'll be the belle of the ball. Now, off you go. Your prince is waiting."

"Much as I'm fond of Kirk, he's not my prince," Suze said.

"I wasn't talking about Kirk." Lola shook her head at Suze and waggled a finger. "But we won't argue. Enjoy the evening. Now go."

Suze took a last look in the mirror and, in a flash of pure silver, was out the door.

Miracle of miracles, Jannie slumbered peacefully all the way to Niagara-on-the-Lake. Aram gave her a tiny nudge to wake her when they arrived. In her hands, she still clutched her barf sack; unused, thank God. She sensed a trace of sleep-drool on her chin, so she wiped it quickly with the edge of the bag before stuffing it into her purse, and prayed she hadn't been snoring.

Aram's face was locked in neutral, conveying nothing at all. Jannie shrugged and got out of his cushy vehicle, emerging into the frosty air of Niagara-on-the-Lake.

"Holy crap! It's freezing," she said and dashed away from the car, leaving Aram to deal with the luggage. He was dressed more warmly, making this the most practical thing to do. Surely he wouldn't mind.

They were staying at the Lavender Inn, a slick, new-made-to-look-old hotel on the main street, half a block away from where Joelle's celebration was being held. As

Aram carted the luggage into the lobby, Jannie rushed to the highly polished reception desk.

"Two rooms. Booked under Jannie Morris."

"Ah, yes, Miss Morris. We have two deluxe chambers reserved for your party: one on the ground floor and the other on the second floor. Both nonsmoking, of course," a female clerk said. She studied her computer screen, flipping her long black hair over one shoulder and revealing her name tag: *Eriko*.

"Can you move them together? Like, make them adjoining?" Jannie whispered, keeping one eye on Aram, who was rolling their bags ever closer.

"Pardon me?"

"Can we stay in adjoining rooms? *Please?*" Jannie muttered out of one corner of her mouth.

Fortunately, Eriko had heard this time. Unfortunately, the news wasn't positive.

"I'm so sorry, Miss Morris. The hotel is completely booked up. I am unable to do this for you."

"That's all right." Jannie sighed.

Well, they'd only be separated by a floor. And maybe, by night's end, they wouldn't be separated at all.

Aram joined her at the desk. "Is there a problem?"

"Nope. Just getting our keys."

"I was telling your daughter I'm sorry we can't offer you adjoining rooms," the receptionist said, totally oblivious of Jannie's dagger-like glare.

"My daughter will have to live with the disappointment," Aram deadpanned. He thanked Eriko, accepted a key and listened to her directions to his room. As he began to heft his overnight bag toward the staircase, he told Jannie to meet him in forty-five minutes back at the same spot. Kind of bossy, not to mention a ridiculously short prep time, but she didn't argue.

Jannie was left to drag her own suitcase, as well as tote the voluminous garment bag, along the ground-floor hallway. As the wheels went clickety-clack, she fumed. The nerve of that girl! Daughter, my ass. Eriko couldn't have missed the sexual sparks flying between the two of them.

But when Jannie opened the door to her luxurious room, with its king cannonball poster bed dominating the space and hinting at pleasures to come, she lost the attitude. Aram had given her less than no time to get ready. Regardless, she planned to be supermodel fabulous by deadline.

Against all odds and in spite of the lingering aftereffect of last night's vodka, she did it. She stood in front of her ornamental faux-Victorian mirror, scrutinizing herself before leaving. In record time, she'd put her hair up in an artless knot, with a few of her dark, trademark curls floating down here and there, as if by accident. Her makeup, which she'd had to daub on more liberally than usual due to yesterday's overindulgence, was a triumph of camouflage. She'd created a sensational smoky-eye effect and a bold mouth with brilliant coral lipstick, and she'd used a dark blush to make her cheekbones appear to jut out like Angelina Jolie's. Very glam.

As for the coral gown: it was a flattering combination of flowy and clingy. Such a nice contrast to her dark hair and eyes. Her shoes were black studded Valentino t-straps with toweringly high skinny heels, and she carried a miniature, beaded evening bag. But, damn, she'd forgotten all about outerwear, so she'd have to schlep to the wedding in a puffy coat. She'd make sure hardly anyone saw her in it. For now she'd just carry it, along with the handbag and their two masks.

As an afterthought, she spritzed herself with Clinique Happy. Yes, it was her mom's old-lady scent, not her own, but Jannie was a spider trying to lure a fly, and this particular fly seemed to respond to that perfume. She'd do anything to get her man.

In the lobby, Aram slouched in a wingchair, gazing into the gas-pretending-to-be-log fire. He was even more babe-like than usual, in spite of the broody look on his handsome, bearded face. Dressed in shades of charcoal, he looked like a zillionaire.

As Jannie approached, his head snapped up, and he started to smile. When he saw who it was, though, his brows lowered and he gave Jannie a rather snippy nod.

"For a moment, I thought …" he murmured.

Well. Whatever. Although a little, *hey, Jannie, you look pretty*, would have been nice.

"Let's go," he said.

Jannie handed him his mask, a black eye covering with a pointy, raised nosepiece and an elastic behind-the-head holder. It might make him look hawkish, but it was the best she'd been able to find last-minute at the costume store.

He stopped her before they left the inn. "Put your coat on. It's below zero tonight."

Jannie hated being ordered about. Normally, she'd refuse to obey. But, damn, it *was* cold out there. And her stunning dress hadn't made even the slightest impression on this man, so what the hell.

She put on her stupid puffy coat and off they went into the night.

25

DO YOU TAKE THIS WOMAN?

*a*s Suze and Kirk walked the short distance from the Hathaway Inn to the historic building where Joelle's wedding reception was taking place, snow began to fall. It didn't come down in delicate flakes; it gusted in hard-edged, pebbly shards that zinged as they touched exposed skin. Conversation was impossible. Suze and Kirk, in unrehearsed harmony, linked arms, lowered heads, hunched shoulders, and hurried as fast as Suze's high heels would allow.

The spectacular, high-ceilinged lobby was swarming with couples dashing in from the storm, peeling off outer layers, and fighting their way across the black-and-white-tiled entrance hall to the coat check. It took Suze and Kirk several minutes to take care of logistics, and by the time they were able to wedge their way into the ballroom, the formal part of the evening's festivities was already in progress.

Suze nudged Kirk and held up her elegant, silver-spangled mask. He nodded, pulled an inexpensive, black Zorro-style one out of his pocket and affixed it to his face, ruffling his spiky hair as he did. Suze felt mysterious and otherworldly, but when she looked at Kirk, with his kiddie mask askew, she chuckled. Kirkie wasn't cut out for subterfuge and glamor, but he was cute, and she reached over and adjusted it so that it sat squarely on his face.

At the front of the room, on a gold velvet-swagged stage, speeches were under way. A bridesmaid, dressed in the kind of deceptively simple black slip dress that had to have cost thousands, was telling a never-ending story about Joelle's undergrad days. The audience, on its feet, was getting fidgety.

Suze paid little attention to the young woman's rambling talk. Instead, she used the time to admire the glittery white and gold ornaments shaped like giant masks and huge crescent moons that hung from the ceiling. They oscillated and sparkled, illuminated by cleverly placed spotlights. The room itself was a large rectangle, and so filled with guests that if the walls were decorated Suze couldn't tell from where she stood. She counted six dance band members, moving restlessly in their niche tucked below the stage, and noted the expansive dance floor that took up at least a third of the room. Glancing over her shoulder, she saw that sleek, metallic counters had been set up and bartenders were readying trays of red and white wine to serve thirsty guests once the interminable speeches were over.

And what a marvelous array of fashions the guests wore! There were people of all shapes and sizes: women arrayed in jewel tones and pearlescent hues; men, mostly in stalwart black, providing a counterfoil. Plus the masks! From behind her disguise, Suze made out cat women, demon girls, and birds of paradise, interspersed with the more stolid, basic eye-coverings of the majority of the men.

". . . and that's why Joelle is ready to settle down and be a great wife," the young speaker concluded at long last, to a smattering of polite applause.

"That was painful," Kirk muttered into Suze's ear.

"Shh!" She gave him a disapproving poke with her elbow.

"And finally, let's hear from our bride, Joelle," a twenty-something man wearing a Chris Hemsworth mask bellowed into the microphone.

The band played a riff from a recent hit as a masked Joelle walked forward, resplendent in her lace-sleeved, tight-waisted bridal gown. Suze recognized the tune. She didn't know the lyrics or who the original artist was, but the young people in the crowd laughed. Oh, to be thirty and understand current cultural references.

"Thank you all for coming to our wedding reception. It means the world to us. We spared most of you the heavy-duty religious part," Joelle said, taking a breath while many listeners gave whoops of approval. She adjusted her gold Columbine mask and continued, "But I can assure you that Ben stomped on the glass, and we're officially hitched." More hoots and hollers. "And now we're all going to enjoy a great big party. In honor of Ben's Venetian ancestors, please enjoy our tribute to the *Carnevale di Venezia*. Let's dance the night away!"

With that, the band started playing something peppy and eminently danceable. Suze and Kirk, caught in the middle of a swirling mass, grimaced at each other, and endeavored to make their way toward the fringe. When this maneuver proved to be a challenge, they settled for a slow shuffle in time to the beat, inching their way along. Sooner or later they'd work themselves out of the crowd, and then they could pay their respects to the bride and groom and their families.

That's why they were there, Suze reminded herself. To show Joelle their support. Not to scan the ballroom for the sight of a certain tall, dark, bearded man.

Still, her head swiveled from side to side as they crept by modest increments toward the outer rim of the crowd. Behind her mask, her eyes stung from a mixture of hope and dread.

Maybe some people in the world enjoyed having slivers of glass thrown in their faces; if so, they'd have relished this icy-snowy weather. Jannie, not so much. Even though she was mad that Aram was treating her like a kid, she was secretly grateful he'd made her put on her jacket. Her dress was protected from the knifelike precipitation and she was spared death by hypothermia, too.

They were a tad on the late side. As they rushed to check their coats, Jannie heard the tail end of the speeches booming out from the hall, then the music starting up. Perfect! They'd missed all that boring lovey-dovey/why we're the perfect married couple crap and now Prince Studly and Jannie could boogie to their hearts' content all night long. Well, not *all* night. They'd need time for other activities later on, of course.

Once her coat was checked, Jannie donned her mask, tying the satin ribbons with care. It was fancier than Aram's black one, but not by a lot. Hers was made of dyed coral leather adorned with a few matching feathers, and it covered the top half of her face, leaving her sensuous lips exposed, all set for kissing.

In selecting it, she'd focused more on coordinating the color with her gown than on showing great originality. She wasn't a fan of the whole mask theme. It seemed kind of a stupid thing for a pretty young lady to wear. It wasn't like she didn't want anyone to see her gorgeousness.

On the other hand, this crowd was full of Jannie-haters. Joelle had invited almost everyone from the office, with one glaring exception. They all wanted to put Jannie on a spit and roast her. It might not be a bad thing to be incognito tonight, after all.

Aram tapped her on the shoulder, to get Jannie's attention without having to yell over the caterwauling of the band. With his mask affixed, he resembled a bird of prey, and he nodded his beaked nose in the direction of the reveling crowd. It looked like a colorful, angry beast with no sense of rhythm. Jannie prayed her gown wouldn't be shredded as they entered the fray.

But, hallelujah! At long last, she was on a date with Aram, and he wanted to dance with her. Maybe he'd just been tired from driving before. Now it was time to get down and party. Cut a rug, shake a leg, and try a twerk. And, at the first opportunity, snaffle a snog. Earl Grey needed to be kissed, and Jannie was just the girl to satisfy his desire.

They inched their way among the compacted, writhing bodies on the dance floor. It wasn't Jannie's fault she had to press her entire frontage up against Aram's back as they made their way into the gyrating crowd. She wondered if it were the masks that made people feel they could do whatever they wanted. There was some downright dirty dancin' going on out here. But those who'd like to participate shouldn't criticize, so Jannie shut off her brain and went with the flow, toward the middle of the floor, losing herself in the rhythm.

She took a firm hold of one of Aram's hands so they didn't get separated. He didn't flinch. He didn't pull away. He just seemed oblivious. His hazel eyes roved, searching the crowd, paying no attention to Jannie at all. At one point he froze and she saw a half smile form on his face, but when she gave him a tug to get his attention he looked down at her with an unreadable expression.

Jannie gazed at her small, dimpled hand in Aram's large, square one. She should have been thrilled that she'd finally accomplished this small first step toward intimacy.

So she wondered why her toes weren't curling in budding lust—why she felt no electric spark, not even a teensy one.

At long last, Suze and Kirk had wriggled their way to the edge of the dance floor. It hadn't been easy to navigate through the undulating huddle without being pushy. Along their path, they'd swayed to tunes from every decade from the last fifty years. The band was doing its best to satisfy the tastes of everyone, young and old, and the crushing mob of dancers was a tribute to its musical versatility.

Still, Suze was glad to be out of the throng. She beckoned to Kirk, indicating they should make a break for the outer hallway. Maybe they could find a back entrance leading to the building's stage where Joelle, Ben and their families were still welcoming guests.

"What a relief! I can hear myself talk again," Kirk said, as they exited the main room. He wiped his brow, nudging his mask off kilter.

"Not much for dance parties, I take it?" Suze asked, as they started nosing around, looking for a likely route to their desired destination.

"Well, not really. Although, maybe . . ."

"Don't worry, Kirk. I get it. Maybe with the perfect partner it would be fun, right?"

"Yeah."

"Understood and agreed. Now, do you think this passageway will take us to—"

But Kirk was making a downward shushing gesture with one hand. Suze looked at his masked profile, then followed the direction of his gaze. How very strange.

Across from where they stood, in a darkened corridor next to the elevator, two men lurked in the shadows. Both of them were dressed in tight black sweats with hoods pulled up. They were wearing full-face, blank white masks, with only the eye holes cut out. Creepy. Suze shivered.

Whatever they were up to seemed odd, too. The smaller man appeared to be keeping a lookout, while the larger, his back to Kirk and Suze, was trying a number of keys or picks, evidently attempting to get through a door marked "Electrical Room. Keep Out."

Weirder yet, when the small, masked man noticed Kirk and Suze staring, he held up a finger to the eerily smiling, unpainted mouth on his mask.

Well, if those up-to-no-good characters thought Suze was just going to stand there and let them break into a room obviously not meant for guests, they were wrong. She started across the hall, with Kirk on her heels, but they were a fraction of a second too late. The larger masked man had already gained access and gone through the doorway. And, before Suze and Kirk could put a stop to whatever shenanigans were going on, the whole building went dark.

For a split second, as the band lost its power source, there was a break from the party's raucous noise. Then, yells of dismay broke out from the ballroom, muffled at first, but gaining in volume as the heavy doors swung open and revelers began to pour out. Many of them had switched on the flashlight features of their phones, and the outer hall now looked as though someone had unloosed dozens of drunken fireflies. From afar, a deep male voice yelled, asking everyone to stay calm and assuring the crowd that power would be restored imminently.

Suze barely heard this announcement, though. While the confusion was at its peak, she found herself seized by the larger of the two hooligans. Utterly powerless to resist, she was now on her way down a back corridor, in the arms of a large, masked man who removed her silver face-covering as he swept her away. With her arms pinioned, she couldn't keep a grip on her clutch, and it clunked on the floor as they clattered into the darkness. Although she cried out for help, there was no response.

Jannie and Aram were fairly close to the front of the ballroom, dancing to some kind of seventies sentimental slop, the kind of thing Mom might like, when the whole place went dark. A few noodle-heads screamed, but those with brains turned on their iPhone flashlights and were able to see the lay of the land well enough to start making an orderly exit. A power outage wasn't much of a biggie, anyway. It was kind of to be expected, what with the raging ice storm going on outside. It likely wouldn't last for long.

Aram held Jannie's hand firmly. He pulled her toward the stage, rather than the hallway doors. It wasn't a bad idea. They were closer to the stairs that led up to where the wedding party was gathered than to the exit. They only had to swim like spawning salmon against the flow for a few seconds, and then they were in the clear.

Only problem was, now Jannie had to face Joelle. She

hadn't seen her since she'd quit work. Kind of abruptly. And, Jannie wasn't exactly an invited guest.

"Jannie? Is that you?" It was Joelle, ethereal in white, the sequins on the fantail skirt of her dress sparkling with fervor in the beams of several tiny flashlights. Her gleaming gold mask made her appear regal and wise.

"Yes, guilty," Jannie said.

Standing behind her, Aram touched her shoulder in an encouraging gesture but he didn't need to. Jannie removed his hand and stepped forward. She had to face up to Joelle sooner or later, and being in near-darkness boosted her confidence. Having a mask on helped, too.

"I'm so glad you're here! You need to meet Ben. Where is he, anyway?" Joelle turned around to find her groom, leaving Jannie with her mouth agape.

How could Joelle be pleased? She hadn't even invited Jannie. And she'd group-shamed her just two days ago, forcing her to quit a job she'd loved.

Aram murmured in Jannie's ear, "Steady, there."

She felt a flash of irritation. She was about to tell him to stop acting like he was her dad, when Joelle reappeared with her groom. The two of them had wide smiles on their faces. Joelle came right up to Jannie, who flinched, until she realized Joelle's arms were outstretched for a hug. Jannie submitted, and Joelle's embrace felt reassuring and, in a way, apologetic.

"Ben, this is Jannie Morris and . . ."

"Aram Krikorian," Jannie supplied. Aram made a small bow, and started to inch away. Perhaps he was trying to be tactful.

"Pleased to meet you both. I've heard a lot about you, Jannie," Ben said. His eyes, behind his solid black mask, revealed nothing. Jannie could only guess the stories he'd heard.

Aram seemed distracted by something that was happening on ground level. He gave a half wave, and backed off toward the stairs.

"I'm not actually crashing your wedding," Jannie said, feeling horribly guilty.

Joelle laughed. "Of course you aren't. Kirk told me he was bringing you." She looked around, maybe for a trace of Kirk, then shrugged. "And I've been regretting I didn't officially invite you, anyhow."

"Really?"

"Yes, really. And, I want—"

But Jannie didn't get to hear what it was Joelle wanted. At that moment, two short men, both wearing black hoodies and weird, featureless white face coverings, swooped out of the darkness and stood on either side of her. Before Jannie could squeal a protest, they lifted her by the elbows and trundled her through a backstage exit she hadn't noticed earlier. Joelle's mouth dropped open, but she made no move to help, as Jannie was carried into the shadows. Likely she was thinking: there goes Jannie, being just as crazy and inconsistent as always and trying to steal the spotlight.

Jannie was far more astonished than terrified. Her kidnappers were the smallest thugs imaginable. They tried to bump her down the stairs, but she dug a stiletto heel into one guy's foot. He yelped and let her go. She punched the other guy in the jaw, using the hand that was holding her phone, and he sat down on a step with a sudden, satisfying plop.

"Aha! Take that, you little weasel!" she yelled, feeling like a warrior princess, armed with right and might and her magic coral mask of power.

Fists up, she was ready to carry on pummeling, but the two men cringed away from her. She stretched out a hand

and grabbed for the smaller guy's mask, but he limboed out of reach. When she tried again, the inept duo clattered down the stairs and away.

But before they disappeared, they threw something back up at her. She flinched but when the object connected with her thigh and bounced off, it didn't hurt. It shimmered on the floor, silvery, under the beam of her flashlight. Jannie lifted it.

What the hell were two wimpy muggers doing with a creamy-silver lady's shawl, wrapped around a gorgeous silver half mask that swooped upward on one side? God only knew, but the items were obviously valuable and must have belonged to one of the guests.

Jannie might as well look for the rightful owner. There was no sign of her cartoonish abductors, so she made her way to the bottom of the staircase. She located the door that led outside, to the back of the building.

It was fricking cold, although the blasting icefall had stopped. Jannie tried to open the door she'd just exited through, reflecting that being warm inside might be preferable to freezing to death out here, even if masked midgets were cavorting in the hallways. Unfortunately, the door must have locked when it closed. Philosophically, she swaddled herself in the found shawl, grateful for its warmth, and started to walk gingerly in her stilt-like heels over the frosty pavement toward the front of the building.

She slipped once, then twice. Each time she was able to regain her balance, but just barely. The footing, particularly in those Valentino t-straps, was treacherous. She forced herself to creep her way along, even though she wanted to gallop toward the comfort of the crowd and the hoped-for restoration of power and light. This was taking so long, and her sense of frustration mounted as she slipped yet again. To avoid a fall, she grabbed the branch of a decorative shrub against the side of the hall, recovered her balance, and paused to catch her breath.

"Suze? Is that you?"

Jannie remained motionless. It was Aram's voice. And he wasn't looking for her.

How embarrassing, not to mention infuriating. What should she do? She was partially concealed by this bush. She'd hide until he went away.

"Suze? Please come out from behind that bush. I know you're there."

This was awful. But in spite of herself, Jannie experienced an unhealthy dollop of curiosity. Nestled in her hiding spot, she pulled her coral face mask off, replaced it with this silvery thing, and draped the shawl around her head and shoulders. At least now he might not recognize her if he got any closer. She crouched further down behind the shrub.

"Suze, I know you're avoiding me," Aram said, his accent making his words sound stilted. "And I know you'll do anything for Jannie."

Rightfully so. Jannie held up a hand to stop him from coming any closer. He paused on the other side of the bush.

"I'll deliver my piece and leave, then," he said, his voice dropping. Jannie inclined her head to hear him better, and a sharp twiglet from her protective plant almost punctured one of her eardrums. She bottled the expletive that leapt to her tongue.

He continued. "I love you deeply, Suze. *You*. No one else. I'm prepared to wait. Forever if I have to. My feelings won't change."

With that, he turned his back and strode away, his shoes clicking against the icy surface of the sidewalk. Jannie followed him with her eyes until he merged with a group of people standing in front of the hall—some smoking, some laughing, all acting as if this were the most normal evening in the world.

But Jannie's world had changed. That was for sure. It had been rocked right off its axis.

As she stood there, wondering if she mostly felt humiliated or bereft or angry, she spied two people approaching. One wore a cockeyed mask and had stick-up, spiky hair. Kirkie! The other, if Jannie's eyes didn't deceive her, was a short guy in a hoodie and a full white face mask. It must be one of her abductors! She had no clue why he was having a comfy chat with her old pal. And why he gave Kirk a nudge toward her concealing shrubbery.

Jannie shrank back. She was too stunned at the moment to have a fun catch-up chat. Like, "Hey, Kirkie, how's that date with my mom going? She appears to have stolen the heart of the man I love. Got any advice for your old pal, Jannie?"

So she stayed quiet and hunkered down. Maybe he hadn't noticed her.

She was wrong, of course.

"Pssst! Suze, that you?" he stage-whispered.

Really? Did every man Jannie knew want to cozy up to her mother? For the love of vodka, which she was starting to crave, she was having a very bad evening!

But Jannie didn't say anything. She'd remain a mysterious silvery figure and leave it up to Kirk to reveal his innermost feelings, just like Aram had done.

When Kirk took a step closer, Jannie once again put up an imperious hand to stop him. Maybe she should consider a career as a traffic cop. She seemed to possess great powers of manual control.

"All right. I won't come any closer," he said.

Jannie gave him a silent thumbs-up.

He continued, "Here's the thing, Suze. I can't find Jannie anywhere. I've been searching."

Well, well, well. Now, this was interesting. Jannie was going to have to fake her best Mom voice so she could get to the bottom of whatever it was Kirk was worrying about.

"Why?" She kept things brief so he wouldn't be suspicious. Mimicry wasn't one of her top talents.

"To tell her I love her. You know. Always have, since high school. Always will."

Would this night's revelations never cease?

She tried to say, "Go on," in Mom's voice but it sounded more like a strangled gurgle. Kirk didn't seem to notice.

"She's so hung up on Aram. I don't stand a chance. I'm so pathetic."

Oh, Kirkie. He'd never been pathetic. He was Jannie's best friend and staunchest supporter. Dearer than dear.

But of course she couldn't say anything.

"Never mind. I'm being an idiot. Like usual. Like when I sent her those stupid Santa gifts and couldn't even tell her. I'm such a loser. I'm going back inside. See you at the bar."

And there he went, into the night, shoulders slumped, head lowered. He reached the front entrance of the hall just as the power was restored. Lights strobed on. People cheered and started to file back into the building.

Jannie stood, brilliantly spotlit in her former hiding place behind the trusty bush. She clutched someone's silvery shawl and shivered, as much from bewilderment as from the subzero temperature. Her mind raced. Strangely, she felt calmer than she had for days.

26

KISS AND TELL

"Don't move. Don't say a word." The speaker's voice was deep and oddly familiar. It didn't have an accent. It certainly wasn't Aram. Who in the world could it be?

"But—" Suze started to say.

"You heard me. Stay here ten minutes. Not one second less. I'll be outside guarding the door, so sit tight. No one's going to hurt you. Got it?"

"Got it."

There'd been no point arguing. The masked, hooded man was much bigger than Suze. And he seemed to mean business. Even though she didn't feel an imminent threat from him, she decided she'd be wise to at least pretend to abide by his rules.

When he closed the door behind him, leaving her alone in a musty basement room, Suze didn't stand idly by. She had lost her cellphone when she'd dropped her clutch, and the room where she sat was too far away from the party to bother shouting for help. But she could check for a possible escape route, and she proceeded to do just that, groping her way in the darkness as quietly as she could, shuddering as she felt cobwebs slinking across her face and arms, and bumping her sandaled toes once or twice on unseen objects.

At last, after completing the spooky circuit and determining there wasn't a second exit, Suze stood by the door and waited quietly in the blackness. She tried to breathe calmly in spite of the sour quality of the air. Mouse droppings? Please, no. Probably just poor ventilation. And now that she was thinking of odors, why had her abductor smelled faintly of French perfume?

As she pondered this, she reached automatically to straighten her mask, forgetting that it had been taken by the mysterious kidnapper. Maybe it was an antique worth stealing. Suze was sorry it was gone, but, what the heck, the important thing was that she was unharmed.

Time passed. After what seemed to be an eternity, she heard the lock click. She grasped the door handle and opened the door.

And that's when Suze walked straight back into the arms of the large masked man. She struggled and called out, but he held her arms tight to her sides. A microsecond later, the lights came on.

"Good girl. Your ten minutes are up." The strangely benign abductor wiped away a bit of dirt on Suze's cheek, then patted the top of her head as if she was his star pupil.

Suze bridled. The masked guy didn't seem to wish her any harm, but where did he get off snatching her away from the crowd and imprisoning her in this murky basement?

"Listen, you—"

"No, Suze. *You* need to listen. I have three words for you and then I must fly. My words are: follow your heart."

Without waiting for her to respond, the man turned

and ran full-tilt down the now brightly lit corridor. He rounded the corner at the end, never looking back.

Suze slumped against the wall, rubbing her temple with a shaking hand.

Why would anyone kidnap her, sequester her for almost a quarter of an hour, and then tell her to follow her heart? What did it all mean? What was she supposed to do?

Well, she knew she loved Aram with all her heart. But he was Jannie's now. Suze had renounced him. Her relationship with her daughter superseded everything. And as much as she craved the sight of him—the *touch* of him— she knew he was lost to her forever.

In the cruel, fluorescent light of the basement hallway, Suze fought back tears. What had just happened, and why would anyone, let alone a masked criminal, give her this advice? What was the point, when she had no future with the man she loved?

Follow your heart. Yes, Aram might be the impossible dream, but there was another person Suze cared for deeply and transcendently. It was Jannie. Jannie, the daughter Suze had nurtured and protected. Jannie, who had thrived in spite of her many childhood challenges, because Suze had been there time and time again to lift her up after each fall. Jannie was the person this stranger must have meant.

Suze was going to find her. Now.

She located the stairs, climbed them to the ground floor, and marched with determined footsteps toward the front of the building. As she turned the corner to the main hallway, Suze stopped short.

A woman was entering the building. She was wrapped in a spangled, silvery shawl that covered her head and upper body. On her face she wore an ornate silver mask.

How odd. Suze was sure that those were her own

possessions. Was this woman in cahoots with the kidnapper?

She intended to find out.

"Stop right there," she commanded.

The woman did as she was told. Slowly, she turned to face Suze.

"Hi, Mom," Jannie said, lowering the mask and unwinding herself from the shawl. Her black curls, released from their confinement, sprang out, surrounding her face, pink from the cold.

"Jannie? Why are you wearing my things?" Suze's eyes widened in astonishment. Her lips formed a perfect circle.

"Your things? Wow! No wonder you're surprised. I know *I* am!" Jannie laughed, but it was shaky, and as she handed the items to Suze, her hands trembled, too.

"What's going on, sweetie?"

"I wish I knew," Jannie said. "It's been the craziest night ever."

"I'll say. And I need to tell you something."

"Mom, let me speak first." Jannie's eyes were serious and pleading.

"All right. If you really want to."

"I do. It's not easy for me. But here goes. I've been a jerk. I tried to make Aram love me. I threatened you. I'm a pig daughter."

"No, you're not. You're my beloved—"

"Nope. I'm a pig. He doesn't love me. Never did, never will. He saw me wearing your clothes tonight, and thought I was you. So now I know, beyond a shadow of a doubt."

Suze was trying to picture the scene. Aram telling Jannie important truths, believing he was talking to Suze. How devastating for Jannie. Her poor daughter.

But she couldn't suppress the rising hope she felt in her heart.

"He loves you. And you deserve to be happy," Jannie said.

"Sweetie, so do you."

"And I will be. Some day. But right now, you need to go to Aram. He's a good man. And he's hurting."

"Jannie, you are my heart's desire. No man can change that."

"I know, Mom. I feel the same way about you, even if I've been such a shitty daughter. But this is different. It's your chance for true love! So, go, already!"

Suze stared at Jannie for a moment longer. When she was satisfied that she read nothing but openhearted encouragement in Jannie's brown eyes, she gave her daughter a tight hug, and hurried into the ballroom, searching for the man she loved.

That was that, then. Jannie hereby renounced all claims on Aram. He deserved someone a bit more sedate. More mature. And Mom fit that bill perfectly.

Still. Dreams were hard to give up.

Anyway, Aram had started to get all bossy. Treating her like a kid. That attitude would have been annoying, had things unrolled as she'd hoped they would.

In any case, Jannie needed to swallow a great big helping of humble pie and move on. And the first place she'd go was off to find Kirk.

The two of them had to set things right. They were best buds. Although there had been those romantic Secret Santa gifts. And that one messy Christmas kiss, fueled by too much alcohol on her part. That episode had been hot, as Jannie recalled. But had it been a mistake? Should they always remain strictly family-friendly, not carnal lovers?

Gah! She was so confused.

She traversed the ballroom, once again lit up with fairy lights. The band wailed away and folks meandered back to the dance floor. Jannie searched for that spiky hair of his, and after a minute—bingo! There was Kirkie, standing at one of the bars, quaffing away. Jannie counted. One shot glass emptied. Two.

She had to stop him before he got to the sloppy stage. It was one she knew too well, after her vodka debacle of the past forty-eight hours. There was that fine line. Now you can talk and walk, now you can't, and Kirk was starting to look a little wobbly.

"Hello there, sailor," she said, gliding up to join him at the bar. She pulled off his mask and tossed it away. Where her own had gone was anyone's guess.

Kirk looked at Jannie. His dark green eyes were clear. His Owen Wilson kissie lips were pursed.

"Jannie," he said. That was it. Her Kirk had never been big on conversation. But Jannie knew his secret now. He fancied himself in love with her. So, Jannie read much more into that single word than just her name. She read longing and love, mixed with a *soupçon* of self-loathing. And the thing was, she related to all of those emotions.

She downed her first drink of the evening, the same kind of shot that Kirk was imbibing. It was sweet and sour, with some kind of peppery after-slap. Ouch.

"C'mere," she commanded.

She grasped him by his jaggedy hair. He staggered forward.

All in the name of science, she told herself, and planted a great big wet one on him. Full, deep kissing, with no feathery warm-ups. All nimble lips and clever, epee-like tongue action. Thrust, parry, riposte. Touché!

And the thing was, she didn't want to stop. She wasn't

feeling a sisterly revulsion for a family member's inappropriate advances. She felt that zinging sensation from the top of her head to the tips of her toes, hitting all the sweet spots in between. She floated on a woolly cotton cloud of desire and experienced electric zaps practically leaping between their two bodies.

Good God. She was deeply in lust with Kirkie!

He surfaced for air. Jannie could have sworn he had stars in his eyes. He cupped her face in his hands and transmitted beams of adoration straight to her soul.

"Oh, Jannie. I do love you so," he said.

Ten minutes ago, Jannie had thought she was head over heels for Aram. She'd considered Kirk her best, platonic friend and never imagined they'd ever be in this place of longing and passion. Apparently, things could change pretty damn quickly at a masquerade ball.

"Kirkie, I know you love me," she finally managed. "And I wish I knew how I feel. Mostly, I'm confused. And stirred, deeply stirred, if you know what I mean."

"Mm-hmm," he said, closing in for another swoony kiss.

"So, maybe we should move slow?" Who was she kidding? She'd never held back in her entire life. Why start now?

She took Kirk by the hand. They collected their coats, and left Joelle's wedding. Whatever happened next—well, Jannie guessed it was meant to be.

And as they departed, fireworks lit up the sky. There was a crowd oohing and aahing as pinwheels spun and rockets flared. Kirk and Jannie looked at each other and smiled. It was a sign, for sure.

❀

She was determined to locate him. Up and down the ballroom Suze moved, peering into the shadows, looking at dancers on the floor, checking the bars. She couldn't spot him anywhere.

She wasn't dissuaded. This was her chance to find love —*her* love—and find him she would. Wrapping her shawl tightly around her shoulders, she ventured outside into the cold, starlit night, joining dozens of others who were milling about, waiting for something to happen.

"Fireworks, I expect," someone said in her ear. Light accent. Bergamot drifting on the air. Aram.

She turned around and looked up at him. His face was lined, his brows straight and severe, shading his eyes.

"It was Jannie you spoke to earlier," she said. "Not me."

"*What?*"

"Yes, Jannie. She told me. I was kind of, well, kidnapped at the time. At the very least, locked up in a dark room."

"Poor darling! You must have been terrified. I'd like to know who . . . but, wait, it's all starting to make sense. Was your abductor, by any chance, a man in black, wearing a white mask?"

"Yes! How did you know?"

"There was a band of mysterious, white-masked men roving around this place tonight. In fact, one of them just handed me this and told me to give it to you." Aram handed Suze her clutch. "Fortunately for us, they seemed to be looking out for our interests."

"Oh, thank goodness! But how weird! And . . ." Suze paused for a moment, choosing her words. "What exactly *are* our interests, Aram?"

He took her in his arms. She didn't resist. As the first Roman candle shot into the sky, leaving trails of incandescent, golden sparks, he lowered his head and kissed her.

It was gentle, the merest brushing of lips. It was a promise of kisses to come, a pledge of constancy, and a declaration of true love. And, as the fireworks continued to light up the night air, Suze and Aram held hands and left Joelle's wedding, eager to start their own adventures.

27

BE MY VALENTINE

*S*pectrum Computing's business was booming and Suze had never been busier at work. She wanted to clear her desk by day's end. Aram had promised her an amazing Valentine's Day dinner, and she was looking forward to an evening of romance.

There were a few things she intended to accomplish before she left for the day. First, she wanted to courier a special package, full of delicious and sexy treats, to Lola Devine. It was only fitting that Suze send her fairy godmother a tribute on this most special of romantic occasions. Perhaps Suze would never be able to repay Lola for everything she had done, but the package would show how much she cared.

"I'm going to catch last delivery. Got anything?" Suze asked.

Kirk and Bruno waved vaguely at her. She surmised they didn't have anything to add, but Tyler rambled over and handed her a few envelopes to stamp and post. She watched him walk back to his desk and wondered where he'd picked up the slight limp. It had been bothering him for a month or so. He might need to get that looked at.

Before Suze left, she called Jannie.

"Happy Valentine's Day, Mom!" Jannie's voice was full of effervescence and anticipation.

"Same to you, sweetie! Do you have plans for tonight?"

"Yes, Kirkie's coming over. We're going to have dinner by candlelight, drink champagne, and then, well, you know."

Suze looked over at Kirk's head, bent over his computer. She felt her cheeks grow warm.

"I think I've got the picture. Well, enjoy yourself! And see you soon."

"For sure! Love you, Mom."

The line went dead, but Suze thought, "And I love you, Jannie. Forever and ever."

That night, over a delicious and languorous dinner in Little Italy, Aram once again broached his favorite topic.

"Move in with me, Suze."

"Not yet."

"Better yet, marry me."

Suze laughed. "At some point, this is going to get annoying."

"I don't know why we need to wait. You know I love you, heart and soul."

"I feel the same way about you." Suze covered his hand with hers.

"Then why delay?"

Suze considered this. She cared for Aram so deeply that sometimes it scared her. They had remarkable chemistry, they treasured spending time together, they never argued.

But this was *her* year of adventure. She'd moved out of

Jannie's condo not so many months ago, intending to forge a new path. On her own, for the first time in her life.

It was too soon to give up on this quest. Maybe in the future, maybe after a year. But not now. And not on someone else's terms, regardless of how madly in love she was with him.

Leaning closer to Aram, she said, "When I met you, it was as if a whole new chapter opened up in my life. I've never been happier."

"Yes, and?" Aram gave her a mock professorial look.

"And I want it to go on and on. I love you. You love me. Let's enjoy every moment of this journey together."

"And you'll think about next steps?" Aram's eyes searched hers.

"I will. Promise."

"Then that will have to do. For now."

Suze smiled. She loved this incredible, honorable, sexy man.

What was more, she'd never had closer, warmer ties with her daughter. And, she'd established herself independently, for the first time in her life.

She could envision changes in the future. But for now, things were perfect as they were.

"Gotta go. Hot date!" Jannie bounded out of her chair and headed for the exit. Five o'clock and she was out of there! Romance and sexiness awaited.

"Happy Valentine's evening," Chuck, her fabulous new assistant, said. He gathered up his own things, likely getting ready to dash off to a crazily lusty evening of his own.

"Have a great night," Joelle said.

Yes. Joelle. Who was now Jannie's second-in-command at BB&M.

They'd all begged Jannie to come back. Not just Shivani and the corporate bigwigs in New York. Her team in Toronto, too. They'd known sales results would suffer if Jannie had gone elsewhere. Worse, they'd been worried she'd be hired by the competition and steal BB&M's top clients. So, they'd promised her she could have whatever she wanted, if only she'd come back.

She'd known exactly what it was, too. She'd wanted a second-in-command she could trust. Joelle fit the bill perfectly. She was honest and direct. And she wasn't afraid to tell Jannie when she was being socially inappropriate. Or idiotic. Jannie appreciated her very much.

She'd also requested a career coach, who understood social skills. Shivani did some research and hooked her up with a top professional, paid for by the company. Jannie was making progress, one baby step at a time.

Like right now. Before she blasted out of there she made an effort to display some of her newly minted sensitivity.

"Joelle, are you and Ben planning a fun Valentine's Day evening?" It wasn't always just about herself. She was asking about what someone else was doing. And listening to her response!

"You bet! Dinner, champagne, the works."

"I have something for you guys."

"Really? What is it?"

"Just some scented candles. They're lovely. Bergamot. It's supposed to rev up your energy level. Not that you newlyweds need it!"

"Jannie, that's so sweet of you. Ben and I will light them tonight."

Jannie liked her new self much better than the old one.

She felt generous and connected. She still kicked ass and took no prisoners, but that was sometimes just what the business needed.

Later, as she lay in Kirkie's arms, her breasts all squashed against his smooth, broad chest, she sighed with sex-glutted happiness.

"Yes, Jannie?" Kirk looked down at her. His lips were plumped out from all their kissing. He looked adorable.

"I don't know what we have here. But you make me happy."

"And I love you more and more."

Jannie hadn't said the *L* word to him yet. But she was starting to feel it might be bubbling up from somewhere deep inside. When it did, she'd likely blatt it out and then never be able to bottle it up again.

There were some things that social skills specialists could teach her. Others, maybe not.

Like, no matter how much training they gave her, she'd always be irrepressible. Spontaneous.

And sex crazed. Absolutely, positively, irredeemably sex crazed.

It was so lucky Kirk and Jannie'd found each other. He had all those years of unrequited love to work out of his randy system. And she needed a young man with high energy and incredible stamina.

Mom had her sedate lover. Jannie had her insatiable stud-muffin. And apart from having great love lives, mother and daughter were both gainfully employed and moving on up in the world. Jannie had even learned to bake Kirk's favorite chocolate chip cookies without burning the condo down.

So far, all was well. It even had the potential to become a happily-ever-after one day. But somehow, being happy right now was more than enough.

ACKNOWLEDGMENTS

I want to thank Jean Lowd and her colleagues at Creative James Media for choosing to publish my novel. They've made this author's dream come true, and I am so appreciative of their patience, expertise, and diligence.

Two individuals in my beautiful town of Niagara-on-the-Lake were particularly influential in the development of this book. If not for the encouragement of Hermine Steinberg, who founded the Niagara-on-the-Lake Writers' Circle, I never would have ventured beyond crafting short stories. Thank you, Hermine! To Susan Barker, who cheered this project on from its early days and never stopped believing in it, I can't even begin to express my gratitude, but I promise I'll do my utmost to demonstrate loyalty to her, forever.

Especially robust thanks go out to my big sister, Nancy Basmajian, for her dexterous and tactful editing skills. She has always been there for me, and I love her so much.

And to my tight society of writing pals—Cat Skinner, Nancy de Guerre, Lena Scholman, and Inge Christensen —thanks for giving me all those bolstering back pats and, occasionally, some much-needed tough love. I adore you all.

ABOUT THE AUTHOR

Sally Basmajian (sallybasmajian.com) is an escapee from Canada's broadcasting business. Before fleeing the corporate world, she was Bell Media's Vice President and General Manager, Comedy and Drama.

In February 2020, she was awarded first prize in both the Fiction and Non-Fiction categories for Ontario's Rising Spirits contest, and she recently placed third in the WOW-Women on Writing short fiction contest. She completed her Graduate Certificate in Creative Writing at Humber College in 2019 and holds a Master of Arts in Musicology from the University of Toronto.

When she isn't walking Parker the Sheltie, or golfing with her tolerant friends, or dreaming up a new story, she's usually tucked away in a flowery nook in Niagara-on-the-Lake, nose deep in a novel.